P.E.A.C.E.

GUY HOLMES

SIMON & SCHUSTER

New York   London   Toronto   Sydney   Singapore

SIMON & SCHUSTER
Rockefeller Center
1230 Avenue of the Americas
New York, NY 10020

DESIGNED BY RUTH LEE

Manufactured in the United States of America

10 9 8 7 6 5 4 3 2 1

Library of Congress Cataloging-in-Publication Data

Holmes, Guy.
P.E.A.C.E. / Guy Holmes.
p. cm.
1. New York (N.Y.)—Fiction. 2. Conspiracies—Fiction. I. Title: Peace. II. Title.
PS3558.O35933 P43 2000
813'.6—dc21
00-038750

ISBN 0-684-87079-7

Acknowledgments

My sincere thanks to David Rosenthal, Marysue Rucci for her excellent editorial guidance, Theresa Park for being the agent I always dreamed of having, Scott Smith for his tireless readings and wonderful suggestions, and Kappy Wells and Sam Mott who make where I live a home.

FOR MY PARENTS,

Judy MacMahon Holmes
and
William Kirby Holmes

In the United States, security cameras observe us in most large stores, airports, and banks. Traffic cameras watch us at highways, tollbooths, and stoplights.

In Amsterdam and other cities around the world, massive installations of video cameras on street corners allow police to maintain surveillance of the populace. In Monaco, large-scale video surveillance has made crime almost nonexistent. In Britain, an estimated 300,000 anticrime cameras watch the public.

Across America, many cities are beginning to explore the use of intensive camera surveillance to fight crime.

P.E.A.C.E.

Four floors below Manhattan in a bunkerlike room, a vast wall of monitors pulses with fragments of a city's picture; images flicker to life then disappear like bits of dream.

On one of the screens Mrs. Franklin Holt does not move, not one muscle. She has not moved in six hours. Crowds pour in and out of subway trains on the platform where she is standing but she stares ahead like a statue. She does not flinch when a teenager waiting for an overdue train dances around her to get laughs from his friends. She does not respond when a young couple asks her if she is okay. She is transfixed by something in front of her no one else can see. Something that will happen soon.

Two blocks away from the subway station where Mrs. Franklin Holt is waiting, Mac Wells leans against the wall of a Korean grocery and watches the flow of traffic. He checks his watch. Sam Mullane is late. They are due on station in six minutes. Mac lets his eyes lose their focus and the taxis speeding by form an undulating river of yellow, the blood of the city.

Mac senses someone lean against the wall next to him.

"You counting cars again?" Sam asks tiredly.

"You're a hundred and thirteen cabs late."

Sam has bags under his eyes, a paleness to his skin.

"You and Lisa overindulge?" Mac asks.

"Apparently I was singing into my hand like it was a microphone. Lisa's pretty ticked off."

"Sorry I couldn't make it." Mac claps his hands next to Sam's ear.

Sam winces.

"So loud noises are bad?"

"You missed your calling," Sam says, starting off down the street, a few feet ahead so Mac can't clap at him again.

"As?"

"I don't know. Colombian death squad member." From a pocket Sam pulls a small skin-colored wireless earpiece and slides it into his ear. He places a two-millimeter-wide wireless microphone patch over his voice box.

Mac, impeccably dressed in a conservative business suit, catches up and falls in step with Sam, who is smeared with grime and dirt, wearing five layers of old, torn clothing and shoes that look like they were found in the trash.

A *block away* a camera in a Plexiglas globe at the top of a telephone pole zeroes in on them, transmitting their images to the watch-room where thousands of images from Manhattan's streets and subways are shimmering, liquid yet constant. The camera zooms in and pictures of Mac and Sam are frozen and outlined in red. Facial characteristics are isolated and in the bottom corner of the screen video photos flip past, an indefinable blur until, a moment later, a match is found; Mac and Sam appear younger and smiling in their police uniforms. In less than a second hundreds of sociological information bits are analyzed, credit ratings to police records to clothing status cues. The scene is determined to have a 100 percent successful nonintervention resolution probability. DADD (Deviant/Antisocial Detection and Deterrent), the most advanced behavior recognition program ever developed, moves on, simultaneously scanning thousands of people, analyzing the most complicated animal behavior on earth: human interaction.

On one of the screens two men in heavy sweatshirts walk into a subway station, their hoods up, their heads lowered. For a brief moment, one of the men looks up, checking out the platform. His face is partly revealed and DADD freeze-frames the image, outlining and enlarging it. A small window appears in the bottom corner of the screen and the identification check begins.

Mac Wells follows Sam Mullane down the steps into the subway. Six months before, the New York underground trains were notoriously unsafe and dirty. Now, no trash litters the platform, no foul odors, urine and worse, assault commuters, no cacophonous boom boxes pound the ears. Instead, a large spotless white sign announces the area as a *Police Enforced Anti-Crime Environment*, and around the station a Strauss waltz drifts through the air from two-inch-thick flat-screen TVs hanging high on pillars and walls. On the screens commercials without sound play—a computer-generated image of a racially blended female, with tan skin and Eurasian eyes, drinks the latest preservative-and-additive-free soda. She smiles, seductive but innocent, holding the glistening can forward. Behind her smile, cameras in each TV silently scan the crowd.

Mac and Sam enter the station separately and take up posts at opposite ends of the platform. Mac sees Lisa Washington, the third member of their team, already on post, sitting on a bench between two old ladies. As per protocol she does not acknowledge him.

A woman with a stroller enters the station and Mac watches her roll the carriage out into the middle of the platform. Mac cannot help but stare at the woman, her back turned, her blonde hair down to midshoulder, just like Eve. Even the way she holds herself is the same as Eve, from the waist up tilting slightly backward, feet turned outward, and it could be Eve standing there, going on an errand with a little baby. Their little baby. But the woman turns, her face larger and broader than Eve's and the illusion is gone.

Mac looks away and the two men in hooded sweatshirts come into view. Trying not to stand out they stand out. Mac doesn't alter his stance, his heartbeat does not even slightly increase. Instead, he casually touches the wireless receiver in his ear and waits for confirmation.

Tony Parks, the taller hooded man, senses he is being watched. But everyone feels that in the subways now. To take the trains is instant paranoia. Still, without lifting his head he glances around the platform. Nearby, a large group of German-speaking tourists laugh loudly over some joke, one of them repeating the punchline, *Sein hund rot und fett trägt jetzt die kleidung seiner frau,* over and over. Across the platform there's a woman with a stroller, a businessman with a leather briefcase, a group of men bouncing a basketball, and, sitting alone, a graduate student type in a ratty tweed jacket. Tony looks at the stairs, considers the street. But the street is a bad idea. Better to play it cool, see what happens. Casually, Tony unzips his sweatshirt to have easy access to his gun.

On the watch-room monitor DADD has a match. Pictures of Tony Parks, a tear-shaped scar below his right eye, and his younger brother, Tommy Parks, fill the screen. Tony Parks's criminal and personal histories begin to scroll across the screen. DADD switches on a Passive Millimeter Wave Imaging system attached to the camera in the subway. Tommy Parks is standing on the other side of Tony and only Tony can be scanned. Variations in electromagnetic rays emitted by Tony Parks's body and all the objects he is carrying, his wallet, a pen, and the gun in a holster under his arm, are measured. Immediately, flashing red images of the gun and the other objects are produced on the screen contrasted against a blue image of Tony Parks's body. DADD bumps the scene to INTERCEPT and a warning tone sounds.

Tom Martinez and Jim Lincoln, the PEACE watch operators, immediately act. Martinez pushes a button that brings the information to a central screen. Tommy Parks has no priors but Tony's rap sheet is endless, a laundry list of armed robberies and assaults. And he is armed.

Lincoln whistles. "A real beaut."

Martinez taps a code on a keypad in his console and leans forward to a microphone. "Watch to seven." Martinez waits a moment. "Mac, you there or what?"

Mac Wells walks to a pillar as if stretching his legs. He speaks quietly, the skin-colored two-millimeter-wide adhesive microphone positioned just below his voice box, sensitive to the softest whisper.

"Mac here."

"The computer's caught two fish there on the platform with you. One's an ex-con wanted for a shitload of stuff. The computer says he's packin' . . . they're wearin'—"

"I've marked them."

"You got 'em?"

"Red and green sweatshirts. Tall one's spooked."

"Okay. Backup's on the way. You take the marks before the train pulls in."

•

Mrs. Franklin Holt can feel the convergence of forces closing in around her. Squeezing tighter. It has been coming a long time and now that the moment is close she feels something similar to relief. The train, the first hint of a low rumble, the sound traveling dimly from a station away, is approaching. People in front of her start to shift toward the edge of the platform. Into her field of view a woman pushes a stroller. That's good, Mrs. Franklin Holt thinks. That's appropriate.

Mac slides into position near the two marks but the men walk forward into a crowd and stand on either side of the woman who looks like Eve.

"No go," Mac breathes. "Innocents in the line. It's gonna happen on the train."

"Okay," Martinez says. "The eighth car is gridded. You know the procedure, Mac. Get them into the grid sector or wait till they're off. No firing on the train."

Mac senses Lisa and Sam moving into position near him.

The sound of the train, less than two blocks away, grows louder as it approaches.

A few feet behind Mac, Mrs. Franklin Holt moves for the first time in just over six hours, her hand, cramped and hurting from lack of movement, gestures toward the crowd. She opens her mouth and begins to speak but at first nothing comes out, just a dry hiss. She tries again and this time the words have form but are without voice, as though she is whispering a secret. "If you saw what God sees you'd think he was mad, lock him up, give him electroshock . . . but God doesn't need to be cured."

She takes a painful step forward. Blood has settled in her feet and she can barely keep her legs from collapsing under her. Muscles are cramping all over her body, and unable to control herself she begins to urinate, the urine spreading down her thick knit stockings, hot against her skin, collecting in her shoes.

She can feel the train vibrating the cement of the platform. She has only a little time left.

Mac watches Tony Parks look up to a mirror on the ceiling and scan the crowd. Suddenly Tony turns toward him and Mac casually looks away. But it is too late. Mac can feel Tony staring at him. Perps sometimes have a way of sniffing out a PEACE officer; Mac knows his cover is blown. He looks up and meets eyes with Tony. There is a moment when they both stare, the predator and the prey.

In less than a second, Tony knocks Tommy to the floor out of firing range, draws his gun, and ducks in the crowd, pivoting behind a teenage girl, holding her in front as a shield.

Mac's gun is out and pointed at the part of Tony's head just visible behind the girl, Sam and Lisa drawing their weapons only a half a beat slower. Mac immediately assesses the situation, some of the crowd backing away but others freezing in place, the armed target visible behind the girl but the other target somewhere out of view. A dangerous situation. Calm the armed target and locate the other suspect. Then take them out.

"Just put your gun down and everything's going to be fine. . . ."

Before Tony Parks can respond the event that Mrs. Franklin Holt has been waiting for happens. A force enters her body, an intense new strength that seems to come from outside her, taking control of her body and pushing her forward, rushing her across the platform. As the train rockets closer, its light just glinting off the tracks of the first half of the station, she shoves the stroller with the baby into the tracks.

Mac, catching the horrific scene in the corner of his eye, responds without thinking, holstering his gun, turning to sprint toward the tracks. But the baby's mother is closer; she leaps in first after the stroller, which sits on end, its large sunguard propped against the second rail, its two rear wheels spinning futilely in the air. The mother lands awkwardly, the snap of her ankle bone audible to those close to the tracks. She falls grabbing at the carriage, pulling at the wheel spokes, screaming desperately for help.

Mac leaps easily into the tracks, the world going into slow motion, his peripheral vision taking in the shower of sparks that shoots from the rails as the wheels of the train grind and slide less than thirty feet away, the driver frantically trying to stop, the squeal of the brakes like a scream.

People on the platform are emerging from their initial shock; some are screaming, panicked, while others begin to scramble forward to help. Mac hoists the mother, his hands in her armpits, in one motion, practically throwing her into people's arms on the platform. With the train less than ten feet away, he reaches into the carriage, snatches the baby up by its little blue pajamas, and dives with all his might toward the middle track. He protects the baby by turning in midair and landing on his side, rocks and wooden tracks jamming into his shoulder as the train misses his legs by an inch and slams into the baby carriage, smashing and dragging it down the tracks. Sparks spray onto Mac as he rolls to his knees, the baby cradled in his left arm like a football, light and dark flashing as the train passes, the fingers of his left hand supporting his weight against the ground just inches from the electricity-carrying third rail.

•

Mac looks down at the crying baby's beet-red face to make sure he is okay. Mac does not see Mrs. Franklin Holt jump into the tracks and go under the train, where her body is severed into two pieces, her cauterized torso tossed up onto the platform. The boy's gumless mouth wails louder than any baby Mac has ever heard. Mac feels a heat growing in his chest, anger.

He stands, drawing his gun, and walks quickly to a space between cars, unaware of the people in the train watching him through their windows. He steps between the cars and sees across the platform the old lady's severed body, Sam motioning with his hands, trying to calm Tony Parks. People around the platform are beginning to gag and vomit, crying and choking sounds fill the air; Sam is doing his best to trade himself for the teenager and Lisa has her gun trained at Tony's head. The mother of the baby, lying on her side, frantically peers between train cars and screams for her child. Mac looks for the other target and sees him, no more than a boy really, standing frozen in place and unarmed.

Mac blocks out the chaos on the platform and raises his gun. He has a shot but Sam and a civilian are standing between him and the target, leaving only a small triangle of space through which to shoot the suspect. He can see that Sam, a few inches at a time, is working himself closer to Parks. Everything becomes slow, Mac's hand is perfectly steady, he begins to squeeze the trigger. Then things go wrong. He tries to pull back even as he is firing, the release of the gun inevitable and dreadful, as at exactly that moment Sam leaps forward to disarm Parks.

Mac watches stunned as the shot hits Sam on the back of the neck, the electropatch releasing its charge, the electricity dancing between the fillings inside his mouth, his body paralyzed as he falls to the ground, his head hitting hard against a metal post.

Suddenly out of breath, the scene losing its focus for a moment, Mac watches as though he is a great distance away, Lisa firing her gun, her first shot hitting Tony in the temple and dropping him to the ground as his teenage captive scrambles into the arms of bystanders.

Mac crawls under the train coupling and hands the baby to a large black woman, who hands the infant to the mother, who begins to sob uncontrollably.

Mac pushes onto the platform toward where Lisa crouches above Sam. He bends at Sam's side when the crowd to his right parts and there stands Tommy Parks, a seventeen year old who looks like he hasn't even begun shaving yet, pointing a .44 at Mac's heart. The teenager's gun hand visibly trembles.

Mac slowly stands, trying to shift gears, to give all his attention to the gunman. The stench of vomit is overwhelming and he involuntarily gags. And another smell, just as sickening, is in the air, like aged cheese but much worse. Mac has smelled it before from dogs when they have been in a fight. Fear and aggression. It is coming from people on the platform, their faces terrified, their brains unable to make sense of the carnage around them. But mostly, it is coming from the boy with the gun.

Mac decides to talk.

"Son, I'm going to lower my gun and you lower yours."

"You killed my brother."

"No, he's just asleep . . . he'll be fine." Mac begins to lower his gun.

"I have nothing to lose," Tommy Parks is breathing out of his mouth, like a caught fish drowning in the air. "I can't go back to juvi court."

"Look, everyone's scared. You haven't done anything that can't be fixed. It'll look good you put down the gun." Mac stands in a relaxed way, his body language conveying total confidence in the situation's outcome.

For a few seconds Tommy Parks nervously glances around then slowly drops his gun hand to his side.

Mac shoots from the hip, the electric patch hitting the boy in the center of the forehead. The boy's finger instantaneously relaxes on the trigger, his eyes fluttering, his mouth jerking into what looks like a smile as he topples.

Mac turns back and stares down at Sam's crumpled form, oblivious to the smattering of cheers and applause that erupt around the station.

2

PEACE headquarters, midtown Manhattan.

Twelve floors of state-of-the-art police investigative operations, from the voice-stress analysis equipment in interview rooms to the subtle beige walls that enhance a sense of well-being among PEACE officers and dampen the violent tendencies of suspects.

Six floors above the subterranean watch room, Sam Mullane sits in a sleek modern hallway and shifts uncomfortably, wondering why the "ergonomically enhanced" modular bench is making his butt sore. Behind him a holographic stencil projects their immediate superior's name into the air, a soft pink luminous LIEUTENANT DANIEL POTESKY. Mac's off getting coffee and Lisa is already being grilled by Dan the Man.

Sam rubs a hand over the bump on the back of his head, still sore, but not bad enough to need stitches. A good thing too; he wasn't going to let them shave part of his head so Wells could call him Kojak.

It was so ironic. Mac, who never screwed up, who won the NIP marksman championships four years in a row, the most competent guy he's ever met, *ever,* whom you could trust to do the right thing in a tactical situation like you could trust the sun to rise each day—Mac had shot him. It was too good to be true. He would get mileage out of this for the rest of their careers. Sam chuckles at the thought of it. From this day on he owns Mac and Mac will just have to eat it.

Sam glances around; no one is looking. He leans toward Potesky's door to see if he can hear Lisa's voice. Not a word. That was the first thing he noticed about Lisa, her voice. Other things, like her eyes, and of course her body, were amazing too. But her voice, high-pitched but soft and with a slight southern accent that caused her to roll some of her words, made him engage her in conversation just to listen.

He smiles to himself, thinking of her, thinking of the day before on his way home from work, finding himself in a jewelry store pricing an engagement ring. When you found yourself looking at rings, it was a pretty good indicator of where things were going. Of course fraternization among PEACE officers was seriously frowned upon and with a team member, forget about it. Not even Mac knew.

And there was the race thing; Lisa was black and his Irish family would never go for it. But he didn't like going home anyway, too many bad memories of not enough food and too much religion, too many relatives hanging onto the past as though it was all they had.

"You sure you're okay?" Mac holds out a cup of coffee.

"Best sleep I've had in a while." Sam smiles, clapping Mac on the shoulder to let him know he's okay. Mac hasn't been this solicitous since he dropped a cinderblock on Sam's foot when they were eleven.

Mac sits, sneaks a glance over. He doesn't care what happens with Potesky; the only thing on his mind since the subway is that Sam is all right. He has known Sam almost all of his life. They were inseparable as kids. With little money, countless siblings, and a drunk absentee father showing up a few times each month to make life miserable, Sam spent so much time at Mac's house that Mac's mother began setting a place at the dinner table for him and Mac's father built bunkbeds in Mac's room. When Sam was thirteen his father went through him to get to his mother and Sam showed up at Mac's house with blackened eyes and a broken arm. Mac had never seen his father so angry. After taking Sam to the hospital Mac's father took Sam's father for a "drive" and from then on, Sam's father came around less often and never laid a finger on his children or wife again. By the end of junior high with his mother thankful for the help, Sam just stayed with Mac and his parents most of the time. At their high school graduation when Sam's name was called, Mac's mother cried and Mac's father, beaming, wiping his eyes, continued to clap long after everyone had stopped.

"You're not getting weepy on me, are you?"

Mac focuses and Sam's staring at him.

"No." Mac looks away across the hall to the flat-screen TVs high on the walls of the holding room that are just switching from the normal soft undulating pink and beige color patterns to the recently finished PEACE promotional film. "Just wanted to make sure the impact against your head didn't injure your small brain."

Sam laughs and Mac sees Tim Dimpter, a fellow PEACE officer, appear out of the holding room and head their way. Mac frowns. Dimpter, an excellent cop but so anal and competitive he isn't well-liked, finished second to Mac in a few annual city-wide shooting competitions and just can't get over it. Mac watches Dimpter pick up speed, locked onto them like a missile, his mouth twisted into a smirk.

"Here comes winky-boy . . ." Mac says under his breath and Sam laughs as though it is the funniest thing he has ever heard.

The laughter knocks Dimpter's swagger down a notch.

"Nice shooting today, hotshot." Dimpter's cold colorless

eyes drive unwavering into Mac. Mac turns to Sam as if Dimpter isn't there.

"You hear about Dimpter?"

"No." Sam plays along, wrinkling his forehead in mock concern.

"That new dispatcher, Barb? She went out with him. Said he's got the tiniest pecker she's ever seen. Like a baby's."

Sam laughs and waves his pinkie at Dimpter. Tom Martinez opens the office door, cutting short the talk. He motions to Sam. Dimpter makes a gun with his hand and fires it at Mac.

"See you 'round, Wild Bill."

Mac walks through the holding room, restless, waiting his turn. Sam's been in with Potesky ten minutes, and Lisa took off without saying anything, standard protocol after a debriefing. Mac stops at the candy machines and scans the entries for granola bars. His reflection, bent in the Plexiglas window, seems blue and foreign. The granola bar falls with a thud and he imagines Sam's head hitting the metal pole. He leans heavily against the wall. Had he made a mistake at the subway? Getting into position to take out the mark, holding the defenseless baby, he felt anger and usually during emergencies of any sort, no matter how violent or chaotic, he did not feel emotions, the adrenaline surge, the fear that most people experienced. It was a genetic quirk. He was emotionally normal except when something bad was happening. Then he was different.

The first time he realized this was when he was eight and a car smashed headfirst into a tree across his street. Mac was hanging out with Sam and other kids on his front porch when the sound of the impact spun him around, the air suddenly turning clear, snapping into focus. Everything began to unfold like a dream where you are at once wholly yourself but also floating above, separate from the scene, telling yourself what to do. As he approached the driver's door, fire beginning to flicker under the car, he felt absolutely nothing. The driver had to get out. It was simple.

People rushed out of their houses, a mother screamed, but their terror and panic was inconsequential to what had to be done. Mac calmly undid the seat belt and struggled to pull the driver out. Soon he was joined by Sam and a middle-aged neighbor who dragged the man up onto the grass and safely away. The car, a souped-up Falcon with an exposed gas tank, exploded seconds later, blowing apart half the tree.

Mac was surprised by all the attention he received afterward; neighbors, newspapers, and a swarm of TV people wanted to ask him questions. Early on in the media frenzy one of the newspaper reporters asked him if he had been afraid and Mac didn't really understand the question; what he had done had simply been the obvious thing to do. It was then that he realized he was different. He learned eventually to lie to the reporters and his parents and pretended that he had been afraid. Everyone said how courageous he was, but he knew that what they meant by courage had nothing to do with it.

And so, his split-second tactical decisions were always lucid and accurate. He was the ideal cop; in just ten years he won most of the commendations the police department had to give.

One of the TVs up on the wall cuts to a picture of an extreme close-up of a tranq-gun being fired in slow motion. Around the room a lot of other PEACE officers are sneaking glances from their computer screens to the TVs, morale high, smiles and jokes going through the room. The day before, the official half way results of the system's test run in New York were released at a White House press conference by President Harris himself. With the election a little over six weeks away, the results had to be glittering for the president to step up to that podium.

Mac grabs up a folded *New York Times* and a tabloid paper off a desk and glances at the glowing quotes. "Crime down sixty

percent in PEACE-controlled areas."; "A city's faith restored.";
"Tourism booming in the Big Apple." A slew of favorable front-
page articles; Mac remembers when every day there was a crush of
victims, when the papers all carried stories of gang growth, school
shootings, and random, horrific violence by teenagers.

Mac looks around and even some of the suspects being
processed are watching the monitors, impressed. Up on the
screens a two-millimeter-wide patch shot from a gun hits a target.
A soothing animal kingdom voice-over speaks, confident and reassuring. The patch, the voice says, induces a safe temporary sleep,
making the old, violent, destructive standbys, the handgun and the
nightstick, tools of a barbaric past. Mac sees one suspect actually
nod at the screen as if he wants to buy one for $19.95. Mac is al-
ways surprised at how easily people accept new technology.
Maybe there's a little kicking and screaming at first, but in the end
most of us are marching in lock step, blissfully unaware of how
the machines that control our lives work.

The electropatch, a modern miracle of 8,000 volts and a
sleep-inducing skin toxin, was like that. People were scared of the
tranq-guns at first but quickly came around. It was painless to be
shot with one. The electrical charge momentarily disabled the nervous system while at the same time scattering and carrying the
molecules of a toxin through almost any kind of clothing. The
beauty of the toxin—a synthetic chemical called DX-4 that instantly increased a sleep-inducing substance in the body, muramyl
peptides—was that no matter what dose you got the effect was the
same. As you fell to the floor, the excess DX-4 in your body immediately became inactive, recognizing appropriate sleep-state
levels of various neurotransmitters such as norepinephrine and
serotonin. An amount of toxin the size of a speck of dust was
enough; whether a patch connected with bare skin or was partially
diffused by clothing, it was lights out.

The image on the TVs changes to the subway, a man and

woman beset by thugs. The screen splits and we see on one side of the TV the watch room, where a PEACE officer monitoring the scene pushes a button. On the other side of the screen back in the subway, a light goes on in small disclike antennas high on the walls. Every person in the crime scene freezes and falls to the ground. The voice-over does play by play. With Rhine Corporation's new Grid Electrostasis system, it says, PEACE officers will be able to literally stop criminals in their tracks.

Incredibly good-looking actors in PEACE uniforms sweep onto the screen, arresting the criminals, helping the woman and man to their feet.

A little boy wearing a PEACE officer outfit steps in front of Mac.

"Are you a real sleeper? I have all the action figures." Before Mac can answer, the boy draws and fires his toy sleeper gun at Mac, the laser sight zeroed in on Mac's heart.

"You got me," Mac says.

3

Lieutenant Dan Potesky puts a hand over his stomach as the leftover chicken cacciatore his wife brought home from her bingo club meeting rises in his throat with a burst of heat. She probably put poison in it. He tilts back in his chair and downs a recyclable cone of water. He hears Wells shift in the seat across from him but doesn't look up. This is the last thing Potesky needed, a big mess. He can usually judge the magnitude of a mess by the severity of his heartburn. He reaches into his top drawer for the bottle of Tums. Standing a few feet away with his back turned, Captain John Codd drones on and on into Potesky's cordless video phone.

"Sure, sure you have my word," Codd is saying.

Which word is that? Potesky wonders, opening a folder behind his desk. One of the two suits Codd brought with him from Rhine to help sort out the situation shifts in his seat and clears his throat. Potesky pages through Mac's report like he is doing something but all he can concentrate on is the pain in his gut. The Tums are losing the battle.

Mac glances over at the two men he has never seen before, one smiling with an air of oiliness, the other expressionless behind thick, square, black prescription glasses. There is something odd about the man wearing glasses. A lack of movement to his face, as though it is a mask. Mac can feel him staring, examining him really, but when Mac looks over the man just looks away.

Mac wonders why Potesky keeps avoiding his eyes. It's Codd's show; maybe Potesky wants to hang back, not show any solidarity. But why is it Codd's show? Codd rarely involves himself with day-to-day departmental affairs. Codd has been quiet a long time on the phone. He's the kind of guy who'd be more comfortable at a fund-raiser with VIPs than with regular cops. Certainly, had Potesky been in charge, he'd never have made such a big deal, calling everyone in one at a time. Mac expected a reprimand but the mood of the room seems more serious than a smack on the hand.

Codd hangs up and Potesky begins.

"Mac, of course you know Captain Codd, our liaison to Rhine Corporation, and this is Mr. Smythe." Potesky motions to the smiling oily man on the couch. "A representative for Rhine."

Mac looks at the expressionless man, waiting for someone to introduce him, but nobody does.

"Obviously we got everything on tape and your report, so I don't really need to ask you what happened," Potesky says.

"The mark made me."

"You were too damn close," Potesky blurts. His anger takes Mac by surprise. "The ACLU drags the city into court every day, Mac. We can't be zapping innocent bystanders, and certainly not cops, for chrissakes." Potesky's face reddens like it might explode.

"I should've seen the old woman."

Smythe leans forward. "The grid, when it's fully operational, will remove human error from the equation."

"Well, until then." Potesky turns to Smythe. "While we're still in the equation and not just sweeping up the garbage identified by microchips. . . ."

Codd puts his hand on Potesky's shoulder, smoothly cutting him off.

"The point is, Wells . . . you're an exemplary officer, top of your class, one of our standard bearers. Ever since that hostage incident in the Bronx years ago, the press has pegged you as a hero. What's important is that we maintain a unified front on what happened today with Sam. There's no reason to talk with the media, to let them blow this incident out of proportion, distort your record."

"No, sir." A moment of silence. Mac can feel the expressionless man examining him again. He waits for Codd to continue speaking, feeling as though he has missed something. When the PEACE program was started, it was a foregone conclusion that lawsuits would be filed by noncriminal civilians who were accidentally shot and had somehow hurt themselves falling. Cases were already pending in the courts. It was an acceptable risk, but according to department doctrine it would be a managed risk; the department did not want any cowboys.

Still, fear of lawsuits and bad press didn't seem to justify the inclusion of Codd and the Rhine people, the tension in the room.

"Any questions, Wells?" Codd asks.

"No, sir." Mac glances at the Rhine man who this time stares back, his expression still blank, his mask still in place.

The photographer adjusts her position, leaning back against a tree. Elbows propped against her body, she waits for the target to arrive. Hidden in a stand of trees above a parking lot for police vehicles in Central Park, she zooms in on a man and a woman kissing on a park bench one hundred yards away. The action is escalating, the couple losing control of their hands, losing sense of where they are, perhaps not caring.

The photographer swings her zoom, supported by a retractable metal rod, back to the target area. She does jobs all around the world, most of her work from long distances, shooting photographs of people who don't want their picture taken.

The target pulls up in his car and the photographer snaps a picture. The target steps out of the car, his back to her, and the photographer freezes another moment of time. She is an artist whose work will be seen by only a few people; the frame of the shot, tree limbs dangling into the top of the photo, is nice.

Making sure to get a face shot, she lines the crosshairs of her lens on the target's head as though she is a sniper.

•

Mac stands a moment by his car, enveloped by the smell of rotting leaves. Autumn has always been his favorite time of year. Early fall is just right, cool but not too cold, a sense of change, of excitement in the air. He begins to walk to the stairs leading into the park along a wall of election posters plastered on a wooden fence—President Harris, a strong-featured, handsome man with a thick head of brown hair, smiles a warm and reassuring smile above the words HARRIS MAKES PEACE. A corner of the closest campaign poster showing Harris's hand has come unglued and flaps back and forth, waving. Mac hears footsteps on the pavement behind him and turns.

A heavy-set man with glasses limps toward him. The fat man motions to his knees.

"Bad knees. High school football coaches are dangerous to your health." The fat man extends a puffy, stubby hand. "Marty Salmon, freelance for *Newsweek, People.* . . . You name it, they all buy or steal from me."

Mac doesn't extend his hand and Salmon pulls his back.

"Heard there was a fouled bust on the IRT today. A sleeper got nailed."

Mac notices tomato sauce around the fat guy's mouth. He feels a familiar unease he often experiences with people in the press, as though they're trying to sell him a car.

"You probably think I'm a sleazeball but the people really running things, they're the sleazeballs. . . ."

Mac turns to climb the steps into the park. The fat guy is getting hyper, maybe he only thinks he's with the press.

"You think Nixon tripped himself up? He was screwed for getting friendly with the Chinese. . . ."

Mac is walking up the stairs while the fat guy labors behind, talking the whole time.

"Woodward was spoon-fed by these people. Reagan was just a front man for them. C'mon, help me out. These people got all the angles. . . ."

Mac gets to the top of the stairs and continues on into the park without looking back.

Marty Salmon stops near the top of the stairs and feels the frustration of the story walking away. "They get away with murder," he calls out as Mac disappears from view.

Salmon looks up and down the stairway, his voice still lingering, a bit too loud in the empty park.

The photographer packs up her camera and lenses, an easy day's work. She has a feeling that getting the fat guy on film is a good thing, that the photos will please her superiors. Presumably, someone else is on the job now, following the thin guy or the fat guy, or maybe it was just the meeting that was important. She does not know and does not need to. She will develop the film, deliver it, then meet her boyfriend who thinks she's in town between assignments from *National Geographic*.

A charity baseball game is in full swing on one of the fields in the heart of Central Park, PEACE officers playing against local radio and TV personalities. The "personalities" ham it up in the field as reporters clog the sidelines. A pretty, blonde, too-thin woman does her spot.

"As you know, many of these dedicated men and woman spend their days keeping our streets and subways safe, but as you can see in the distance behind me, the members of the elite PEACE patrols, popularly known as Sleepers, are winning over the public with more than just the prevention of crime. All proceeds from this game will go to the Have a Hope Foundation . . . "

A hundred yards away, on the far side of a tree, Sam leans forward and kisses Lisa.

"Cut that out, big man. Someone will see." Lisa can't believe how comfortable she feels with Sam. She knows he's dated a lot more than she has, and that makes him a bit of a wild card for a long-term relationship, but she trusts him, doesn't worry for a moment when a beautiful woman walks by. Somehow she just knows that he is hers. When they first met, he was onto her right away, flirting like a child. Though interested, she had never dated a white guy. And there was the problem of them both being PEACE officers.

Sam pushes against her hands and when he reaches out to pull her close, Lisa doesn't fight hard.

"I don't care if they see," Sam growls in her ear. "Tomorrow I'm going in to the lieutenant . . ."

Lisa pushes Sam back a couple inches. "You're going to tell him?"

"Not in so many words."

"What, honey? You just gonna grunt and Dan will grunt back?"

"I'm going to work it so you and I can be together as much as we want."

Lisa smiles, looks into her lap. "You are my man," she says quietly, "aren't you."

Sam tilts Lisa's face up with the tips of his fingers and he and Lisa look at each other, staring as if they can't get enough of each other, an exchange no passerby would mistake.

At the tables of burgers, potato salad, rich desserts, Mac piles his plate high with salad.

He starts off toward a group of trees where he can see Sam's jacket on a fence. Halfway there Sam and Lisa come into view and

Mac stops cold at the sight of his partners kissing in an open-mouthed scorcher. They disengage and go back to eating. Mac starts forward, stunned, fighting the urge to laugh. Sam and Lisa? How could he have missed them together? When he gets close he plays dumb.

"Hey."

"Hey, Dirty Harry." Lisa is smiling.

"How'd it go at the station, Wells?" Sam's mouth is full of fries. "You grounded without allowance?"

"They asked me why I didn't use a real gun," Mac sits, balancing his plate on his knees, his mind still racing, thinking back. Were there signs? Lisa always in a good mood? Sam always busy in the evenings?

Sam motions with his beer. "They asked me about my drinking. Can you believe it?"

"They put me on drug detail," Lisa says.

Mac motions to himself. "Me too. No *love affair* those drug busts."

Lisa nods, oblivious, and Sam isn't paying attention. Mac smiles and stabs a cherry tomato with his plastic fork.

Sam turns to sneeze into his napkin and feels a twinge in the side of his head, an intense pressure in his veins. He closes his eyes and rubs the area just above his temple, the pain subsiding as quickly as it came. He opens his eyes and suddenly the world is in double. He blinks again and his normal vision returns as though nothing happened. He glances from Mac to Lisa but they haven't noticed.

5

On the top floor of a run-down building in the upper reaches of East Harlem, a large loft full of equipment identical to the PEACE watch room monitors the city.

Owned by an off-shore import/export concern, EXCO, the building appears empty, a dilapidated shell. Disintegrating bricks and broken windows, plywood nailed over every opening, everything looks old, even the new entrances, where steel doors have been treated with chemicals to make them match the rest of the building.

The building was picked precisely because of its deserted neighborhood. The cops never cruise; the homeless people stay away. No one was in the area one year earlier when, in the dead of night, large moving trucks pulled into a loading dock at the back of the building. No one was around to see the huge crates transported into the building. If someone had happened to wander in, a homeless person or someone who had made a few wrong turns, he would have been watched. If he had lingered too long, he would have been strongly encouraged to leave by a group of men, dressed like a gang, but not a gang, waiting in the shadows at either end of the building's block.

Except for pencil-thin cameras that have been hidden at key points throughout the building—the entrance to the garage, the elevators, at every door to the outside—the first seven floors of the building have been left the way they were when acquired, dirty and full of trash. City officials, elevator and fire inspectors and the like, whose job it is to make sure the building is safe every six months or so, often complain about the bad smell and leave after only a cursory glance. The most conscientious make it to the second floor before turning back, chuckling to EXCO's representative, "So your company bought this as an investment?" They leave with a laugh and a signature on the dotted line. The building is structurally sound, just disgusting. The inspectors never see the pristine top floor, as the two elevators in the building have been fixed so they will not go there. It is accessible by one entrance only, a set of stairs behind a locked steel door that unlocks when the right code is entered into a hidden panel along its side.

Today, the man with no expression from Potesky's office straddles a puddle at the door and enters the code. He absently rubs his face where the nerves in his cheek don't work. As a child people always asked him why he was sad and he developed the nervous tic of covering his face with his hand. By force of will he does it only rarely now. The door unlocks. The man enters the stairs, shuts the door, and climbs one floor to the room of monitors. The two men sitting before the screens glance up.

"Mr. Schorr," one of the men says. "No recent movement. Everything's copacetic."

Schorr leans forward to one of the screens where the camera is fixed on the entrance to an elegant red-brick apartment building on Park Avenue. Every time someone emerges from the building DADD automatically does an identification check.

•

Inside the Park Avenue building a television is turned up to an unbearable volume. In a large third-floor apartment Reece Timmons, a successful high-level investment manager on Wall Street and the man DADD is looking for, numbly watches the news on a big-screen TV from a leather couch.

"Campaigning today before veterans in Columbus, Ohio, President Harris touted the recent positive numbers for PEACE, his popular anticrime program currently being tested in New York City, and urged its swift implementation across the country. With just over six weeks left until the election, President Harris has increased his lead to fourteen points ahead of billionaire Independent candidate Bert Pickens."

The screen's image, the president at a podium in front of flag-waving crowds, reflects off Reece Timmons's glasses.

"We are retaking the country," President Harris says in his best bass-voiced oratorical style. "Criminals, from street thieves to sophisticated crime syndicates, better find a new line of work . . . *Because* . . ." He pauses and there is a ripple of laughter in the crowd as people anticipate his next line. He points to the crowd and cups his ear as fifteen thousand voices shout the line in unison with him. " . . . *there's a new sheriff in town!*"

The crowd erupts in wild applause.

Reece Timmons, impeccably dressed in a Brooks Brothers suit and Italian handmade shoes, gets up and goes to the window. A young blonde-haired woman passes below on the sidewalk. Reece Timmons closely watches the woman as she bends to tie her shoe. He stares, dumbstruck, as if there is some mystery to be discerned in her, some answer in the way she double-ties the knot, then stands, straightening her skirt. Then it clicks, the answer, like a cold fire in his head, a cool blue flame that burns away the paper-thin connections and courtesies that bind him to his life, to other people. Action is demanded. Valiant, irreversible action. There will be meaning in that. The blue fire spreads to his hands.

He slides a letter opener off a nearby desktop and casually heads out the front door.

DADD freeze-frames Reece Timmons exiting his building. The identification is almost immediate. A soft tone sounds and the two operators and Tom Schorr all focus on the screen.

"Christ, what's that in his hand?" Schorr says and one of the operators zooms the camera in, the letter opener looking like a knife.

"Tip off PEACE. *Now!*"

One of the operators punches a few buttons on his console, removing an override order, erasing the command that allows DADD to be shut off from PEACE operations in certain parts of the city while appearing to be on. Miles away in the watch room, suddenly able to operate freely, DADD switches the scene to intercept status, a call going out to the closest PEACE patrol.

Schorr watches as the camera loses sight of Reece Timmons, walking slowly, calmly below a group of trees still holding enough of their leaves to block the view. He prays the PEACE officers get there in time.

Reece Timmons catches up to the girl while she waits for the light to change. She must sense him, because she turns and, for an instant, looks into his eyes, but he has nothing to tell her, nothing to explain. Fate is unexplainable.

She does not scream, her face frozen in surprise as she slides to the ground. A moment ago here. Now gone.

When the nightmare comes, Mac is able to struggle up out of it into the bedroom, into the early evening. The clock glows only twenty minutes later than when he had shut his eyes to catch a nap before Eve got home. He walks to the bathroom and splashes water on his face.

It was a decade before, the summer of his rookie year, at the Cuomo Municipal Building, the day that turned into his nightmare. A worker who had been fired from one of the judge's courtrooms had threatened to get even with the judge. They had a picture of the man and Mac had memorized the face. His job was to scan the few people climbing the steps to enter the building. The threat was over a week old and the latest information was that the suspect had left town; the other unit had been recalled the day before, leaving only Sam and Mac posted.

It was a slow day and Sam was taking a bathroom break inside the building. A few feet up the street a pretty Hispanic woman, maybe twenty years old, was selling food from a corner stand. Since opening the stand a half an hour before, she had been watching Mac, staring at him. She wiped her forehead with the end of her apron and gave Mac a long look. With Sam gone it was a good time to make a move, to avoid the running commentary Sam would inevitably resort to if he saw Mac was interested in the girl. Mac tipped his hat and smiled. She smiled back in a way that made it absolutely clear she wasn't just being friendly. Mac glanced around the vacant block, the suspect was probably in Ohio or something. He walked over.

The woman at the food stand laughed when as an opener Mac asked what she recommended on the menu. She was not at all shy, knowing full well why he was there at her counter. Mac glanced down the block again and it was still empty; he turned his full attention to the girl. But the moment he turned away a car door opened far down the street. While Mac was making time with the girl, a man in a ratty trenchcoat walked up the long steps to the courthouse entrance.

The first shot was like a backfire and turned Mac around, to hear the second shot, followed by screams. He launched full speed up the steps, gun unholstered, immediately registering the guard inside lying in a pool of blood, a woman screaming from down the hall. Mac saw Sam, his gun drawn, coming out of a bathroom far down another hall. More shots exploded from Mac's side of the building and Mac sprinted down a long hallway toward them, bursting through a door just in time to see a small girl in a floral, multicolored beret and her mother falling to the floor, wounded.

Just ahead the gunman's voice echoed down the hall, "It's not like I wanted to hurt anyone . . ." and Mac ran toward the voice, past the girl and her mother to where the gunman was standing, lording over a small group of people with his gun pressed to the head of a tall, shaking man. Mac aimed his service revolver and as the gunman turned toward him, fired once, the bullet hitting the gunman in the forehead, crumpling him, suddenly lifeless, to the floor. People began cheering and crying as Mac raced back to the mother and her little girl, lifeless silhouettes on the floor. He desperately tried to stop the bleeding and gave the girl mouth to mouth but it was too late. What happened after that was a blur, his body wracked with nausea so he could barely stand, Sam taking him aside, telling him what to say, chaos in the halls of the building as scores of police and emergency services people descended on the scene.

The brass didn't care that Mac had disregarded protocol and taken out a gunman with a hostage when no negotiations had been initiated; everyone was so glad it wasn't worse, the guy had enough ammunition in his knapsack to kill hundreds. Sam, heavily connected through his father's four brothers, every one of them a cop, had protected Mac, finding an unguarded side door that was supposed to be locked but wasn't. The video tape of the surveillance camera was being changed at the time of the incident and it was assumed that the gunman had gained entry at the side door. More convenient for everyone if Mac was the hero who saved uncounted lives rather than the cop responsible for three deaths.

Mac looks at his reflection in the mirror, the heaviness, the shame, the guilt from that day still in his gut. It took a long time after that day to not just go through the motions. But, as he gradually returned to a normal daily routine, he was a different person, more careful, more thoughtful, no longer taking things in his life for granted. While Sam continued to date women like it was a full-contact sport, Mac was married within a year. It was strange the way the worst thing that had ever happened to him led to the best thing that had ever happened to him, his marriage with Eve.

He dries his face and looks out the window, the lights of his neighborhood coming to life. People returning from the city, home from work, to their cul-de-sac, one among hundreds in the northern New Jersey gated community, FarQuar Park. Aluminum siding, perfect square green lawns, a neighborhood where little happens that isn't expected.

The window's glass fills with clouds from Mac's breath, obscuring the cul-de-sac as he leans too close. He tilts back and Far-Quar Park reappears, Shangri-La emerging from the mist.

He walks through the downstairs flipping on lights. Each light turns the windows a shade darker. Inevitably Eve will go through the house turning off many of the lights, but dusk has always made Mac slightly uncomfortable, so he flips every switch.

In the kitchen, Mac cuts open a tofu package, Eve's choice for dinner. He carefully chops garlic and mushrooms on a cutting board, making neat piles. He smiles at a framed black-and-white picture on the counter of himself and Eve standing in front of the Hudson River, the light on the water broken into sparks, a group of sparrows caught in midair. It was taken the day they met; Mac remembers exactly the way Eve looked the first moment he saw her, the way her hair fell over her eyes and the way the light pink shade of her lipstick contrasted with her pale skin when she glanced up from a psychology book as he approached the park bench where she was sitting. It was the strangest, most wonderful experience; before either of them said a word, before they spent all afternoon talking and laughing together, before their first kiss later that night, he felt as though he already knew her. And she felt the same way.

Of course, as days went by, then months, they got to actually know each other, the way he always slept with a bathroom or hall-way light on, her need to always answer the phone and to make endless lists, but their differences and idiosyncrasies only deepened their need to be together. Her parents, well-to-do and from Washington, D.C., were a little put off at Eve's decision to marry a cop; they had expected a lawyer or a doctor. Eve had read books in college he had never heard of and enjoyed opera and other things he had never been exposed to. They were from totally different backgrounds, but when they looked at each other, they were always from the same place.

Mac glances outside the large bay window. Leaves skip across the lawn and the young maple trees stand against the fading sky like shadows. Back when they first bought the house, after Eve was done with school and her practice was up and running, he would stand outside in the dark watching Eve move around inside, amazed that she was there, waiting for him. She had a way of often laughing aloud to herself when something struck her as funny and once, on one of those nights, standing at a window she had suddenly smiled then laughed and out in the yard he had laughed too, connected in the dark and the light.

He wipes a bit of dust off the frame of the photo and turns back to the cutting board, not hearing the lone call of the day's last bird, just then disturbed by Eve's car in the driveway.

Eve sits in her car. The house is all lit up and she knows Mac is making dinner. She takes her hand from the shift and rests it on the gym bag beside her. She lets her head go back against the headrest and looks out the window, the clouds still catching light, stretching across the sky like exposed human ribs. A thin child lying across the horizon.

It is silly to sit in the car, to not go right in and see Mac. She knows this. But she can't move.

At her self-defense class that night, the instructor had applauded her fury, telling the rest of the class to watch her as she defended against the attacker in the padded suit, as she delivered disabling blows to the man's knee, neck, and groin so that, despite his padding, he went down.

"That," the instructor said, "is controlled anger. We must, in a defense situation, forget our natural empathy." The women in the class had all nodded and looked at her and later, after class, congratulated her, given pats on the back as though she had struck a blow for womanhood.

Eve watches Mac's shadow pass by a window. She tells herself she won't cry, that she is done with that.

"Sam was definitely okay, though?" Eve says, concerned, across the dinner table.

"Fine. I'm being reassigned."

"God, I hate your job. Those cameras everywhere."

Mac takes a breath, looks down at his food, doesn't get into it. Eve had marched against PEACE even while he was one of the first to be recruited from the NYPD. He glances up at Eve, her eyes fixed on her plate as though she is trying to decipher something in its design, pink flowers and soft yellow spirals. The way her head is tilted down accentuates dark circles around her eyes, marks out of place on a beautiful, still unlined face.

"Maybe we should try tonight," he says.

Eve looks up from her food. "It's not a target day. I'd rather conserve you, if you know what I mean."

"There's more than enough of me." Mac smiles, reaches across the table, takes Eve's hands. "It's going to happen for us, Eve. One way or another."

"I know." Eve squeezes Mac's hands. "God, I'm just so tired of waiting! Remember how great Maine was; we always used to talk about living there. I could start up a practice in Portland, always room for another pyschologist. And every sheriff's department in the state would love to have you."

"If you really want to move let's talk about it but it's *going* to happen for us, whether we're here or there." Mac gives her a little tug as though he might pull her across the table and make it happen right there and then. "How long do I have to wait?"

Eve smiles, looking at their hands together. "My temperature was up this morning so I'd say my cycle begins in a day or two."

Just a few feet from where they sit a laser beam is directed against the outside of the bay window. Invisible to the human eye, the laser measures the vibrations of Mac and Eve's voices from the glass. In a Nissan Quest minivan with tinted windows, the vibrations are turned back into voices and are recorded on a minidisc in a portable computer. Two men listen in silence as Mac and Eve do the dishes.

In the middle of the night Eve wakes up. She goes to the bathroom to get a glass of water and stops at the bedroom door at the end of the hall. She opens the door and steps into the small bedroom, turning on a light, everything waiting perfectly in the interior, the crib, the music-making toys and stuffed animals. Above the crib, the glow-in-the-dark mobile, stars, planets, and a crescent moon hang motionless.

She returns to the bedroom, shuts the door, and quietly slides into bed so as not to wake Mac. The phones are turned off, so neither of them hears the answering machine in the downstairs hallway quietly click to life, picking up the late-night call.

They do not hear Lisa, anxious and tired, leaving a message that Sam is in the hospital

There is a repetitive sound in Sam's head like water dripping from a faucet, drip, drip, drip. . . . People have come and gone, giving him shots, too many shots. Faces leaning over him he doesn't recognize. Lisa's face was there but now she is gone. Drip, drip, drip. . . . A hospital room looms around him, his arms feel as if they're tied down. His head hurts and his brain doesn't feel right, as though he's having a conscious nightmare, thoughts racing too fast, whispering back and forth. On the wall across from the bed there seems to be a pattern in the white paint, subtle but unmistakable, a large leering face looking down on him. Drip, drip, drip. . . . He can feel the pillow behind his head soaked through with sweat. A male nurse comes in, awfully muscular to be a nurse, and frowns at him. The nurse adds something to the IV bag. There is a flash of light from behind a mirror next to the bed. Sam does his best to focus on the mirror and there is another flash. Whatever the nurse added to the IV is making him drowsy.

•

Mac knocks open the double doors and jogs to the desk nurse. She is on the phone and he interrupts her.

"Sam Mullane's room?"

The nurse looks up, irritated; Mac already has his badge out.

"It's two-twelve, but it's before visiting hours, officer."

"Thanks." Mac turns for the rooms. The nurse puts her call on hold and punches a button on the phone for security.

Sam is asleep. Mac is shocked by how pale Sam's face is, as though he's been in the hospital a week. He sits next to him. The 6:00 A.M. news is on the TV. A detective Mac knows only by reputation is talking to a reporter on Park Avenue. The camera pans down to a chalk outline on the sidewalk and the detective is talking. "No, as far as we can tell, this individual just went berserk, picked the victim at random, the letter opener has been traced to his apartment . . ."

Sam opens his eyes and Mac leans over him.

"Hey, buddy." Mac pats Sam's arm. "A lot to go through just to get workers' comp."

Sam smiles but his eyes close again. His face looks too relaxed, too flaccid.

"They must have you doped up pretty good."

Sam nods weakly.

"God. I'm so sorry, Sam."

"Mac . . . ?" Sam's voice is barely a whisper.

"What is it, Sam?"

"Some . . . something's not right."

"Yeah, because of me, you have a concussion."

"No . . ."

Mac watches Sam move his lips but nothing comes out. He pours a cup of water and puts it to Sam's lips. Sam drinks. "Something else is going on." Sam tries to move his head to the right but

can't do it. He motions with his eyes to a large mirror on the wall.
"The mirror . . ."

"What about the mirror?"

"Something's . . . a light . . . behind it."

"You want me to check the mirror?"

Sam nods.

Mac walks to the mirror and runs his fingers along the edge,
which is glued to the wall. He taps the mirror, solid, flush against
the wall and turns back to Sam but Sam is asleep.

Mac goes back into the hall. There is a door right next to
Sam's and Mac tries the knob but it is locked.

In the room behind the door Tom Schorr places his cigarette
in an ashtray next to the two-way mirror and undoes the button
to the holster of his gun.

"Excuse me."

Mac looks up and a young doctor with a clipboard is approaching, the nurse close on his heels.

"May I help you with something? Visiting hours don't begin
for another two hours."

"I want to speak to the doctor handling Sam Mullane's
case."

"Dr. Preston will be here at nine A.M.," the young doctor
says coolly.

"That's not good enough . . ."

"The patient's been hallucinating during the night, doctor,"
the nurse says.

The young doctor looks at Mac then pages through his clipboard. "Yes, here. He's on anti-inflammatories and they can cause
aberrant psychological behavior."

Mac looks at Sam's door, unsure.

"He should be fine," the doctor says firmly.

"He'll be okay? It's just routine then?"

"I don't see a problem. He suffered a concussion. The effects were delayed, that's all. We're keeping a careful watch."

Next to the elevator Mac takes a long drink from the water fountain. He doesn't usually perspire much but sweat is dripping off his forehead. He cups water in his hand and splashes it on his face. He tells himself everything's going to be fine. It's just a concussion. Concussions are a pain in the ass, he's had two himself, but Sam will be up and around in no time.

One hour after Mac has left, the elevator doors open and Lisa steps out.

The desk nurse has bent over to retrieve a pen and Lisa walks by. She knows she is early for visiting hours, they had made her leave after Sam was admitted, but she couldn't wait any longer. All the doors along the hall are open, revealing unused rooms. A surprisingly empty floor.

Ahead a door is ajar and she can hear muffled words, Sam's voice saying, "No, no . . ." but it is too indistinct to be sure. She walks quickly to the door and opens it; two male nurses are leaning over Sam, just putting a syringe away.

"What are you giving him?!"

"Anti-inflammatories, ma'am. Are you family?"

"No—I just heard him speaking."

"Couldn't have, ma'am." The nurse's tone is matter of fact. "He's been sleeping like a baby all night. That musta been us." The other man gently tucks a blanket up under Sam's arm.

Lisa relaxes, looks at Sam's face sound asleep. "Will he be awake anytime soon?"

"Couple hours, maybe." The first nurse smiles, turning to leave the room.

Lisa slides a chair next to the bed.

•

Not long after Lisa leaves Tom Schorr exits the room next to Sam's and takes the elevator to the ground floor. He walks out into the street to an old phone booth. He looks around, opens the door, and the booth light flickers on. The phone is antiquated, no video, perfect. He had left his encoded portable back at HQ and was worried about finding an old phone. With the right attachments, phones without video signal were actually more secure than any encoded wireless communications. The booth smells of rotting food. He unscrews the mouthpiece and inserts a small, black scrambler. He punches a code into the phone. The phone rings once and a cool, businesslike female voice picks up.

"Travel number?"

"Ten, twelve, sixty-five."

"Securing line. Please wait . . . line secure. Contact?"

"William K."

"Hold. Transferring the call."

There is a click on the line, the call being transferred.

"What's going on in the zoo?" a deep voice asks.

"The zoo is a zoo."

"I thought the situation was being contained."

"We need more room to maneuver." Schorr opens the phone booth door a crack to get fresh air.

"That's a negative."

"It's getting busy. Secondary targets have been mobile and have been contacted by the media. . . . And we have a leak."

"Christ."

"We think we know who it is."

"Just hold tight. I'll get back to you."

The line goes dead.

8

William Kane folds his portable phone and sits back in his chair. He stares out the bay window of his study, his daughter Elizabeth sitting at the edge of the heated pool tilted over a copy of *Seventeen,* enjoying the Indian summer October day. Off to the side the Redskins are driving for a score on the big-screen wall TV, but William Kane pays no attention. He has a previously scheduled debriefing with George Angelson, known affectionately around the office as "the old man," in two days but two days will be too long. The contact in New York had sounded uncharacteristically edgy, as though things needed to be fixed. Soon. William Kane, a man who has participated in many covert programs over the years, who has slipped out of countries under collapsing operations, eluding capture that would have meant certain slow and painful interrogation before death, feels a rising unease. His instincts tell him to move. The ball is too big. Elizabeth drops her magazine and lies back in the sun, not a care in the world. Kane picks up the portable phone and dials a number he does not want to dial.

A minute later, Martha, his wife, pops her head in.

"Okay to come back in?" she says, eyeing the portable phone on the desk that rarely rings.

William Kane nods.

"Isn't it great about the Skins?" Martha says.

He absently glances to the TV. "Marth, I gotta go to the office. Something's come up."

She nods, slightly frowning, another Sunday without her husband. She turns to pack him a sandwich for dinner and does not ask when he will be home.

The traffic is light on the highway and it takes William Kane less than a half hour to get on the exit ramp for Haddonfield, an exclusive suburb of the capital, vast, new houses built around golf courses. A list of the owners would read like a roster of who's who from the Washington power scene, if there were such a list.

An armed guard, six feet five inches of muscle with a Glock .44 semi-automatic strapped to his side, steps out of a spacious wooden hut at the gate to the old man's neighborhood and asks to see Kane's identification. Kane is on the list, his call to the old man an hour earlier making his arrival expected. The guard steps back into his building and pushes a button and a titanium-reinforced steel gate opens. Kane slowly swerves through large anti-terrorist cement blocks and heads into the neighborhood. The houses are mostly low-slung and long, set back from the road at the ends of long winding drives with few big trees. Another security measure.

Kane gets to the end of a cul-de-sac and turns up the gravel lane through another smaller steel gate, then drives between two perfect lines of dogwood trees. He pulls next to a Range Rover in front of a sprawling white-brick ranch house. The front door opens. George Angelson smiles a smile as if he has no worries in the world.

"William, let's take a walk," he says.

For a while they walk in silence. Kane waits for Angelson to take the lead, but Angelson seems content to follow a path through tall hedgerows without a word. They pass walled gardens, partially hidden fountains, and bronze statues posed behind closed wrought-iron gates. Kane studies the back of the large balding man in front of him, a man well into his sixties who moves better than a man in his forties, a man he knows little about, a man of tremendous power who very few people, outside of certain extremely small circles, have ever heard of.

Angelson steps out of the hedgerows and walks across a small field to a man-made pond. "I had carp put in this pond but they all died. Came out here to fish and found them floating." He turns to Kane. "We can talk here. I take it there are developments in the zoo."

"The program has a leak." Kane pauses, trying to gauge what the old man already knows. But the old man's expression is blank. Kane forges ahead. "We have another situation unrelated to the leak, things may need to be contained."

"Contained?"

"Cleaned up."

Angelson looks across the pond, the afternoon sun shimmering diamonds on the water, the day, the scene eminently peaceful, entirely pure and separate from the two men who talk of murder.

"Are these subjects truly a danger?"

"That's being evaluated. One was definitely compromised and the concern was that questions would be asked. Another subject met with media. Our contact has asked for leeway. Good opportunities may present themselves, it might be a good time to move. A preemptive strike, if you will."

Angelson looks thoughtfully at his hands and Kane notices that even for his relatively youthful appearance, the old man's hands, soft and unblemished, are bizarrely young, like a teenage boy's.

"Well," Angelson says, meeting Kane's eyes, "we don't normally correct what's not a problem."

"No, sir."

"I have no trouble loosening the reins. If things need to be done, then they need to be done. But let's look into it. Bottom line, the zoo must, of course, be kept clean."

There is a splash out in the middle of the pond and Kane catches the flash of a leaping fish in his peripheral vision.

"There's still one left," Angelson says.

9

Lisa Washington is trying to focus on what Tim Dimpter, the task commander, is saying, but all she can think about is Sam. It's been three hours since she left the hospital and she wouldn't even have come if she could have taken the day off but there were co-ordinated drug busts all over the city and everyone was needed. She, Mac, and eight other PEACE officers crouch behind a Dumpster outside a run-down warehouse.

She can tell Mac isn't in much better shape than she is. Normally so focused and calm, he keeps adjusting his night-vision goggles as though they won't fit right.

"Washington," Dimpter says, "I want you to take first lead. Wells, you're in second." Mac nods but Lisa doesn't respond right away, in her mind's eye an image of Sam all doped up.

"Washington, you got someplace else to be?" Dimpter hisses.

"No, sir."

"Good, you're the first one through the door. Got it?"

"Yes, sir."

"Okay. . . . People, let's take it to them." Dimpter raises his hand, then lets it fall and the unit is running toward two large sliding doors held together with an old rusty chain. The chain is cut and the unit pours into a dimly lit hallway. Muffled voices filter through a red metal door. Lisa lines up beside the door, feels the adrenaline rush, the surroundings, the slightest rustle of her clothing, coming into sharp focus. Mac is next to her, his breathing maintaining an easy, calm rhythm.

At the other end of the building at a huge fuse box a PEACE officer waits. Dimpter nods to the unit and everyone flips down their night-vision goggles. Dimpter counts a slow three with his hand in the air and gives a terse "*Go!*" into a radio to the officer at the fuse box who flips a row of switches, knocking out the lights of the entire warehouse. The unit bursts through the red door into a vast central room where eight men, who had just been closing the sale of twenty-five wooden crates of heroin, fumble to pull out their guns in the dark.

The PEACE unit unleashes a blaze of fire, Mac and Lisa go into a crouch next to each other, the world through their night-vision goggles bathed in an orange glow, laser sights from the other sleeper guns dancing thin red beams around the room, electrical bursts from the stun patches brilliantly lighting the air. Mac and Lisa fire at anything that moves and the suspects are put down with precision, two on the right, four on the left, and two behind a large table where, moments before, money was being counted and high-grade heroin sampled.

There is a pause. Slowly, carefully they rise. Suddenly there is a flash of movement behind the table. One of the downed suspects, playing possum on the floor, unleashes a barrage of automatic gunfire. Lisa hears the officer on the other side of her grunt and fall to the floor. As the unit scrambles for nonexistent cover, the suspect turns and runs up a set of stairs. Lisa, Mac, Dimpter, and three officers run to the foot of the steps. They snap air filters into place over their mouths and a tear gas canister is fired through the doorway to the next floor. Nothing happens. Lisa charges the stairs with Mac just behind, and bursts into a long empty hallway. The second floor is a warren of interconnected broken-down hallways and rooms. The sleepers gather at the entry and Dimpter splits them into three pairs with hand signals. Mac and Lisa are sent down a wide, pitch-black passage.

They search the rooms one by one, kicking open closets, picking their way through broken furniture and stacked wooden slats.

Lisa's breathing, loud and echoey through her air filter, is the only sound she can hear as she edges down the long hallway. The search seems endless, the air dark and tense. There is a sound behind her and she whips around, dropping to a knee, her gun aimed. Mac reacts too, but it is only a rat dragging the sole of a shoe. Lisa sighs, relaxing. A floorboard creaks behind her. Both she and Mac freeze. There is the sound of a gun clicking and in one movement Lisa drops behind a box and Mac dives to the side as bullets shred the floor between them.

Lisa is protected but Mac lands hard, unable to break his fall, his night-vision goggles shoved down on his chin so he can only see out part of one lens, a shadowy momentary image, orange and grainy, of what looks like a uniformed PEACE officer disappearing down the hall.

He pulls on his goggles and the image is gone.

10

The hospital room is dark, the curtains drawn. Sam lies in bed, groggy and sweating, and slowly rubs his hand back and forth against the sharp metal edge on the back of the bed to stay conscious. He looks at the clock but the numbers are blurry. There is a flash of light for a moment in the mirror and Sam is careful to keep his hand moving beneath the covers where it will not be seen.

Hours pass. Though his body is sluggish, Sam's mind is becoming clearer; he knows what he must do when the male nurse who is not a nurse comes. As if in answer to his thoughts a beam of light shoots from the hallway as the door opens and Sam closes his eyes, pretending to sleep. Without turning on the light the male nurse comes to the side of the bed and begins preparing the injection.

"Just one more shot, my friend." The male nurse lifts the syringe to the light of the doorway then begins to lower it to Sam's arm.

Sam grabs the man's wrist. He pulls him forward onto the bed, the needle hovering between them, glancing off Sam's skin. Sam yanks the man's hand over the side of the bed and they roll onto the floor, Sam landing on top of the man, the man grunting as the wind is knocked from his lungs and a rib cracks in his chest. Sam edges the needle closer and closer to the man's neck. The man headbutts Sam, dark and white squares filling Sam's eyes, his hands reaching out wildly, grabbing a lamp from the table. He feels the needle jab into his shoulder and slams the lamp down on the man's forehead, knocking him out. He pulls out the half-injected syringe from his shoulder.

Sam groggily enters the hallway in the man's white shirt and pants. They are two sizes too small. The female desk nurse reads a paperback.

Sam walks past, in his peripheral vision seeing the nurse look up, her expression dimming. He turns back to her as she is punching a button on her phone. He rips the phone from the wall.

"Mr. Mullane, we're only trying to help you."

Sam squelches the urge to punch her in the head and turns toward the stairs.

From a side hallway the other male nurse steps out in front of Sam.

"Mr. Mullane, just go back to your room."

"I have enough poison in me, thanks."

The door to the stairs is a few feet beyond the male nurse. Sam steps toward the nurse and the nurse pulls a small stun prod from his pocket and goes into the crouch of someone trained in the martial arts. Sam grimly smiles. This is no nurse.

The man lunges but Sam is ready. He dodges to the side, clamps on the man's arm, and delivers two punches to the side of the man's head. The man drops to his knees then falls forward onto the stun prod. The electrical screech continues for a few seconds as the man's body bounces and vibrates. The smell of burning cloth and flesh fills the air.

Sam leans dizzily against the wall, the floor is rocking, the deck of a ship. Behind the buzz of the overhead fluorescent lights there is a whispering sound, running water, a group of children telling secrets. Sam struggles to the stairs. He just needs to make it to a phone and call Mac. He wavers at the top of the landing, the metal-edged steps heaving in front of him and for the first time he is not sure he will make it. Something is not right inside him, he can feel the drug they've given him making his heart heavy, his breathing tight, there is a pain in his arm. Vaguely he hears the sound of a door opening and closing behind him. He thinks of Lisa and takes the first step but tilts backward, bumping into something soft just behind him. He feels two things like hands on his back, an angel's hands to steady him, but then the hands shove him forward, or maybe he just loses his balance, and he knows it's going to be a bad fall. He wants to put out his hands to catch the railing, to block the floor, but they just won't work and he falls headfirst down the full flight of stairs.

There is no pain. He can feel himself blinking and something wet coming out of his mouth. He thinks of Lisa and tears fill his eyes.

A pair of small nurse's feet step down into his line of sight. Then everything goes dark.

Mac sits at his dining room table, staring forward, seeing nothing. Twenty-five years he's known Sam. It was Sam, bigger and a natural fighter, who protected him from bullies in the neighborhood when they were kids; Sam who always used connections in the NYPD to keep them together; Sam who was the witness before the justice of the peace when Mac and Eve got married; Sam who was inconsolable at Mac's mother's and father's funerals.

Sam who was found with a broken neck at the bottom of a hospital stairwell.

Mac feels an awkward turning, a thickness in his chest. He keeps going over the events that led to Sam's death, examining the sequence. But each time he replays the sequence the image that freezes in his mind is the instant Sam was struck by the patch. If he hadn't shot Sam on the subway Sam would still be alive.

Eve comes in with a plate of food. Mac feels her hands on his arm.

"It must have been the drugs the hospital gave him, Mac, for him to talk that way, to fall like that." Eve reaches around and hugs him, used tissues in her hand.

Mac turns to her and looks up into her eyes, which are red and puffy. She sits next to him and the turning awkwardness inside him turns too far, snapping, a heat releasing.

"He was like a brother," he says, the heat in his chest rising, filling him until there is no more room. He buries his face into Eve's neck.

In the middle of the night Mac finally gives up trying to sleep. He slips out of bed, dresses, and goes out for a drive. Sam's death makes no sense. Driving through the peaceful, puddle-strewn streets, it seems some unreal nightmare, something that when he returns home won't have happened.

Earlier that day with rain coming down in torrents he brought Lisa home from the morgue. They sat in front of her mother's place, a tidy Brooklyn row house, and Lisa did not cry. Her expression frozen, lifeless, she stared out the windshield, rainwater pouring down the glass, streaking her face.

"You knew we were together?" she said, her voice flat.

"I figured it out yesterday," Mac felt numb to the bone, barely able to speak.

"We were going to get married. He hadn't asked me yet but he was going to."

Mac looked at her and she had the briefest glimmer of a smile. Then the smile evaporated and her face turned vacant again.

"I had this strange feeling at the hospital this morning," she said.

"What do you mean?"

"I thought I heard Sam calling for help."

"Was he?"

"No. It was just my imagination. Weird though, for it to happen the same day."

They sat for a long time in silence, unable to talk anymore, neither of them able to get their minds around what had happened.

When Lisa's mother stepped out onto the porch, Mac opened Lisa's door and walked her through the rain. Though the downpour was thick and blowing onto the porch, Lisa's mother didn't make a move to go inside. She opened her arms and Mac watched Lisa put her head onto her mother's shoulder and dissolve, her back heaving, her fists clenching and unclenching behind her mother as though reaching for something she would never hold again.

Mac drives for hours until at dawn he finds himself parked out front of Sam's dark and empty house. The nightmare is real. He slips the key in the lock and the door creaks, pierces the stillness. He enters slowly, hesitantly, and flicks on a light. At the end of the hall hangs a board full of tacked pictures: Sam on an outcropping of rock hiking somewhere in the Appalachians; Sam at home plate during a softball game predicting a homerun like Babe Ruth; Sam, Lisa, and Mac in undercover outfits at the precinct; and an old picture of Sam with his arm around his mother. Mac untacks the picture of Sam and his mother.

In the living room the big-screen TV Sam had been so proud to win a few months before in a precinct raffle sits in the corner. On a side table a huge mug with BIG KAHUNA on the side still contains stale beer. Mac turns toward the kitchen and for the first time notices a stream of light from under the door. He pushes open the swinging door. A box of donuts from the softball game is open and on its side on the kitchen table. A half-eaten powdered donut lies near the edge of the table. A sound comes from inside the pantry and Mac turns. The door is ajar. Mac unholsters his tranq-gun, clicks off the safety. He flicks open the door and crouched in the dark is the fat press guy that pestered him at the park.

"*Out!*" Mac wants the fat guy to swing at him. "Out, you fat sonofa—"

"Okay, okay, take it easy." Salmon struggles to get to his feet, the pain in his knees obvious. Powdered sugar rings his mouth. He has a donut in one hand.

"Sit!" Mac motions the fat press guy to the table.

Salmon sits.

"Name's Marty Salmon, remember? I'm in the press."

"Why are you eating Sam's donuts?"

"What do you care? They aren't fresh."

Mac considers smacking the guy in the head with the pistol handle for being in Sam's house. He settles for jamming the gun hard into the fat man's stomach.

"I'll say it slowly so you can understand. What—are—you—doing—here?"

Salmon glances at the gun pushed into the folds of his mid-section and looks into Mac's eyes.

"You want to arrest me, fine. I'm not telling you jack squat till you back off."

Mac pauses, staring into Salmon's bloodshot weasel-like eyes. He pulls the gun back, sits on the other side of the table, and slowly sheathes it. Salmon begins to eat the donut in his hand.

"I eat when I'm nervous. Actually, I eat all the time."

Mac looks at Salmon as though he might kill him. Salmon gets the message.

"The problem is, I don't know what side you're on."

"Side?"

Salmon starts to speak, then pauses, sizing Mac up.

"I got a call . . ."

"A call?"

"A tip that something's rotten in the sleeper corps."

"Someone's pulling your chain," Mac says, irritated. "Guys like you think JFK was wiped out by Jacqueline."

"Kennedy was assassinated. So was Sam Mullane."

Mac looks hard at Salmon. Ever since he got word of Sam's "accident" his brain has been filled with details that don't make sense: Sam at the bottom of the stairs with his gown on inside out, the desk nurse telling detectives she never saw Sam pass her desk. But bizarre accidents often left questions, threads of story that would never lead anywhere, riddles that could never be deciphered.

Salmon pulls out a small beat-up pad. He jots something at the bottom of a page full of notes. Mac sees the word *Birdie* underlined three times at the top of the pad, question marks encircling it.

The sound of a car pulling up comes from outside. Salmon turns toward the front of the house.

"I've been followed since the day I talked to you at Central Park."

Mac frowns at Salmon and Salmon shrugs.

"Stay!" he says to Salmon. He goes to the front of the house. A Chrysler Sebring with tinted windows is parked on the other side of the street. A light flashes through the driver's side window.

Mac eases out the front door and down the sidewalk, unbuttoning his holster, taking out his badge.

Inside, Salmon moves to the front of the house and watches Mac out a window.

When Mac gets within ten feet of the Chrysler it pulls away quickly.

Salmon watches Mac try to make out the receding plates of the car in the dark. Nothing conclusive, but probably Wells isn't on their side.

Mac heads back into the house, thinking of the brief retreating image of the PEACE officer he had seen at the warehouse. Maybe it wasn't, as he decided earlier, just a trick of the lighting.

When he enters the kitchen Salmon and the donuts are gone.

(12)

Late morning. Across the street from O'Malley's, a bar near PEACE HQ, Mac sits on a wet bench and waits. The day is gray and damp but the sun is burning it off. People hurry along on their lunch breaks, heading out for food, doing errands, the daily tasks, and Mac feels separated from them, unstuck from the day. Twenty-four hours before, Sam was still alive.

Above Mac's head on a telephone pole one of DADD's cameras slowly pivots inside its opaque protective Plexiglas bubble in silence, taking in the street. In his mind Mac replays the part of the drug bust when he and Lisa came under fire, the image vague and skewed at best, half-blocked by the thick lip of his goggles.

Across the street Potesky turns the corner. Among the crowds he looks pale and anonymous. He stops and looks in an electronics store window. Mac notices a man in a long gray raincoat looking in a bakery window twenty feet behind Potesky. The man keeps glancing in Potesky's direction. When Potesky starts toward O'Malley's the man starts forward also. But when Potesky enters O'Malley's the man walks past without stopping. Mac watches the man fade into the crowds up the street.

Mac crosses the street to the bar.

O'Malley's does a thriving lunch-hour business; waitresses hurry to and fro with sandwiches, baskets of fries, and salads. Potesky is sitting alone in his usual spot at the back of the room. Mac picks up two beers at the bar and walks back to Potesky's table. Potesky looks up.

"I'm so sorry, Mac."

"You alone?"

"Yeah, yeah. Sit."

Mac sits and slides the beer to Potesky. They each take a sip. Potesky looks into his glass.

"The good stuff."

"Sam drank it."

"To Sam."

"To Sam." They clink glasses.

Potesky looks into his beer. After a while he looks up at Mac. "What's that place you and Eve went years ago?"

"Bar Harbor, Maine, on our honeymoon."

"Maine, right. You oughta take a week or two off. Take Eve to Maine. Get outta this place for a while. You're gonna be deskbound for at least a month anyway. Standard protocol you lose a partner." Potesky takes a long draught of beer.

"You know Sam had his gown on inside out."

Potesky looks at Mac, his eyes even. "There's nothing there, Mac. I went over it with a fine-tooth comb myself. Just a crazy thing, the whole mess." Potesky takes a handful of pretzels and pushes the bowl toward Mac. Mac takes a breath, comes to a decision.

"You read the report on the heroin bust?"

"Yeah, good work."

"Lisa and I came under fire and it seemed like maybe it was friendly."

"Meaning what?" Potesky is suddenly attentive.

"Meaning maybe I saw another PEACE officer take a shot at us."

"Did you or not?"

"I don't know."

"Mac, no way one of our people fired on you, you all had goggles on. It's not like the perps were wearin' clothes that looked like PEACE uniforms." Potesky is implacable, his tone dismissive. He leans forward. "You got time coming up, right? Get outta town and relax. Sam's accident is getting to you." Potesky finishes off his beer and Mac watches him, a solid guy, a guy he has known more than nine years and suddenly Mac's suspicions seem like deranged fantasies, his meeting with Salmon a bad dream.

"You know," Potesky is saying, motioning to a waitress, "soon we're all gonna be dinosaurs. Grids and computers need technicians, not cops. I'm gonna take early retirement next year, maybe sail the boat down the coast. . . ."

"Thought you were a lifer," Mac says, surprised. He lowers his voice. "You gonna take that woman, sail off into the sunset?"

Potesky looks around as if Mac has shouted his question to the entire room. "You're the only one knows about her. . . ."

"Mum's the word, Dan. You never said anything before about bowing out your first year eligible."

Potesky's face seems suddenly puffy, deeply lined, and tired in every sense of the word.

"You get put in an office, Mac, and the shit pours in so thick you can't shovel fast enough. It's up around my neck now." Potesky looks at Mac in a meaningful way but Mac doesn't know what he means. Then abruptly Potesky's again trying to get the waitress's attention, as if his life depended on it.

Early afternoon. Lieutenant Dan Potesky steps out of O'Malley's into the sun. He is drunk but after years of drinking hides it well.

Potesky starts to walk back toward the PEACE HQ, hoping fresh air will change his mood, turned dark since talking to Mac. Sam's death, the whole mess a bad business, and he can tell Mac won't let it go. He knows Mac's instincts, his determination won't allow him to stop until he has an answer. Since the moment the call came through from the hospital, Potesky has felt like a building has been collapsing on top of him, floor by floor. The sun and walk aren't helping.

A limo pulls up along the curb and the rear window lowers. John Codd sticks his head out.

"Dan, get in."

Potesky almost flinches. The building above him sways. The door opens and he slides in, looks at all the gadgets and runs his hand along the soft leather seat.

"You swipe this from the mayor?"

Codd doesn't say anything but presses a button and a tinted window silently rises, separating them from the driver. Codd takes a white handkerchief from his pocket and presses it to his nose. Potesky notices the handkerchief is silk.

"Someone's leaking to the press. They're saying it's one of us."

"Just what we need." Potesky looks Codd in the eye; Codd seems on edge. "You're not worried?"

"We have to be careful."

"Of course." Potesky looks out the window at a group of little boys fighting over a broken hockey stick, pulling it this way and that.

Codd stares at Potesky a few moments, measuring his words.

"Dan, I know you've been unhappy with this system."

Potesky turns back. "What's that supposed to mean?"

"Nothing. Just, at this juncture, we have to be careful."

"If you're gonna say something, say it."

Codd reaches over, pats Potesky's arm. "It's nothing personal. I have to ask around. It's just . . . it's shaken some people up, what happened with Sam Mullane."

"Christ, it's shaken me up."

Codd looks over and Potesky can feel him examining him. Potesky looks out the window and watches Mac leave O'Malley's and walk up the street.

More floors crash down.

13

The late afternoon sun has disappeared behind clouds, turning everything gray at the Bronx Zoo. The zoo was full of schoolkids before, but they have left and the zoo is largely empty. Marty Salmon arrived early to get the lay of the land, to scout exits, ways of escape. He checks his watch, twenty minutes to go. He heads back into the Trump Building for night creatures to do one more run-through.

Stepping inside the main doors is like stepping into a cave, the black lights along the ceiling illuminating the walkways but keeping the entire area suitably dim. Salmon can see why Birdie picked this place for their meeting but it gives him the creeps. He has always hated zoos; the idea that humans put animals in cages to preserve their existence is unbelievable. Even when he was little and his mom insisted on dragging him to the Central Park Zoo Salmon had hated it, watching the bears stalk back and forth in their enclosure, their eyes fixed on the people looking back through the bars.

He remembered a tiger at the zoo, a rare one, one of a hundred or so of its kind left in the world. A groove had been worn a half a foot down into a slab of rock from the tiger's pacing over the years. To Salmon that animal seemed as though it were grieving. Better to die in the wild from a poacher seeking its hide than to spend its life in jail, an exhibit. He remembered when he was in high school and he had read in the paper that the tiger had finally died, that the zoo surgeons had tried to keep it alive but it had died on the table. For years the tiger's health had been declining. Tigers were supposed to live to be a lot older than this one had but Salmon was surprised the tiger had lasted so long. Perhaps it harbored a small hope of escape or had waited for the opportunity of taking out a keeper, dragging a small child through the bars, the feeling of a fresh kill. Probably it just paced, its mind numb until in the end its heart failed. Salmon was so angry he wrote a piece for the school newspaper. It was his first article.

Behind the floor-to-ceiling Plexiglas the African bats are darting in a frenzy, swooping and changing direction so that they don't look so much like they are flying as falling, dropping in every direction. Salmon hates bats. He has read how they are beneficial, how they are misunderstood just like sharks. He hates sharks too. He walks along the corridors, stopping for a moment at an exhibit of snakes, two snakes intertwined in a tight spiral rolling around in what looks like a death struggle. The snakes have a cream-colored covering over their eyes and it occurs to Salmon they are having sex. He does not bend to read the card about the snakes but continues on. The fact that snakes have no hands and feet, that they are one long undulating muscle, upsets some standard of design to Salmon's way of thinking. He dislikes them even more than sharks and bats.

He stops at a dim corridor that leads thirty yards to an emergency exit and for the second time marks the spot in his mind. He traces his steps back but the bats have disappeared up into their perches along the roof of their enclosure. Two tourists, a middle-aged Asian man and woman, stop to look at the inactivity of the bats. The man points to the ceiling and begins to speak in a language that sounds like Japanese. The woman asks a question and the man flaps his arm. They move on. Salmon shifts his weight from foot to foot, regretting his decision not to use the bathroom he saw down the hall. He looks at his watch and his hand trembles. His contact, his informer, is a few minutes late.

He could go for the emergency exit, just beat it from this dark, desolate place, just be home with a large pizza and a ball game on the tube.

But he needs a story. Badly. And any kind of cover-up in PEACE would be hot, would get him back in the fold. Very hot, very back in the fold. Five years of chasing gossip and writing fluff pieces, not knowing where the next check would come from, would fade like a bad dream. He would have redemption. Christ, the gutless editors at the paper, living proof that everyone can be gotten to, said his production was slow, that he was chasing conspiracy fantasies, that he was paranoid. But it was punishment for getting too close, for playing his own game, for not letting a story, a substantial story, disappear. A story he simply walked into. Just fate.

Five years before to the month he had stood outside a midtown bar, a decently rising reporter with reasonable expectations of some fair scoops, with dreams of a down-the-road book deal, debating whether he had time to go in and get some lunch and still make some crappy assignment downtown. He had this feeling that he should go downtown, that he should ignore the siren voice of his appetite that was calling for a turkey club and fries, but instead thumbed his nose at intuition and went into the bar.

Halfway into the turkey club, a man had come into the bar and sat one stool away. The man was neatly dressed, gray-haired with a crisp military-style haircut, and had obviously been drinking all morning. The man kept rubbing his eyes, which were full of water. He turned to Salmon.

"What business you in?"

"Insurance," Salmon lied without hesitation.

"Well . . . that's a pretty stable life . . ."

The man rambled on and on like a speaking autobiography, starting with his childhood, blah blah blah. Salmon only half listened to how the man had been dumped into a military academy for accidentally burning down a barn full of animals when he was thirteen, how that led to the naval academy and then to Vietnam. Salmon was watching a talk show about men and women transsexuals who had gotten married. Then the man mentioned drugs. Salmon turned away from the TV.

"That's when the drug running got started, or anyway when I got involved. I was recruited a few months after I got into Nam . . ." The man looked over. "Say, what'd you say you do for a living?"

Salmon ordered the next round of drinks. The man went on and on, drug running with the CIA through Laos and Cambodia, then later through Nicaragua and countless other countries, a highly organized cartel within the military, dealing to its own soldiers. Salmon's microrecorder was taping in his breast pocket from the first mention of drugs. Then the man announced he had to go. Salmon tried to stop him, got his name and address and asked the man if he would ever consider going on the record with his story. The man stepped back as if someone had hit him in the face. He looked Salmon up and down and hurried out the door. Salmon followed but lost him in the crowd.

Later that day Salmon tried to track the man down but the address was bogus. There was no record of the man's name in the military. Salmon dug for weeks and turned up a few articles about drug dealing on bases in Germany. Though none of the articles even hinted at the scale of drug dealing his barmate had referred to, one mentioned a suspicious suicide. Digging further, Salmon found a string of suspicious military "suicides" and "accidental deaths" dating back to the late sixties. Not unusual in an organization the size of the U.S. Armed Forces to have unexplained deaths. But among these files he found a colonel, much decorated for his service during Vietnam, who was discovered hanging in his New York City hotel room. The photo enclosed was of the man Salmon had met in the bar.

For a few months that was it. Then the call came. Someone wanted to meet him to talk at a small motel forty-five minutes outside Fort Carter, Georgia. Salmon got to the motel early and went across the street to a diner to get something to eat. Again, food and fate were linked. While on his second piece of key lime pie a maid entered his motel room and it exploded.

The whole way back to New York, Salmon looked over his shoulder. Within days he was fired.

At the sound of feet approaching on the carpet Salmon slips his hand in his pocket around his .38. A young, attractive dark-haired woman walks by and Salmon lets go of his gun. He checks his watch.

"Where's Hal Holbrook when you need him," he mutters, his voice louder than he intended it to be.

Something drops, a thing soft and heavy back toward the main corridor and Salmon whips around.

"Birdie?" Salmon whispers.

A cleaning man appears out of the gloom pushing a cart. He walks slowly by. A group of teenagers, shoving one another and laughing, stops to look at the bats. The area, deserted a moment ago, is suddenly very congested. Salmon feels the end of a gun pressed hard into his back.

"Take your hand slowly out of your pocket," the voice, gravelly, says from behind him. Salmon lets his hand fall to his side.

"This is no good here," the voice says, the accent north Jersey, maybe some Long Island. "I wanted to talk to you but there are too many people around." The person behind him clears his throat. "In an hour I'll have something to help you. At the southeast corner of Forty-second and Sixth the phone will ring. Answer it."

The pressure against his back releases and Salmon hears someone walking away.

Salmon heads in the other direction, then jogs to the emergency door, setting off a small alarm when he opens it.

(14)

Queens. A narrow tree-covered street.

Mac hasn't seen Sam's mother since she moved while he was in college. He walks up the front steps to the small two-story house in need of a fresh coat of paint and raps the big brass knocker. The door opens immediately and an old face appears in the crack.

"Yes?"

"Mrs. Mullane, it's Mac Wells."

"Mac. C'mon in."

A red-faced man, a smaller stockier version of Sam, whom Mac recognizes as Sam's older brother, Pat, opens the door wide from behind Mrs. Mullane and suspiciously eyes Mac up and down.

"Hello, Mac." His voice is gruff.

"Patrick, be a good boy and get us some tea," Mrs. Mullane says, gesturing toward the kitchen.

The house's interior is full of photographs and religious icons; color photos of Sam and his siblings in grade school next to Jesus bleeding from the cross.

Mac sits on a worn red antique love seat in the living room. Sam's mother talks continuously, a nervous chatter, about when Sam and Mac were boys. In the light Mac can see her eyes are rimmed with red.

"Sam and I weren't much in touch lately," Mrs. Mullane is saying. "Things get in between people. You know?"

"I know," Mac says.

"But then they're so small once . . . you lose someone."

Mac can see the old woman's eyes are beginning to tear.

"You ever meet this colored girl he was dating? She a nice girl?"

"A very nice girl."

Mrs. Mullane looks at Mac, unsure. "I don't know. I guess the world has changed so much since I was a young woman."

Mac wants to say the right thing. Mrs. Mullane looks beaten down, as if Sam's death is just the final blow in a long series. He remembers the photograph in his pocket and pulls it out, handing it to the old woman. "Sam had this up in the hallway." Sam's mother looks at the photo, her face quivering, about to lose her composure. Pat comes in with tea.

"Two sleepers were here already," he says, the same gruff voice as at the door.

"Here?"

"Wouldn't even show me ID. Sat parked out front for hours before I got here. Scared Mom. Asked questions about whether or not Sam 'drank often'. . . ."

"Now Patrick." Mrs. Mullane turns to Mac. "We also had a visit from a very nice heavy fellow."

"With a limp?"

"Yes, poor man. Told me how he got that in Harlem on a mission with Sammy. He brought flowers." She motions to a vase of flowers. "Said Sammy saved his life once."

Sam's mother pours out her memories of Sam for an hour;

Mac tells her stories and details about Sam's life in the city for a while and she seems to appreciate them a great deal, as though she is learning about his world there for the first time. Then it is time to leave and Mac is glad to go. Being around Sam's mother makes him feel worse, even more responsible for Sam's death.

The green landscape gradually turns to bricks and cement as Mac gets closer to the city.

He looks in the rearview and notices a Mercury Cougar a few car-lengths back.

Swinging onto the FDR Drive, Mac looks in the rearview and the Cougar is still there. He switches lanes.

The Cougar switches lanes.

Mac turns the wheel hard right, pulling the car from the left lane onto an off-ramp into East Harlem. He speeds ahead to a stoplight and turns in his seat to look back at the off-ramp.

No Cougar.

The light changes and Mac pulls ahead.

15

William Kane unlocks one of the fireproof file cabinets in his office, a sparse room, a computer he never uses on a desk that is empty except for a small American flag on the corner. A paper shredder is pushed against the wall on a stand above a large plastic-lined trash can. No photographs, no personal effects.

Kane sits down behind his desk and flips through the folder to the report on Mac Wells's subway incident from a few days before. The fax machine beeps and Kane punches in his personal identification number to release the incoming file. A fax detailing all subsequent contacts and related events since the subway incident emerges.

A few more weeks and all the headaches, the worries, the vast amount of details will be someone else's to fret about, someone else's ball to keep in the air. President Harris must get reelected first. Without Harris in office the future of PEACE became less certain. When the election was secured and the project safe, Kane would take early retirement, perhaps a job teaching one history class a year at some top-flight university, with a little recruiting and consulting his only real duties until Elizabeth heads off to college.

Then, perhaps, he'll leave the "life" altogether, traveling with Martha, playing golf and the stock market with the substantial nest egg accrued in two South American countries years before, the accounts Martha doesn't even know about.

Just one more program to run successfully, the largest and most important of his career, and Kane will go out on top. He smiles to himself. The fax stops with a soft beep and Kane scans the material. His smile disappears. The shredder slices the fax into countless pieces.

Kane walks down one of fifteen sterile, central hallways in the vast main complex of a government agency in rural Virginia, one hour outside the capital; an agency not mentioned in the official government budget. Kane turns a corner into another long hallway. Angelson had been cautious: allow the people in place to respond decisively if necessary but, short of that, check things out, follow guidelines, pursue inquiry and surveillance. If the inquiry turned up what Kane thought it would, well . . . things would be done immediately, conclusively.

The project would remain a tight ship. Kane was picked to run the day-to-day operations because of his reputation for running near-perfect programs, because of his need for all operations to be clean and efficient. Mess bothers him and the idea that there might be complications, even a leak, up in New York unsettles him, as though his perfectly shined black wing tips have just stepped in something unpleasant.

Kane taps in his six-number security clearance on a keypad at an unmarked door. A computer asks him for a voice sample and Kane speaks his voice ID code, "ESAC one." A square white plate in the wall glows to life with an orange light. Following the computer's instructions, Kane places his hand on the plate and his palm is washed in the scanner's light. The door silently slides open. Kane walks into a room with two armed guards sitting behind a desk. One of the men holds out an electronic clipboard and

Kane dips the metal edge of his ID card into a slot at the bottom of the board. His name and the time of his visit is electronically recorded.

"Thank you, sir," the guard says. Another door slides open and Kane steps into a huge room with a house-size computer at its center, a room that intercepts telecommunications from around the world. At desks radiating in concentric circles back from the computer, hundreds and hundreds of technicians sit at consoles and wear light headphones. Kane walks up to a man sitting at a large keyboard terminal near the center of the room.

"I have a priority buzzword watch list."

"Go ahead, sir."

"Rhine Corporation space, PEACE space, Sleepers space, Mac Wells space, Eve Wells space, Martin or Marty Salmon space, Sam Mullane space, Lisa Washington space. End."

The man types the buzzwords into his keyboard.

"Done, sir."

"Reports every half hour to my office."

William Kane walks back to his office, the thick carpet absorbing his footsteps, as though even the sound of his shoes gives away too much.

16

Marty Salmon sits on a bus stop bench at the corner of Forty-second Street and Sixth Avenue. A chili dog with sauerkraut and cheese is coming apart in his hands. Two wrappers from previous chili dogs blow onto the ground from the bench. Salmon never takes his eye off the pay phone ten feet across the sidewalk. In fifteen minutes a handful of people have used it, and now a reasonably attractive woman, who was once much more attractive, long thin legs rising into a painted-on leather miniskirt, steps up to the phone and begins to make a call. She fumbles for a piece of paper from a large leather shoulder bag and then turns toward the phone so Salmon can't see what she's doing.

Salmon finishes off the chili dog, staring at the woman's perfect hips. It's five minutes till Birdie said to pick up the phone. The woman hangs up and saunters away and Salmon watches her, imagining things that will never happen.

"Hey, mister."

Salmon turns and a little tan-skinned boy is holding out a crumpled cardboard box of candy bars.

"Want to buy a candy bar? Only two bucks. It's for my school."

"I'm full. You'll have to get me next time."

"It's your civic duty." The kid flashes a smile a mile wide and Salmon fishes in his pocket for two dollars, handing the crumpled money to the boy.

"Thanks." The boy flips the chocolate bar into Salmon's hands and walks away.

The phone rings and Salmon is like a charging bull toward it, cutting off a teenage girl.

"Hello."

"This Salmon?" A high-pitched woman's voice.

At this moment, at the word *Salmon,* two hundred sixty miles away at William Kane's place of business, the massive computer, which simultaneously scans many tens of thousands of phone calls a second, bumps Salmon's call up to a human operator and automatically begins to record.

The sound of traffic and a passing siren echo over the line. Salmon hears the same siren a few blocks away. They are nearby.

"Where's Birdie?"

"Uh, it's gotten hot for Birdie. I'm his voice now. . . ."

Salmon sees his candy bar salesman down the street talking to two men in suits, one of the men motioning the kid into a gray four-door car with its door open. The kid takes off down the sidewalk and the men jump into the car. Salmon reaches into his pocket and opens the candy bar but it's just a wrapper and chocolate.

"And he wants to know—"

"Uh, look . . ." Salmon looks around to see if someone is staking him out, but there are too many people to pick anyone. "I'm in a tight spot. I gotta move. He said he would have something for me."

There is the sound of muffled voices, a woman's and a man's, conferring. "Check behind the phone." The phone line goes dead.

Salmon pretends he is still talking, and as inconspicuously as possible, using his bulk to cover the phone, he feels between the phone and the Plexiglas housing around it. His hand comes out with a few sheets of paper folded into a small square. He stuffs the paper into his pants and hangs up the phone.

A few blocks away a middle-aged man and a woman with long legs that rise into a painted-on leather miniskirt walk away from a pay phone. They walk hurriedly, the man looking around, until a few blocks later, they slow to a normal pace along a line of small restaurants. The woman turns to the man.

"So. We gonna get some dinner now?"

"In a bit, Ruth. In a bit."

As they walk up the street Dan Potesky glances at the reflection of every store window to see if they are being followed.

Marty Salmon takes a cab to the Plaza Hotel, walks through the front door past the well-heeled guests, the impeccably uniformed staff, then out the side entrance into another cab. He takes this cab up to Riverside Drive where he has the cab park and wait. No following car shows.

Salmon gets out and walks to his car, a beat-up Pinto jammed into an impossibly small space. He slides his bulk into the front bucket seat. Plastic army men litter the dashboard and a Barney doll with a noose around its neck swings gently from the rearview mirror. Salmon pulls the papers from inside his pants. He unfolds them and glances at the first page, alphabetized names and addresses of people in and around New York.

Salmon's doorman, a middle-aged guy with a pile of papers in his lap, looks at Mac's PEACE credential, then gestures toward the elevator. Mac pushes the number for Salmon's floor. The fact that PEACE sent some officers up to Sam's mother's house isn't that surprising. Just covering all the bases, watching out for lawsuits, bad press. Typical stuff. And the inconsistencies at the hospital could easily be the same thing.

Maybe Eve is right about Maine. It won't ever be the same with Sam gone.

The elevator doors open and Mac walks to Salmon's door, 7E, and knocks. There is the sound of movement, of someone leaning to the door, looking through the eyepiece.

"You alone, Wells?" Salmon's voice is muffled through the door.

"No, I brought Sirhan Sirhan."

A series of locks unlock and bolts slide. The door swings open and Salmon moves back from the door. Mac steps inside and Salmon quickly shuts the door. Mac watches Salmon turn two massive locks and slide two thick heavy bolts into place. The door and the door frame are metal.

"Afraid of burglars?" Mac asks.

"Nope. Someone tried to blow me up once."

"Didn't know Sam saved your life."

Salmon smiles a little.

On the TV, a short piece of the promo film for the PEACE system is being shown as a commercial, a phony PEACE officer apprehending a thug. Salmon glances over and snaps up the remote, raising the volume. A smooth deep-voiced narrator begins to speak.

"Across the country, violent crime is on the rise. The Rhine PEACE System can be a turning point in the war on this scourge that is rotting our society's foundations."

The words SURVEILLANCE, PROTECTION, PREVENTION flash across the TV.

"Implementing the system in metropolitan areas across the country will make crime the exception rather than the rule. Call 1-800-NO-CRIME for further information. Take back your town, your neighborhood, your home."

The local news comes back on and Salmon clicks off the TV.

"Pretty slick." Salmon turns and drops the remote into a pile of clothes and Mac sees the butt of a gun handle sticking out of his jacket pocket.

"So. You being followed yet, Wells?"

"I don't know." Mac doesn't mention the Cougar.

"Oh, by now, definitely. Probably since that day I introduced myself to you out in the park."

Mac wants Salmon to stop throwing around cloak and dagger crap. "Marty, look, the fact is I fucked up on the subway—"

"Hold that thought." Salmon puts his finger to his lips and motions Mac toward a square tentlike structure.

"What is this, a portable shower?"

"Step inside, then we can talk. It keeps what we say private."

Mac sighs and reluctantly steps inside the fabric doorway which leads to a five-by-five square area. The roof, made of the same heavy gray fabric, just clears his head. Salmon steps in after Mac and closes the flap. He flips a switch and a fan in the fabric wall at Mac's feet begins to draw air from the apartment into the space.

"Let me guess, you were in the Boy Scouts and it was the best time of your life."

"No this is a TI-seven, an RF shielded enclosure."

"And?"

"It was originally designed to attenuate emanating signals from PCs and any other type of information equipment, but this one protects our voices as well."

"You think someone is trying to listen to us?"

"I know someone is."

"Why?"

"I don't know that yet."

"Look, I'm here because I feel bad about my friend's death and I want to come clean. There's no conspiracy—it's my fault Sam ended up in the hospital and it was an accident he fell down the stairs. All the stuff since then is just spin control, nothing more."

Salmon doesn't bat an eye and even smiles a little. Wells's demeanor is so sincere. He's the kind of guy who toes the company line but believes in what he is doing, in justice. Kind of touching. If Wells is a plant, Salmon will give up pizza. Things are stalled and Wells might be useful; he decides to bring Wells in. Salmon leans forward. "The fact is I've been contacted now two times by someone in your department."

"Who?"

"Don't know. Someone, I'm guessing high up. This guy's

feeding me stuff, I don't know what the hell it is. But it's something big, something that scares this informant shitless, and not about losin' his pension."

"That could be anyone."

"No, I had him confirm things about PEACE that never've been published."

"Like what?"

"I can't reveal that."

"This is bullshit."

"Listen, on the pay phone today this guy, my informant, is so close to the coals he used this chick to be his mouthpiece. I mean, legs to the moon and a short-as-it-can-go leather miniskirt, a professional. . . ."

Mac has a flash of the tall attractive woman with too much makeup Dan Potesky's been clandestinely meeting for years. He frowns as if he is bored. "You saw this woman?"

"Yeah."

"What color was her hair."

"She was wearing a black wig."

Potesky's woman wore a black wig the time Mac came across them in a restaurant, stumbling in on Potesky's secret life. Mac doesn't flinch, doesn't give the slightest glimmer that the ground below him has just turned to water, that everything he trusted has just been thrown up for grabs.

"You wouldn't know who the bean spiller is?" Salmon leans forward.

"No."

Salmon watches Mac, then comes to a decision. "I probably shouldn't do this. But I figure you lost your friend, you want to get to the bottom of this, whatever 'this' is, as much as I do. Right?"

"If there's something to this, I want to know."

Salmon pulls a Xerox of the list of names and addresses from his pocket.

"My Deep Throat gave me this. It mean anything to you?"

Mac scans the pages. "No."

"I think these names are the key, they're connected in some way. I've already begun a search of databases and I'll finish that soon, but there are some names that never come up in the computers. I need someone do the legwork. . . ."

Mac tries to look disinterested but his mind swirls with images: Sam at the base of the hospital steps; the shadowy figure running down the hall at the heroin bust that looked like a PEACE officer; and Potesky at O'Malley's, urging him to take time off, to get out of town.

Even though her mother's favorite ice cream, mint chocolate chip, is melting in the car, Lisa cannot bring herself to unload the groceries. It is dusk. Exactly two days and three hours since Sam's death.

That morning at the funeral, Mac had been weird, tense, standing apart from the rank and file with Eve who seemed too thin, too pale. Then he left in a hurry. Potesky kept glancing at her during the whole thing and it all felt somehow wrong. More than just Sam's death, more than just the suddenness of it. She blows her nose in a soggy tissue, the skin of her face tight, tears dried in tracks down her cheeks. She feels like a husk, as though someone has just reached inside her and ripped out her life. As though just when her life was going, it was stopped. If Mac was there she could talk to him, share Sam openly with him. She had had to leave the funeral quickly, it was too hard to pretend Sam was only a partner. It was all too hard.

A last beam of sun shoots down the street, making shade from her mother's small maple tree across her legs and feet, hovering spots of dark and light from the hanging yellow leaves. Why hasn't her mother called out the window? Told her to come in? Lisa cannot summon the will to get up and check. A group of boys plays baseball in the street with a broom handle and a crushed soda can. A little girl walks slowly along the opposite sidewalk, talking to a doll she cradles like a baby. A few houses away a man moves boxes into a house from a U-Haul. One of the boys hits a line drive and the soda can sails through the air until it bounces off the windshield of a late-model windowless Dodge van parked across the street. The boys scatter.

Lisa glances at her mother's car and notices for the first time the distorted high-pitched *ping ping ping* the car is exhaustedly making because she left the keys in the ignition and the driver-side door open. She stands and walks toward the car.

Inside the living room of her mother's house a man wearing latex gloves watches Lisa through venetian blinds and speaks quietly, his throat mike transmitting his words.

"Subject on the move."

In the kitchen two men wearing latex gloves position themselves next to the door to the back porch and wait. The lightbulb in the ceiling has been unscrewed and the flowered curtains over the windows have been pulled.

"About time," one of the men says.

In the living room the first man watches Lisa collect two bags of groceries from the car. "Ten seconds," he says into his microphone. There is a sound from upstairs. Something falling, Lisa's mother's voice croaking, like out of a deep sleep, "Lisa, is that you?"

The man from the front of the house is running lightly and silently up the stairs, his hand pulling a small vial out of his pocket. For some reason it has worn off too fast. Lisa's mother is turned away from the door, reaching for her walker from a La-Z-Boy chair. The man hears Lisa fumbling with her keys on the back porch below and before Lisa's mother can again call out, he smoothly moves behind the La-Z-Boy chair and waves the open vial under the old woman's nose. Lisa's mother manages to say "Oh" at the glimpse of an arm coming around the chair before she is sound asleep.

Lisa opens the back door and steps into the dark kitchen. She flicks on the overhead light but the light doesn't go on. She moves forward, a little uneasy, the hair on the back of her neck rising, the whole house dark. Behind her, the two men wait until she puts down her groceries—there can be no signs of struggle, no ripped bag, no dented can of soup. What is about to happen never happened. Lisa drops the bags on the kitchen table and is about to turn when one of the men is behind her, his left arm hard around her, his right arm pressing a cloth against her mouth. She struggles for only the briefest instant.

Lisa sits at the kitchen table, her chin on her chest. Two of the men crouch next to her. One leans against the counter. The first man lightly slaps Lisa's cheek. Lisa moans but doesn't open her eyes.

She is not in the kitchen but instead walks on a path through the woods in early spring near her parents' house in South Carolina, a path she took home every day from school when she was a child. Buds are just opening light green at the tips of tree branches and the smell in the afternoon air is sweet and clean. It should be a place she feels safe but she doesn't feel safe.

A white man in a suit steps out from behind a tree and she sees that two other white men in suits are crouched in the path.

"Give her another dose just to make sure," the man leaning against a branch says.

Lisa feels her arm lifted as though it is someone else's arm. She feels the needle slip beneath her skin there in the woods and yet it does not strike her as odd.

"Tell me," one of the crouching men says, the syringe still in his hand. "How do you think Sam Mullane died?"

"It was an accident. . . ." Lisa's head feels heavy and she lets it fall to one side.

The man puts the syringe in a small black bag.

Lisa opens her eyes and the man crouching in front of her looks exactly like a sheriff from the town where she grew up. "Sam tried to tell me."

The sheriff leans forward. "He tried to tell you what?"

Suddenly, there is a knocking sound, a woodpecker in one of the trees.

One of the men walks quietly to the front of the house, draws his silenced gun, and peers out a window.

Mac stands on the front porch, waiting for Lisa's mother to come to the door. Because she uses a walker he is used to it taking a long time.

Mac had been undecided about coming to talk to Lisa. She had enough to handle and he didn't want to needlessly upset her when there might be nothing to Salmon's investigation. He had come to her house without a clear idea of what he would say. At the very least he would be able to talk to her, apologize for shooting Sam, comfort her. He would start off that way and see how it went. Mac steps back and looks at the dark windows. Where would they be on the day of Sam's funeral? Maybe Valerie had taken Lisa out to a diner or something to force some food into her. Lisa had looked awfully thin at the funeral, as though she hadn't eaten in a couple of days. Mac reaches for the doorknob.

The man inside points his gun at where the door will open.

The knob doesn't turn, the door locked.

Mac knocks again, loud enough so that the sound can be heard in every room. He thinks about leaving a note but instead turns and walks out to where his car is double parked.

The man watches Mac drive away. He sheathes his gun and returns to the kitchen.

Lisa watches the man come out from behind a tree and walk back down the path.

"It was Wells, the other target," the returning man says.

"Did he leave?" the man standing by the tree asks.

"I watched him drive away."

"Will that leave memory?" he asks the sheriff.

"No, we're fine." The sheriff again crouches in front of Lisa. "Now Lisa, what did Sam try to tell you?"

"I thought I heard him say something at the hospital, but he didn't. I think it was a . . . a premonition that something bad was going to happen." Lisa's face tightens and she begins to cry. "We were going to get married."

"Does Mac Wells know you were going to be married?"

"I told him."

"Does he think Sam's death was an accident?"

"He thinks it was his fault."

The sheriff stands and pulls another syringe, a smaller one, from the black leather bag. He kneels beside Lisa and slides the needle into her arm. Lisa feels her face go lax. She stops crying. A tremendous calm flows into her.

The sheriff shines a pen light into her eyes.

"Lisa, listen to me," he says in a soothing voice. "When you wake up you will remember you fell asleep at the kitchen table. Okay?"

Lisa nods. The sheriff's words fall into her mind with an incredible weight, each one a boulder, into a deep, placid lake.

"Lisa," the sheriff says. He holds up a copy of *People* magazine. "You read this and dozed off at the kitchen table. You were very tired."

Lisa nods. If the sheriff told her she was a dog she would bark.

"Have a deep restful sleep, Lisa."

Lisa's head drops to her chest.

Morning. A slew of birds hop around the birdbath, poking through empty seed husks. Every morning at dawn Lisa's mother fills the birdbath with a scoop of bird seed from a large metal trash can. It is now past eight. Three birds sit on the trash can and watch the back door.

In the kitchen, light streams through the windows above the sink and falls in two long rectangles on the checkered linoleum floor. On the counter two empty grocery bags are neatly folded. At the kitchen table Lisa sits slumped forward, her head on folded arms, her mouth open.

A car alarm begins to wail across the street. Lisa opens her eyes and lifts her head, the pattern of her sweater imprinted on her cheek. She looks around the kitchen, trying to collect herself. Her mother's *People* magazine sits under her elbow, open to an exposé on British royalty. She pages through the magazine, remembering reading it, but none of the stories seem familiar. Her arm is sore as though she banged it but there is no bruise. For some reason she looks up at the overhead light and walks to the switch by the door. She flips the switch and the light goes on. She stares at the light. She walks around the downstairs trying all the doors and they are all locked. A wave of nausea passes through her and she goes to the kitchen sink, thinking she might throw up, but the feeling subsides. Her mouth is bone-dry and she suddenly feels dehydrated and drinks two glasses of water. She opens the cupboard to get an aspirin and all the Campbell's soup is on the empty shelf above the medicine, a shelf she never uses because it is too high for her mother to reach. Why would she put it there? She moves the soup to its normal cupboard and hears a bump from upstairs. She looks at the clock. Her mother must have come down at dawn as usual but let her sleep.

Lisa walks to the foot of the stairs and her mother is standing at the top of the staircase, her hair pushed to one side as though she slept in one position all night. She has a perplexed look on her face.

"I haven't slept this late in years." Her mother pauses, staring off, a momentary look of concern.

"What is it?" Lisa says.

Her mother smiles, her normal morning smile. "Oh, nothing. Just a weird dream."

19

Julian Sanders's limo takes the off-ramp from the Long Island Expressway into the Bronx as the sun rises and he tells his driver, a white man named Stevens, to head for his old neighborhood. Stevens clearly does not like the idea of driving the shiny Lincoln with the TV antennae into the bombed-out South Bronx and Sanders does not reassure him. Shifting deeper into the soft leather seats he smiles to himself as the driver electronically locks the doors and turns on the antipersonnel devices that complement the double-plate metal and bulletproof glass. A moving fortress. Outside the tinted windows the early morning light almost makes what passes for a business district, a few bodegas, an off-track betting place, and a fast-food joint with heavy bars on the windows, look clean. Sanders glances up at the telephone poles. No cameras here.

The driver follows instructions to a neighborhood of row houses, once a government low-income housing program that was heralded as an answer to the drug-and-crime-infested high-rise projects. You give a person a home and a tiny patch of grass and asphalt to call his own and pride blossoms, cohesive and clean neighborhoods take shape; the program was wildly successful but it wasn't a big moneymaker for the developers, building costly high-rises were financial gushers and pressure to kill the "neighborhood" approach was immense. After a few years the government abandoned the program. Julian Sanders's mother was one of the first to get a house. Julian was in his senior year of college on partial scholarship at Morehouse then. He had almost no money and usually only returned home once a year, but he took on a third job and largely did without sleep for three weeks to scrape enough money together for a house-warming gift and a round-trip ticket to the Port Authority in Manhattan so he could see the look on his mother's face when she walked through the door into the first home she had ever owned. Six days a week for twenty years she had commuted an hour to Macy's in Manhattan and worked on the cleaning crew to put food on the table and clothes on his back.

Before she even got through the front door she began to cry and he and his two younger brothers covered their faces and hurried inside so no one would see the tears their mother had brought into their own eyes. Six days a week for twenty years his mother had swept around the dish and table settings, washed the floors around evening gowns and coats that cost many times her weekly salary, but the only thing she had ever talked about was the crystal display she dusted at the end of her rounds, the glass paperweights and figurines glistening inside the locked cases as if from another world, a world his mother kept clean but never touched, never felt in her hand, never was a part of. She would always update Julian on the new figurines that were added, the ones that were taken away, as though it were her private collection and she had made the decision herself. When he decided to give his mother a house-warming gift he knew it shouldn't be something useful; the occasion did not call for a good toaster or a vacuum, both of which she needed. It called for something which wasn't a necessity, which was pure and beautiful and a luxury. So the first place he went from Port Authority, a small beat-up suitcase in his hand, was to Macy's, to the crystal department. His mother was deeply religious and the crystal piece he had heard his mother mention most often was a small angel figurine, but it was twice the money he had. He asked to look at it anyway. The only piece he could afford was a small, plain candy dish. He was terribly disappointed and was about to buy the candy dish when the young white saleswoman asked him who he was looking to buy the gift for and he told her about his mother, about how it was her first house, how she had cleaned the store for twenty years and always talked about the crystal and particularly the angel because she was so religious. The saleswoman smiled and he said he would take the candy dish. She said it would only take a minute to wrap. After wandering around the store he returned to the crystal department and the saleswoman had wrapped the box so beautifully, with layers of white tissue paper and long tied ribbons, that he no longer felt bad about giving his mother the candy dish and hurried out of the store to catch the subway.

After everyone had checked out all the rooms of the house, Julian presented his mother with the wrapped Macy's box and said it was from both him and his two younger brothers who had no money. She started to cry again and at first didn't want to unwrap the gift because she said it was the most beautiful thing she had ever received, a cardboard box wrapped in white tissue, and he had no doubt that that was the truth. Finally after much cajoling she slowly opened the gift, gently putting aside the ribbons and paper, careful not to crease the tissue, every piece of which she eventually put in an old antique tin from her childhood on a table in the living room. When it came time to open the box she was breathing so heavily Julian was afraid—his mother back then had been a big woman—that his gift would knock her dead on the spot. She closed her eyes, slid her hand into the box, and tilted her head to the ceiling, and with the words *Thank you, Lord, for my boys, my angels,* she pulled from the box the small angel figurine, its head tilted toward heaven in her hands, its shoulders catching the light from the front window.

His mother was stunned. She knew exactly what the little angel had cost and would have been overwhelmed with the candy dish or even a toaster. Of course she began to cry again and hugged the three boys, getting the shoulders of their Sunday best all wet. Julian was glad to have his face hidden so she would not see his own surprise, which was considerable, and in that moment a light touched Julian that changed his life. Ever since he was little, his mother had brought him up not to hate, to take people as he found them on an individual basis, to never be a racist. But it was hard; what he had found was that things weren't fair, that the deck was stacked against black people. Even if many white people didn't consider themselves racist and were basically good people, racism was in the fiber and bloodstream of the country and had been for three hundred and some years. In his short life he had little real interaction with white people; his life in the Bronx and in church did not offer any variety and when he got to Morehouse, stunning in its freedoms for a young man with an overprotective mother, most of the faces were still black. So every interaction with a white person made a deep impression on Julian, a cabdriver passing him by, a housewife looking at him nervously and clutching her bag just perceptibly closer to her body in the aisle of a store. More and more each day Julian had seen the world as black and white, us and them. Nothing in his experience had yet contradicted this. Until now. Perhaps it was easy for the saleswoman to switch the angel for the candy dish, but perhaps it wasn't and she had made up the money with her own. The specifics didn't matter. Her kindness set off a change in Julian. So moving was his mother's emotion, such a pinnacle of prayers answered and of so many years of not having, of doing without, that the gesture of the saleswoman made the moment perfect, suffused the small new house with a light more powerful than anything Julian had known in his life, a light that washed all previous slights away, that made him feel sympathy rather than anger for the white cabdriver, the woman clutching her purse in the store.

As the years went by, as his small civil rights law practice grew to be an influential firm with offices around the country, as his stature rose to the national stage and he became a powerful voice in the country for the disenfranchised, for those left behind, no matter what their color, on his own talk show on CNN, or in private lunches with three presidents, or in constant speeches to the youth of the country, one white woman's beautiful gesture guided his way.

As the limo approaches his mother's street, Julian watches the trash-filled yards pass. Each year it gets worse; some of the houses of the neighborhood becoming drugstores, junkies lying around the small front yard, high or waiting their turn, other houses dingy and broken down. When the government had pulled out and stopped screening applicants it had all fallen apart. The already entrenched people who wanted a clean neighborhood had fought back, but the war hadn't lasted too long. After the drug dealers shot a few husbands and burned down a few houses the once sparkling neighborhood, the diamond in a sea of coal, had been drawn back into hell.

And through it all his mother had refused to leave. Julian could buy her a house anywhere in the country but she wanted to stay. She would, she said, grow old and die in the house and would rather die of a gunshot wound if the Lord meant to take her that way than of the broken heart she would have if Julian took her out of her house. The limo turns onto his mother's street, a bit rundown but trash-free and in far better shape than the other streets; when his mother wouldn't move Julian had bought as many houses on the block as he could and had given them free to people he knew would keep them up and keep the drug dealers out. Actually his mother's block had become quite safe. The drug dealers kept their hands off because it was Julian's block. When he made speeches about the disenfranchised they knew he was talking about them, defending them, and Julian was a powerful man and they respected that and knew that if anything happened on Julian's block it would be bad business. So a kind of peace was achieved.

The limo pulls in front of his mother's house, the tiny yard immaculate and neatly planted. Julian looks through the tinted window at the front door and takes a deep breath. His mother had wanted to grow old and die in the house and that is exactly what she was doing. The chauffeur comes around the back of the car but Julian has already opened his door. The front door of the house opens and Roderick, a large black man in a dark suit, who, along with his younger brother, Ben, has served as a guard at the house, nods toward Julian and smiles. When his mother passes away Julian will have jobs at his side for both Roderick and Ben. He has never used personal guards before, but the hate mail increases all the time and there have been a few close calls.

"Mr. Sanders." Roderick extends his hand, formal as always. Julian takes the firm handshake, Roderick's massive forearm flexing impressively.

"Julian to you, Roderick. Ben coming tonight?"

"Yes, sir."

"I'm making the TV stops, giving a speech at an outdoor rally in a few days. Can your brother cover here?"

"I'm sure he can."

The day nurse comes down the stairs into the small living room.

"I thought I heard your voice, Mr. Sanders. Your mother will be so glad to see you."

"How is she?"

"She just went to sleep. She's as comfortable as she can be."

Julian climbs the stairs to his mother's room, leaving everyone behind and lets the mask drop. He pauses before going into his mother's room and can feel his hands trembling at his sides. His mother has been gradually slipping away these last two years, her decline greatly accelerating during the last few months, to where he has made inquiries to her doctors about the possibility of one last morphine shot if her pain becomes too great. By now he should have expected to be resigned to her leaving, he has had so much time to come to terms with it, but he finds it hard to enter her room. It is as if her impending death has come from a sudden accident or illness, as if she is being struck down in her prime. And in a way she is. She is his prime, the primary adult figure in his whole life, his whole reason for achieving what he has.

He steps into the room and she has lost even more weight in the last two weeks, her cheeks sunken, her breathing raspy and shallow. She has stopped eating altogether and an IV drip cord runs from the back of her wrist to a bottle hung from a metal stand. Julian sees his mother's tattered Bible sitting on a chair next to the bed, torn bits of paper sticking out of the top to mark her favorite places. His mother no longer with the strength to lift the book, the nurse reads to her whenever she is awake. His mother is not afraid to die. She is far more at peace with her death than Julian is. Julian sits at the side of the bed, the Bible in his lap. He looks down into his mother's face, the first face he saw in life, now at once recognizable but so different too.

He takes hold of her hand, which is cool and no longer warm as it has been all her life, her body so close to being left behind. He covers his face and begins to cry.

(20)

Mac sits in his car and looks at the clock: only 8:35; no civil servant would show up at someone's door before nine A.M. He pulls a thread from the cuff of his tweed jacket, a jacket he had to dig deep in the closet to find, and looks in the rearview mirror, adjusting the glasses he borrowed from the Props Department at HQ— silver rims, studious-looking but not too nice, the kind of glasses an earnest but underpaid social worker for the city would wear.

The neighborhood, Sixty-third Street between Fifth and Park, is well-to-do, mostly privately owned townhouses and elegant brownstones. A few children toting knapsacks, one boy actually has a briefcase, are led down the street to private school by a woman who is probably their nanny. Right in front of Mac a van from a flower store pulls in and makes a delivery of flowers, an old man and a boy carting in fresh arrangements and bringing out the flowers they delivered a day earlier.

A PEACE maintenance van pulls up to the curb a half block down from Mac. He watches the men in blue jumpsuits begin to unload gear. Mac looks up to the top of a telephone pole and sees that the Plexiglas camera globe is covered by a large REAL

PEACE sticker, a two-by-two-foot smiley face with the words REAL PEACE in black letters along the top. The REAL PEACE vigilantes had begun their stickering campaign almost from the day the program started, blacking out official PEACE surveillance units all over the city. Wearing rubber masks or flags over their heads, no one had been identified yet, but a task force had been created to catch the anti-PEACE group. In the meantime, the PEACE maintenance crews were kept constantly busy restoring DADD's sight. The Plexiglas of the globes was designed so that you could hold a spray paint can to it all day and the paint would never adhere to the plastic. But large smiley face stickers were another matter.

The story had been picked up nationally and REAL PEACE members, incognito of course, had appeared on various talk shows and on CNN. Mac had watched one of the interviews and the two representatives of REAL PEACE, one wearing a rubber Scooby Doo mask, the other appearing as Shaggy, were articulate and passionate but sounded, to Mac, like naive, overeducated college kids. Other than the inconvenience of losing sight and removing the stickers, brass at PEACE HQ were most worried about the vulnerability in the PEACE system that REAL PEACE was exposing. Engineers were already hard at work on ways of diminishing access to the globes at the tops of telephone poles, the easiest targets. It will probably, Mac guesses, be a game of cat and mouse for years to come.

Mac watches one of the installers climb the pole. He begins to go over the whole thing in his head again. If Potesky is really feeding Salmon information, there has to be a reason. But what? The PEACE department is often touted as the cleanest police force in the country. If corruption existed enough for Potesky to be talking, Mac had a suspicion it must be in the upper echelons of the force rather than in the rank and file—some sort of kickback scheme, or possibly illegal use of the system beyond the law, some kind of spying. A perfect system was only as good as its imperfect master; Mac had always known the system would eventually be abused, it would be naive not to expect it. But what would that have to do with Sam? Perhaps he didn't know Sam as well as he thought. That had to be considered, but it seemed an unreasonable stretch. What would some kickback scheme or covert operation have need of Sam for? Perhaps Sam had stumbled into it in some way and had to be eliminated. The hospital had provided a good cover, his death a crime of opportunity. But if Sam had come across something he wasn't supposed to in the weeks or months before his death, surely he would have said something.

There was always the possibility that Sam's death and Salmon's "Deep Throat" information were unrelated. But in Mac's gut he knew something was wrong with Sam's death. And that was enough to go on. What would his father, a career cop in northern New Jersey, have done? Would he have been sitting here on his day off waiting to go knock on someone's door he had never met? If his partner had died, he would. His father, who took early retirement rather than go on the dole or rat out his buddies and be ostracized by the whole department, had never approved of Mac's choice of profession. He was bitter about the police, the department brass leaving him out in the cold, preferring to let one honorable cop go than to clean up and suffer the bad publicity. But it was more than that; Mac had been a good student and his father and mother had always wanted Mac to be a lawyer, a banker, to move up in the world, so when Mac finished at Rutgers and applied to the New York City Police Academy instead of law school they had been deeply disappointed. But Mac knew he would feel confined in an office, had known since he was a child that he wanted to be a cop like his father, and his parents never got over it. Even years later, after his marriage to Eve, right up until his parents had died within the same year, they were still hoping he would give up the force and go back to school.

The maintenance man at the top of the telephone pole pulls a can from a utility belt and begins spraying the exterior of the sticker. After a few moments he pulls at the corner of the sticker and it lifts easily, leaving no mark. He crumples the sticker and stuffs it in one of his oversize pockets. Mac notices for the first time a Grid generator already installed just below the Plexiglas bubble. Across the street two more Grid generators are affixed to poles.

It seems everywhere Mac goes in the city, Grids are in place or going up, but he prefers the target acquisition discrimination of the tranq-guns to the grenade effect of the Grids. Why take out a whole sidewalk when you are after one person? It is simple math—the Grid zones will cause more inconvenience to the civilian population, not to mention more lawsuits from them.

A stray cat pokes its head out between two cars and begins to strut across the street. Nothing else moves in the zone. The maintenance man at the top of the pole pulls a remote from a case attached to his belt. He pushes a button and a low buzz fills the air as the Grid is activated. Mac feels the hair stand on his arms, an electrical charge in the air as out in the Grid area the cat freezes midstep, then falls slowly to its side. The worker at the top of the pole shuts down the Grid. The cat shakes her head and stands to her feet. She looks around once, surprised that she decided to lie down in a dangerous place like the street, and scurries off between parked cars.

Mac looks at his watch, ten minutes after nine. He opens the car door and steps out into the street. The maintenance guys are packing up their stuff and take no notice of him as he walks by. He glances at the top of the clipboard under his arm and stops at a spotless, light lemon-colored four-story townhouse. He takes a deep breath, steps down to the door, and rings the bell. There is no sound for a while until he hears a voice muffled through the door.

"Sonya! Where are you? There's someone at the door!"

The door opens and a well-dressed middle-aged woman stands in front of Mac talking into a cordless phone. She gives Mac the up and down with her eyes and smiles in a perfunctory, formal way. She turns slightly away to talk into the phone.

"No, honey, it was dreadful. Hold on a sec . . ." She turns back to Mac. "Yes?"

"I'm with the city's Human Resources Department. May I speak to Fred Harriman?"

The woman's smile tightens. She turns away to the phone again. "I'll call you back." She clicks off the phone and turns back to Mac. "You're not with the press?"

"No, I'm with the city. We're conducting a survey . . ."

"Yes, well . . ."

"It will only take a minute."

"No, it's not that. He, Mr. Harriman I mean, has gone away." The woman taps the long lacquered nails of the hand not holding the phone on a side table.

"When would it be convenient—"

"No, he's away indefinitely." The rhythm of the woman's nails speeds up. "I don't mean to be rude, but you'll have to excuse me."

The woman shuts the door before Mac can say another word.

In the car Mac looks at the Xerox of the list Salmon showed him in his apartment. Mac has grouped the names geographically. For the morning he has scheduled the Upper East Side. The next address is on Ninetieth Street, toward the river. Mac moves past the PEACE installation van, one of the maintenance men standing on the sidewalk talking into a portable phone.

The traffic uptown isn't bad for the time of day and Mac pulls up to the next address, a decent high-rise with small square balconies on each side all the way up to the fifteenth floor. Mac parks in the circle next to a sign that says NO PARKING—VIOLA-

TORS SUBJECT TO ABUSE. He flips his PEACE pass onto the dash and heads past a small dry cement fountain into the building's lobby, a long hallway with brass-potted ferns on either side of a red rug that has seen better days. Behind a large wooden desk, a dark-skinned young man in dark green janitor-type work clothes watches Mac approach.

"Hi, I work for the city's Human Resources Department. I'm here to see Suzi Danilovic."

The man, probably an assistant super, smells strongly of a cheap cologne and looks startled for a moment. "She no longer lives here, man."

"Any forwarding address?"

The man looks around to make sure no one is walking through the lobby. "The thing of it is, she's dead." He stops as a young attractive woman exits the building. "She jumped off the balcony of her apartment." He looks around conspiratorially. "She landed in the fountain right out there. Came from a rich family, I think, 'cause it was all hushed up. No cops, no newspapers." A door closes and the guy clams up as an older man in a doorman's uniform approaches. Mac turns and goes.

Mac starts the car and heads to the next two addresses, as luck would have it, on the same street and same block, 100th Street just off of Fifth. The houses aren't as nice as farther down but are still well-kept and affluent. Mac gets out of the car and walks up the street, looking for number seventeen and doesn't see half a block down an elderly woman slowly pulling her front door closed. The old woman carries an antique black metal lunch box and begins to make her way slowly toward the park. A young woman, a neighbor on the street, stops her and they begin talking.

Mac climbs the stairs to number seventeen, a worn brownstone, and rings the bell, which fades in and out as though it is low on batteries. There is no answer. Mac tries the bell two more times but the house is silent, the blinds pulled. Probably they're in the

Hamptons. Mac turns to leave and doesn't see behind him a subtle movement of the curtains, a shaky hand pulling them open a few inches, a figure watching, a thin layer of sweat above and below a rapidly blinking eye.

Mac heads down to number nine. Ahead of him the old woman with the black metal lunch box has just reached the corner and is waiting for the light to change. Mac climbs the steps of another brownstone which has seen better days and raps the wolf-shaped antique brass knocker, his hand on the wolf's ears, the back of its head knocking against a worn spot in the heavy wood door. The door is opened by an old woman.

"Margaret Williams?"

The old woman lifts glasses hanging from her neck and holds them over her eyes to see Mac clearly. "No, no, that's my sister. She just started for the park. Maybe you can catch her."

The old woman steps out onto the stoop and she and Mac look down the block toward Central Park, but the light has changed and Margaret Williams, the woman with the lunch box, is gone.

Marty Salmon sits at a NEXUS computer terminal in the basement of Columbia University's main library. The large room is dark, the air thick with the smell of old books, rows of ceiling-high bookshelves stretching almost from wall to wall. Way back when, Salmon went to Columbia's prestigious School of Journalism for a semester and every several years since then, for some reason, he has been given an alumni library card. He never paid off his school loan, so it has been a good investment. Though he can still call in favors from some friends at the city's papers, the Columbia library system is his main source of information and research. And right now it is paying off big-time. He punches a button and a printer starts spewing out newspaper articles from the last six months. Salmon puts stars by seven of the names on Birdie's list and smiles to himself. A big, fat, juicy story.

Somewhere many shelves away there is the sound of a book falling. Salmon's blood goes cold, sweat begins to drip down from under his arms. He listens to the room but there is nothing except his breathing and the printer, which stops. Salmon turns slowly in his chair and looks up and down the dim hallway. The buzz of the overhead lighting and an indefinable hum from inside the walls seems suddenly quite loud and Salmon hurriedly gathers Birdie's list and the stack of articles he has printed and begins to move toward the exit. He peers down each dark aisle as he goes but there is no one. He opens the door to the stairs and hurries up the two flights, breathing heavily until he is at the door for the first floor. In the crack above the floor he can see the shadow of two feet standing, waiting. The sound of one of the heavy fire doors opening and clos-ing echoes up the stairwell from below and he yanks the handle to the first floor, startling a female librarian, who makes a small "oh" sound and lifts her hand to her heart. Salmon does not pause to apologize as he hurries in the direction of the main entrance.

At that moment across campus, Mac Wells enters Columbia Uni-versity's main gate. Young people walk by with backpacks and books and though he is only a decade or so older, they seem like kids. Mac walks toward the central courtyard area without much hope of finding his target. All day he has knocked on doors, twenty-two visits to be exact, and he's only talked to one person from the list, a retired plumber who was wary and unhelpful and wouldn't let him in the door; everyone else was out or moved or dead. Three dead to be exact: two suicides and one "accident." A man had driven his car up an off-ramp and been hit head-on by a tractor trailer. Sounded like a third suicide. Three deaths on a list of thirty people in a six-month period.

Mac enters the large concrete campus formed by the brick university buildings built along the perimeter of a couple of large city blocks. A Frisbee whizzes passed Mac's head and lands nearby. A young bearded boy with hair down to his shoulders calls out, "Hey, sorry, bossman."

Mac picks up the disc and flings it side-arm dead on target to the chest of the youth.

"Yo, good toss, boss," the student says, in one motion spinning the disc to a woman far across the field.

Mac discovers a Heather Duncap after flashing his PEACE badge to a couple groups of students.

One girl, a cigarette dangling from her mouth, points out a pretty blonde girl sitting on a bench listening to headphones. "You're in luck," the girl says. "Normally this time of the day she's shacked up with her man."

Heather doesn't look up until Mac's shadow covers her face. She doesn't remove the headphones until he motions he wants to talk. A rebel every step of the way.

"You Heather Duncap?"

"Who are you?"

"Name's Bob Langley. I work with the city's Health and Human Resources Department."

"I already told you guys, everything's okay."

"Someone from Health and Human Resources already visited you?"

"Like a million times." Heather Duncap twists around, looking for someone, an expression at once of supreme boredom and irritation crossing her face.

"About what?"

Suddenly Heather is all attention, her eyes focusing on Mac's face. "Shouldn't you know, if it's your department?"

Before Mac can answer, a muscular kid trying to look tough in a leather jacket walks up. "Hey, Heath. What's up?"

"Thank you, Ms. Duncap." Mac turns to leave. "You've been very helpful."

After he is safely near the entrance gate under a canopy of orange- and red-leafed trees, Mac turns around to make sure Heather hasn't called campus security and is relieved to see her perched in the muscular guy's lap, their heads together as if they are not in public, as if it is the only kiss they will ever have.

The day is cold in the park. Margaret Williams glances around, then lifts a small silver flask from her antique lunch box and takes a dainty sip. The flask was her father's, probably worth a small fortune, just for the silver alone. Dad tilted it back a few times in his life but he was a grand man, never an unkind word, never a stumble, a gentleman drinker. Margaret used to pour the whiskey in her tea and drink out of the Thermos but she has dispensed with all that, at least now that it's cold, now that there are less people around, just a few walkers and a group of children, a class from one of the private schools playing kickball. It doesn't bother her if someone sees. She used to be so self-conscious but lately it doesn't seem to matter.

She strokes her fingers across her cheek. The cold air feels good, seems to be helping her keep her thoughts clear, to help her be free of the confusion that has gripped her during the last few days. God, how could she think those thoughts! When that kind young woman across the street brought her new little baby over she had imagined doing the most horrible things. And it had seemed so real. Like she was doing them and at the same time cooing with her sister over the baby that slept in her arms.

Neither her father nor her mother had had Alzheimer's before they went, she did not even have the genetic precursors for it, but perhaps this was the beginning. The night before she had had to prop a chair under the doorknob of her room to get any sleep at all. She kept seeing the knob turn, her sister coming into the room with a large knife. And when finally Margaret had calmed herself and turned out the lights it was as if the dark were alive, swooping shapes, phantoms, and garish faces transforming and twisting, taking form in the air around her.

She closes her eyes and feels her mind drift, feels herself suddenly moving, drawn along as though on one of those moving sidewalks at the mall, her body pulled backward in time, not an unpleasant sensation, part of her still in the present but the rest speeding backward in time through different people until finally she can feel herself as an animal, scared and alert in a herd of animals like herself, the danger invisible, but filling her nostrils, getting closer, closer. . . .

She opens her eyes, all the parts of her zooming back into the present moment. She shivers. She must have dozed off, but it felt so real. A boy, the fattest boy in the kickball game, boots the ball over the heads of his classmates and starts to lumber around the bases. Margaret wonders if Alzheimer's is always this frightening, if those she has known in her life who have had it were constantly and deeply terrified beneath their non sequitur conversation, trapped in an unknown world and unable to express the true horror of it. When she gets home she will have to tell her sister. She had almost broken a hip the night before when she leapt out of bed, the demons swirling in the blackness around her. It was still sore. At least here in her favorite spot in her favorite park everything is normal.

Margaret takes another sip from her flask, pleasantly slipping into a fog when out of the corner of her eye she sees the kickball booted in her direction. The ball bounces and rolls until it stops at her feet. A tall angular boy is jogging across the square to retrieve it and Margaret feels herself beginning to perspire. She should run, drop her lunch box and try to make it to the edge of the park, but she can't move. The boy approaches closer, within touching distance and stoops to pick up the ball. Margaret has no time to react as the boy shoves the ball into her face, pressing the pink rubber over her mouth and nose so she can no longer breathe. She tries to scream and grabs at the boy's arms but he is surprisingly strong. She begins to cry.

Ten feet away the boy watches the old woman flailing at the air in front of her. Because it scares him, he will remember this moment forever. But as the woman's lunch box clatters to the ground, he hears his teacher's call and runs back to the game.

Eve looks out the kitchen window again, anticipating Mac's car. That morning he was deliberately vague about what he would be doing in the city all day. Eve sprinkles flour on the top of the dough and begins to knead it with her fists. The dough is warm and soft, enveloping her hands. The phone rings and Eve picks up, expecting Mac, but instead it is Dr. Knowles's secretary who asks Eve to hold on a moment, the doctor would like to talk to her. Eve feels the bottom go out of her stomach. Why would he call one day after her visit? Tests usually took a couple of days. But if it was bad news he wouldn't do it over the phone. Maybe tests for him came back faster because he was so high-priced.

She thinks of him in his examining room, a small, highly regarded, fastidious man in his fifties with a close-cropped goatee, a man she had only gotten in to see because his brother's wife was one of her professors, her mentor really, in grad school.

He had been enthusiastic about her chances to have a child but wouldn't commit himself until the tests came back. That was enough to send her emotions through the roof. She and Mac had been trying for almost two years. Mac had already been checked and came out with flying colors. Now it was her turn.

The phone clicks and Dr. Knowles's high-pitched voice comes on line.

"Ms. Wells, I have good news . . ."

Across the street a little boy stands guard while his baby sister crawls around the front yard and the entire time the doctor talks, Eve watches the little girl. When Eve starts to cry Dr. Knowles asks Eve if she is okay but Eve can't answer. There is Dr. Knowles's voice, uncomfortable and nervous, away from the receiver, asking someone to pick up the phone and then the secretary with the calm voice is on line and Dr. Knowles is gone. When Eve has assured the secretary she is fine the phone call ends and she stands for a long time at the sink.

Across the street the little boy picks up his sister and carries her inside like a fragile toy.

Mac comes in the front door and hears the water through the pipes, Eve in the shower. Good. He goes to the kitchen phone and dials Salmon's number but the machine picks up. Mac hangs up, leaving a message a bad idea. He goes into the garage from the kitchen. At the back is a small metal lockbox. He takes it over to the door. Taped to the top of the door frame is a key. Mac slips the key into the lockbox and takes out his father's .45-caliber handgun. The gun is shiny, in good condition, and has a nice worn feel to it.

The first time Mac shot a gun it was this .45. He was eight and with his father at a shooting range, the heat in his stomach and the feeling in his chest like it was pumped up with air and he couldn't breathe, his father behind him, his arm along Mac's arm, his hairy hand lightly resting around Mac's. The kick from the gun knocked Mac's arm up and to the side, smoke rising into his nostrils, power and exhilaration filling him as he saw a small hole near the center of the target and his father straightened and laughed. "Nerves of steel, little man. Hell of a shot."

After carefully placing the gun on a small table, his father, not normally an expressive man, wrapped an arm around Mac and Mac felt something shift between them, as if in the moment of firing the gun and hitting the target a bond had grown between them, a bridge between men, wordless and eternal. At that moment he could still feel it in the weight of his father's gun in his hand.

If he had been interested Mac could have pursued pistol shooting at a higher level, international competitions, maybe the Olympics; he had the gift, perfect aim and a hand that had never known nerves.

In the walls the pipes suddenly cease their cadences of throbbing water; Eve will be down soon. Mac does not know what he will say to her. He does not know what to tell himself yet. He has always approached events in his life logically, made order, measured eventualities. So what did it mean that the people on the Birdie list had off-the-charts incidences of accidents, death, and suicide; that the Columbia University girl had been visited before him by someone supposedly from city government; that the evidence pointed to Potesky as Salmon's informant? The whole thing, aside from Sam's death, could easily have been orchestrated— Salmon gave him the list and his description of Potesky's mistress would be easy to obtain. But to what end? An article on how to dupe a PEACE officer? Mac had done his own checking and Salmon was the real thing, he had been a hard-news investigative reporter until a few years before and had done easily traceable freelance stuff since then, nothing hinting at paranoia or the confabulation of stories. The logical conclusion was that something was going on. His father would go to Potesky and demand an explanation. His father, a no-nonsense guy, wouldn't have waited until he had overwhelming evidence. *A rat is a rat is a rat* were the words he uttered the last day he came home from his job, never to be a cop again.

In the kitchen Mac tries Salmon's number but the answering machine picks up again. The gun and a dusty box of bullets sit on the kitchen table. The soft tread of Eve coming down the stairs sounds from the hallway and Mac suddenly wants to stash the gun and bullets, but Eve is already standing in the doorway in a bathrobe, the belt untied, the robe falling open. Her breasts are mostly visible and her legs are slightly apart. Mac forgets the gun on the table. And then he is moving toward her, the action of his legs and of his arms reaching for her involuntary, a buzz in his muscles and heavy heat in his chest as he is kissing her. They are fierce together, in an instant he is half out of his clothes and her robe is on the floor as he backs her into the hallway, their hips moving against each other, her fingers scratching his shoulders then locked behind his neck, his hands wrapped around her bottom, pulling her hard against him as they slam into the hall closet and he hears something crack in the wood but it is nothing to him, and her hands around his neck are dragging him to the floor and he is inside her, their kissing mouths all over each other's face, their grabbing and touching hands moving without conscious thought. Their voices stab the air, their bodies hit against each other as though the goal is obliteration, as though they want to force themselves totally inside of each other, to no longer be separate, the violent, unconscious rhythm between them, nature's friction, an explosion of waiting a month since Eve's last ovulation.

The ending is a unified scream.

"I hope no one looks through the mail slot," Eve says, laughing on her back, her hands locked under the backs of her knees, pulling them close to her chest so that she and Mac will have maximum chance at conception. Mac runs his hand through her sweat-slicked hair.

Later, he follows into the kitchen and watches her shudder at the sight of the gun on the table. "Mac, what's going on?"

Eve hates to sit through long stories without hearing the point first, so he lays it out. "There may be a problem in the program. I got the gun out for your protection when I'm not here."

She nods for him to continue. Mac recounts the story from the beginning, sticking to Salmon and leaving out Sam. Eve doesn't say a word but her expression of disbelief says enough. When he is done she looks at the gun and back to him.

"Mac, you would never have gotten that gun out unless this story were credible. Who do you think the informant is? Do I know him?"

Mac hesitates, not wanting to draw Eve in. But he looks at her and she is not frightened. He can tell by the way her pupils are darting back and forth that she is synthesizing what he has told her, that she is figuring something out.

"It's Potesky," he says.

"Well, that's it right there. That gives you an indication of where the corruption is."

"How's that?"

"Every time I've seen Dan, he's either played down the accomplishments of PEACE or made a disparaging remark. An odd thing for someone in his position within the program. Potesky's old-school, NYPD through to the bone. Whatever's going on here originated with the new school, the PEACE people. Dan wouldn't rat on his own."

Mac smiles. When it comes to psychological cues and motivational assessments Eve is a steel trap. He'd trust her more than his own senses.

"Wait a minute."

Mac watches Eve thinking. Her eyes rise to meet his.

"Does this have to do with Sam's accident? Do you think someone killed Sam?"

"I don't know."

Suddenly it is no longer a psychological profiling session for Eve, no longer an abstraction, no longer a game. Her color fades.

"You don't know? Mac, are we in some sort of danger?"

"I don't know."

"Were you involved with Sam in something? I have a right to know."

"No."

"This is why you wouldn't tell me about where you were going today in the city, this thing?"

"Yes."

Mac tells her about his attempts to visit people on Salmon's list.

"And here I thought you were buying me a present."

"I wish I had been."

Eve looks solidly into Mac's eyes. He can see that she is not afraid. She reaches across the table to take his hand. "Well, what do we do?"

"*We* do nothing. I don't know who I can count on at the department so I have to figure this out quietly on my own. Then I'll know where to go with it. Hopefully the papers will handle it and I can stay clear of any fallout." Mac gives Eve's hand a squeeze. "Meanwhile, be a little more wary, even here. I don't think there's any problem but don't let anyone in to fix the phone or anything. Just to be safe, I'm gonna put the gun in the table by the bed where we used to keep it. You okay with that?"

Eve picks up the gun and it seems heavier in her hand than when Mac used it to teach her how to shoot. She checks the safety and pops the chamber, which is empty. She snaps the chamber back in place and puts the gun carefully back on the table. She looks into Mac's face and is seized with a sudden premonition of fear. She looks back at the gun and it has moved, it has grown larger, as though it has a life of its own.

(22)

William Kane stays late at his desk, reviewing the recent report from New York. It is not good news. He reads through the report again knowing his conclusion will be the same. The old man will still be at his desk but Kane doesn't want to go in just yet.

Kane had planned on being an educator like his father when he was recruited out of school by a history professor who had taken notice of his papers, his removed but confident demeanor, his ability with languages. When he married Martha he did not tell her at first exactly what he did, but she was smart and after a few positions at various consulates, and then later long trips to the Mideast, she knew he was a spook.

They did not discuss his profession openly. Just one night a few years after Elizabeth was born she asked him point-blank what the chances were that she and Elizabeth would receive a visit from some anonymous man who would give his condolences and then disappear. He downplayed the danger. And then Elizabeth wobbled in from her bedroom and ended the conversation. She was three and having trouble sleeping almost nightly. They went and checked under her bed and in the closets. Martha never brought up the subject again.

Kane drops the fax into the shredder. It has been a long time since he has been the point man on a decision like this. He thinks of Elizabeth talking to friends and to boys on the phone too much, a perfect cross between Martha and himself, outgoing, highly intelligent, comfortable with herself, but innocent. The order he is to give will leave other Elizabeths suddenly without a father, without a husband. They will be in their familiar life one day and the next day in a world without someone they love.

He reaches to pick up the phone to call the old man, but it rings first. He has waited too long. A mistake. He picks up the phone immediately and Angelson's secretary is on the line. Angelson wants to meet.

After a quick mental once-over of the office, everything locked and put away, Kane grabs his jacket and heads into the long antiseptic hallway. Walking down the corridor is like walking in a vacuum. He heads in the opposite direction from the Telecommunications Interception Room. Angelson's probably got the latest report, knows as much as he does. Probably knows more. He gets to an unmarked door. He taps his six-digit ID number. A pleasant female voice that Kane knows is a computer requests a voice sample.

"ESAC one." Kane finishes the security clearance and the door opens on another hallway. Kane knows that as he walks down it he is being filmed, scanned with infrared and metal detection devices. The "pictures" taken now will be automatically compared with those taken when he leaves. A strong deterrent against smuggling anything out.

After passing through four more checkpoints, he reaches Angelson's spacious reception area. Angelson's personal assistant, a middle-aged stately woman named Mrs. Kehough, is nowhere to be seen and Kane waits.

A veteran of talks and planning sessions with Angelson, Kane has never gotten used to Angelson's office. Though it is only two average-size rooms, Kane knows, or thinks he knows, what it represents. And knowing that is intimidating. The space feels massive, the deepest corridor of power.

He was recruited by Angelson himself ten years before from the CIA's oversea ops to this organization, nameless and so secret it made the transfer of information at other government agencies seem like Internet bulletin boards. Prior to joining the group Kane had never known it existed. Eventually he grew to understand it was more than just a department of the NSA that handled various large off-the-books operations, as Angelson originally described it. It is its own self-contained agency. As far as he can tell the funding is huge, monstrous even, but he does not know what the money goes for outside his own programs, nor from where it comes, certainly not Congress.

Everything is compartmentalized. No one but the top people know anything more than what they need to. And the only "top" person Kane has ever met is Angelson. Even though Kane is running a large domestic operation that is potentially changing the history of the country, he has absolutely no idea what the guy in the office next to his is doing. He has never met any of the other midlevel people. Teams for domestic programs are culled from other agencies and then kept on or dispersed back to their original agency with a fat promotion when the job is finished. He had worked with one guy five years and the day the program they were working on no longer needed maintenance, the guy was gone and Kane had never seen him again.

But Kane knew he himself was considered a keeper. Now on his sixth program in ten years he can deduce that the large programs the agency runs are mostly domestically based, highly illegal, and geared toward political and financial manipulation of the country; he had been personally involved with systemic computerized and noncomputerized tampering with the economy through manipulation of the Federal Reserve and the stock market. Capitalism is still the country's financial system, America is still a place anyone can make it, but Kane has come to learn that the economy is a boat with a deep rudder. He understands that there are people who usually know the direction prevailing winds will blow and that it has been that way in some capacity since shortly after the creation of the Federal Reserve System. What he quickly suspected after joining the organization, what eventually he knew to be true but would never breathe a word of, is that the "shadow government" hinted at in movies or touted by fringe conspiracy buffs does in some form really exist. It has for many decades. Kane is sure of this. He is working for them.

Mrs. Kehough steps out of Angelson's office and says, rather formally, "He will see you now."

Angelson looks up from behind a massive walnut desk with only a paper shredder at one end and a small mobile of hovering white and black birds at the other. The birds are bobbing in a slow circular motion. Every time Kane has come to the old man's office the birds have been moving. On a dark mahogany tray on a stand next to the desk is a pitcher of orange juice and two empty glasses.

Angelson pours himself a glass. He takes a sip and motions Kane to sit. "Some juice, William? It's freshly squeezed."

"No thanks." Kane takes the soft leather chair to the right of the desk, as usual. He notices that the plastic trash can below the paper shredder is full to the brim. Angelson follows his eyes to the can.

"Do you—" Angelson takes another sip of the orange juice as though his throat is dry, "—have a course of action in mind?"

"Yes."

Angelson pulls a slim folder from his top drawer. He opens it and Kane can see photographs of all the targets in New York, three women and three men, clipped to the top of a field report. In one glance he can see the field report is one he hasn't seen. As usual, Angelson has his own team. People watching people watching people. Kane has the thought he always has with the old man: What more does he know than me? Angelson fingers two of the photographs. "So attempts were already made. Two failed but the most important was successful?"

"Yes."

Angelson holds up the photographs, studying them. "We're sure this is the one?"

"No doubt."

"And her too, a prostitute?"

"Yes."

Angelson drops the photos on his desk. "You know how cops are. There can't even be a whiff of anything but an accident or they'll go rabid."

"Understood."

Angelson pulls another photo free, shows it to Kane. "Do we even need to discuss this guy?"

"No."

Angelson flicks the photo onto the desk. "And these two." Angelson unclips two small color photos. "A handsome couple. He was asking questions?"

"Yes. He is compromised. She is now too."

Angelson holds up the last photo.

"She's clean. We have to be careful or this will turn into an epidemic and get noticed."

"Keep an eye on her."

"Of course."

Angelson drops the final photo into the pile. "If this is taken care of, will contamination be ended?"

"That is our analysis. My gut feeling is we've been pretty lucky so far and should take immediate action. I have people in place."

"I'm bringing in an independent."

"Is that necessary?"

"For reserve. A backup on retainer. Just to bring in if things get out of hand." Angelson smiles, finishes off his juice as though it is from a rare bottle of wine. "You know, the oranges are shipped fresh from Florida. Less than half a day goes by before I am drinking them." He swoops up the stack of photos and dumps them into the shredder.

Images of Potesky, Ruthie, Salmon, Lisa, Mac, and Eve are chopped into over a thousand unrecognizable pieces.

(23)

The independent arrives in New York at 2:00 A.M. He leaves his rental car at the Port Authority parking lot and takes a taxi to the Paramount. He is using the name Scott Joyce. One would think it better to choose a last name like Johnson but people will as likely remember you for a common name as a name less common. The key is to strike a balance, a place of invisibility; over the years he has perfected that ability, a knack for fading in, for being the face that no one can remember. He is neither tall nor short, neither good-looking nor bad-looking, just straight brown hair cut in the short style of the day and no distinguishing features except for gray eyes that change color according to the colors of his clothes. An added bonus in his profession. Of course, it is sometimes necessary to disguise features. If he is going to be on camera and can't avoid it, he will use a pair of glasses, maybe a mustache, but usually he does not need to; he was born with the talent for being anonymous and has cultivated this ability so that he is able to walk among police, drift through a roadblock, through life itself unnoticed.

He walks through the lobby, his gait uneven, his shoulders

slightly slumped, and memorizes the general layout, emergency exits, the number of elevators. As he steps into the elevator with the bellhop, one could ask the desk person, a woman who has worked hotel front desk jobs for twenty years, who prides herself on her ability at recalling names and faces, to describe the man who just checked in and she would be unable to.

The moment the bellhop leaves with a generous tip, but not so big it will attract attention, he straightens to his full height, his back ramrod straight, his movement around the room perfectly balanced like a cat. He checks out the room, the bathroom, the closet, the sight line from the windows.

He carefully places his passport, wallet with credit cards, and New Jersey license, all under the name Scott Joyce, on a bedside table. The last time someone addressed him by his original name was more than fifteen years before. That name, the name his mother gave him, seems far away, almost nonexistent.

He sits on the bed and takes out a bag of white pistachios from his jacket pocket. He begins to crack them one by one, laying the shells carefully back on one side in the bag. The call had come through unexpected channels. A rush situation. For most jobs he had time to plan. New York was difficult because of the cameras. It was a risk, but the money was way above top dollar and the targets were, as far as he could tell, just normal people. No bodyguards to get past. No security. Just wait by the phone and their location will be called in. Then he will do it. The job is a cleanup, more than one hit. As is often the case, he does not know exactly for whom he is working. But whoever it is they have wired most of the money in advance, enough to retain his services for a week. And this has never happened before. It occurred to him that the job was a setup, that he was the target, but the verifications were sterling. The money worth the risk.

He pulls his suitcase over and puts his thumbs on the fingerprint locks. They snap open and he removes the schematics for the surveillance setup in the city. A useful thing to have, the kind of thing a lot of people would pay significant amounts of money for. And he had. He is tired but will not sleep until morning; the call could come in four days but it could also come in ten minutes and he wants to be ready. He looks at the map and begins to memorize camera placements.

Dan Potesky walks to the end of the pier and looks down at his pride and joy, *Dorothy Said Yes*. Small waves gently rock the hull of the thirty-two-foot sailboat. When people see the name on the boat they always smile, the kind of smile that runs through a crowd when a marriage proposal is made in a restaurant or the birth of a baby is announced, the kind of smile people have when they feel an invisible thread between themselves and strangers, between themselves and what has gone before and what is to come. They always assume that the title of the boat is referring to his and Dorothy's marriage, that after twenty-seven years he is still the buoyant, bubbling husband. What it really refers to is that she let him buy the boat—for a brief glorious moment she released her greedy iron-grip hands from the purse strings when he convinced her that the boat was a good investment and allowed her to redo the kitchen she never cooked in. The name of the boat was a mistake but he decided to keep it as a secret wish, that he would ask and receive from her a divorce.

For years the kids had kept him from asking, but now that they both had families of their own, he was preparing to finally separate himself from her. His son had gone so far as to ask him point-blank why they stayed together. Potesky realized it was his son's way of saying that it was okay to move on, that he no longer needed to do the responsible thing, that after decades of leading two lives and feeling trapped he could be free.

He and Dorothy had been married in a shotgun wedding; she trapped him, one careless night at a local singles dance, and before he knew it a reception was being planned. Jeff was born and for a while that was enough. Potesky threw himself into his kids, their soccer matches, their triumphs and setbacks in school, and because of that it was as fulfilling a marriage as a loveless union can be. During the whole marriage he had slept with her maybe a handful of times. If he could have left her and taken the kids with him without fear of reprisal he would have. She was only a barely adequate mother on her best days, but at that time, barring an act of God, custody went to the mother. Secretly he wondered if she even liked men, if she was a young woman now she would probably have short hair and be dating other women. She had a group with whom she surfed the home shopping and electronic bingo networks, and whenever he came home the air in the TV room would go cold and quiet, as if he were an outsider, an alien.

He could not be blamed when after a few years he sought solace in the arms of women whose company he paid for, or another ten years later when he started a regular relationship with one of these woman, Ruthie Mardell. He had lived two lives ever since.

Ruthie was a peach of a girl who had had no breaks. Her life until she ran away to the streets was one unbroken string of dysfunction and abuse. She had looks and a body that was the kind that men appreciated and had clawed her way up to a midlevel prostitute—not a girl on the street, but not one in the Plaza either. On their first "date," Potesky found he was unable to sleep with her and they went out to dinner instead. After that he became one of her regulars, but they did not sleep together until their fifth visit, and though he paid her for the first few years they both knew that he was not a client. He had now seen her almost ten years. If he wasn't in such a bad marriage he probably couldn't have put up with her vocation. But because his home life was so broken, Ruthie fit right in. And now maybe, finally, they would leave together, sail away on the boat, live in different ports in the South. One could stretch the dollars a long way by living on a boat. He knew she had been saving, probably had a lot more than he, though what he had was enough. They would head south and leave their fractured lives behind.

Potesky steps from the deck into the boat. She is almost ready. Step by step, over the years he has restored and improved her interior, beds and a kitchen in the cabin below, new electrical wiring, a microwave, TV, and DVD. She is as comfortable as a small cushy apartment. A self-inflatable dinghy and all the latest safety and navigation equipment: G.P.S., a true motion radar, a gyro compass, and radio telephone had been installed. He has replaced the deck and all the brass fittings so that she looks new. A floating home. He runs his hand across the smiling wooden whale screwed into the slat above the hatch. Ruthie bought it for good luck for their trip.

A knocking sound comes from the pier and Potesky turns and looks down the dock. There is no one. Ruthie would not show up so early in the morning. Her idea of waking up early is before noon. She'll come at least a half an hour after he asked her to, sauntering down the dock, her hair perfect, nothing out of place, nothing to suggest it is only an hour after dawn. She does not go out in public without the look, the makeup, the whole thing.

He filed his early retirement papers the day before. Get out while the getting is good. Only five days before, prior to Sam's death, he would have been shocked if someone suggested that he'd be here this day preparing to leave. He had to talk to Ruthie, they hadn't planned on going for another two years, but she has nothing holding her. She'll pack her mountains of clothes, raid her safety deposit box, they'll step onto the boat and go. That will be it. The knocking comes again and he looks over the side of the boat and a piece of driftwood taps against the hull. His leaving would raise a few eyebrows but he would sail off and keep his mouth shut. Let that fat reporter do what he could. Potesky had picked Salmon only because he had met him years before at a police news conference and saved his business card; and because Salmon was from the *New York Times*. Maybe he should have spread the information around but that might have exposed him. No, he had done what he could while maintaining his own safety. Anything more would have drawn too much attention.

Something falls over in the cabin and Potesky jumps and sees a float cushion fallen to the floor. He chuckles to himself at being spooked by a cushion. He bends over to pick it up and feels an arm hard around his neck and a gloved hand pressing a wet cloth across his nose and mouth. He struggles for only an instant, the last thing he sees the Jersey City skyline through a cabin window, a tall building reflecting squares of white light. The light dims.

The man holding him gently lays Potesky to the deck of the boat and glances around the pier, not a person in sight. He quickly takes a lifeline and ties it around Potesky's waist, then takes a blunt square object from his pocket and hits Potesky once on the forehead. Before blood can get on the deck, the man easily lifts Potesky and dumps him over the side of the boat. He looks around the dock again and when he is sure it is deserted, he starts the boat's motor, leaving the throttle slightly forward. He undoes the tie lines and pushes the boat out toward the river.

(25)

Mac wakes at dawn and looks at Eve, her forehead against his shoulder. Images of making love with her floating through his mind, he closes his eyes and pleasantly drifts in and out of sleep; it hadn't been like that in many months, the desperation to be together. He carefully sits up in bed so as not to wake her and slides out from under the covers. He looks back at Eve to admire the way her hips and breasts curve under the blankets but the night table next to her side of the bed with the loaded gun inside looms in his field of vision.

For a few minutes in the fog of the early morning he has forgotten that his best friend is dead.

Ten minutes later, down in the kitchen, dressed and sipping a cup of coffee, he writes Eve a note and tries Salmon for the third time. No answer. Mac heads out the front door and gets into his car. As he backs out of the driveway he does not pay attention to the new dark green minivan parked across the street. There are a lot of minivans in the neighborhood and this one doesn't stick out so he doesn't notice a shadowy figure sitting in the front seat watching him drive away.

•

Salmon glances behind him as he makes his way up the sidewalk to his building. It was silly to go out of the apartment unnecessarily but all he had left to eat were frosted flakes that looked like they were a decade old. So he went to the corner Korean place for supplies, bagels, donuts and coffee, papers, the works. Salmon was in the mood for celebrating. He had scanned the papers first and there was nothing. According to the *Times* and everybody else, everything in Denmark was as it should be. He knew the story was easily the biggest he had ever gotten so far and was afraid that one morning he would see it all splashed across CNN. Only one more day or so, he just needed a few more pieces, a bit more confirmation, and then he would make his pitch.

He takes one last look up and down the street before entering his building. The doorman anticipates his question.

"No one unusual came in while you were out, Mr. Salmon."

"Thanks, Marv."

Salmon heads for the door to the stairs instead of the elevator.

"Doin' the stairs for your health, Mr. Salmon?"

Salmon smiles, opening the door. "In a manner of speaking, Marv."

Though it is seven floors to his apartment and his knee kills him, Salmon goes up one more floor, walks down the long hallway, and steps into the emergency stairway, which can only be entered from the inhabited floors and not from the lobby. He takes the stairs to his own floor and peers out the small square window. His hallway is empty. He pushes open the heavy metal door and walks to his doorway. No one has gone into his apartment. The toothpick he left wedged in the upper left hand corner of the door is still there. He pulls the keys from his pocket. When he feels the person standing behind him in the hall it is too late. He pretends to drop his keys.

"Hi, Marty."

Salmon whirls, facing Mac, the gun in his hand dropping to his side.

"I could have shot you."

"No. The safety's on."

"You shouldn't sneak up on people. Especially paranoid people." Salmon undoes his locks and Mac follows him inside.

After Salmon relocks the four locks on the door, he drops his bags on a table and begins pulling out bagels. He tosses one to Mac and they're still warm. Mac hasn't eaten so he doesn't toss it back. Salmon tears into a donut and gulps a large coffee.

"You know, I did some checking on you . . . pretty interesting stuff," Salmon says, his mouth full. "You're a one-man wrecking crew the last decade or so, since a girl and her mother were killed in the Bronx."

"Let's get to business."

"Just two months ago you traded yourself for hostages. Took out two bad guys. You have a death wish or has something just pissed you off?"

"Reporters piss me off."

Salmon washes down the last chunk of a jelly donut with a swig of orange juice and smiles. He motions Mac toward the RF-shielded enclosure. Mac frowns.

"It's the only way we can play show-and-tell."

Mac steps into the TI-7 and waits for Salmon to grab a folder out in the living room. Salmon zips up the entrance and turns on the fan.

"So you find anything interesting?" he asks, as if he already knows the answer.

"Yep." Mac shifts his weight. The enclosure's hardly big

enough; it's getting warm and Salmon smells like powdered sugar. "Most of the names on the sheet are hard to get hold of. A few are dead, two confirmed suicides—"

"Suzi Danilovic and Byron something."

"How'd you know?"

"Morgue records. Anything else?"

"Heather Duncap's been visited by the city a lot, the Health and Human Resources Department to be specific."

"She say why?"

"I ran out of time but she said something unusual, that she had already told us that everything was okay. When I asked her if we had visited her before, she said a million times."

Salmon hands Mac the folder, Xeroxes of newspaper articles from the last six months. Mac glances at the top few, the headlines reading like local TV news leading stories: "Lawyer Shoots Hot Dog Vendor, Self"; "Woman Plows Car Through Park, Kills Two, Injures Six"; "Train Track Suicide."

"So what do these mean?"

"Those mean that the people on the list are having a bad year."

The phone rings dimly from out in the apartment and Salmon visibly jumps. Mac looks at Salmon, who doesn't move.

"You aren't going to answer?"

"No. First rule. Never verify your location. Someone's been calling and hanging up when the machine picks up."

"That was me."

"Oh." Salmon unzips the entrance enough to hear the machine pick up the call, the sound of someone fumbling with a phone. A female voice comes on.

"Uh, Birdie has to call off tonight. You should get outta there. They know you're in the apartment."

The line goes dead and before the machine begins to rewind,

Salmon is slithering out of the TI-7 and gathering stuff into a knapsack.

Mac reflexively glances at the door, then at the windows, which are covered with blinds. "Did you recognize the voice?"

"It was my contact's sidekick, legs to the moon and all, and she didn't sound good."

26

Inside the phone booth Ruthie fights to stay calm. In her profession she has faced more than a few uncertain situations and found that the best way to get through them is to bluff, to show no fear; it takes the opponent by surprise and before they know what hits them you are either in control of the situation or gone. Probably this is okay. The guy met her at the end of the pier and knew everything about her and Dan and what Dan had been going through with all this undercover business at work. Said he was part of it, and that Dan couldn't make it because he had things he had to take care of and had asked him to meet her and have her make a call. They would be leaving that night on the boat. Said he was an old friend of Dan's.

"Just a sec," she says glancing over her shoulder to the man who waits outside the booth. She calmly ducks down and looks at her reflection in the pay phone's chrome surface. Her face looks uncertain as she applies a fresh layer of lipstick, but when she stands and steps out onto the sidewalk the uncertainty is no longer visible. She smiles and looks right into the large sandy-haired man's eyes.

"That okay?"

"That was great. Very helpful. Can I give you a ride?" The large man motions to his car, a four-door slightly old Oldsmobile. A cop's car, a family car.

"No, you know my favorite diner in the whole world is up at the corner. Dan and I always eat breakfast there. I think I'll get some coffee."

The man looks at his watch like he's got somewhere to be. He waves and starts to back toward his car. "Dan's a very lucky man. You guys take care on your trip."

"Thanks."

The man gets in his car. He waves again as he drives past.

Ruthie looks up and down the empty street. Total relief. The big guy was for real. Dan is okay. She begins to walk toward the diner and thinks about what she must do to get ready for leaving. Her clothes are already packed, the rest she would give away to friends, and she could give most of the stuff in her apartment to this newlywed couple who had just moved in across the hall and had only a futon. They would think they had won the lottery but she had gotten most of the things in her apartment free over the years from a few steady clients who were "involved" in electronics and furniture stores.

Taking care of the bank stuff, something she has been putting off, opening her safe deposit box to put some extra traveling money in her checking account, will be the hard part. The thought makes her stomach turn. She knows it is irrational, that she has more than enough money to support both her and Dan until they are old. She has worked hard, rarely turning down a job, spent little and compulsively saved for twenty years. Now is her moment of freedom, to enjoy her life. But the thought of touching the money makes her feel as if she will run out, as if she will never have enough, reminding her of when she was a kid and had nothing and lived on the street, her mother taken away by the police, the Social Services people prowling around the house.

A car pulls up behind Ruthie and the hair on her arms raises as the car just rolls slowly behind her. The diner is only a few buildings ahead. She quickens her pace. The car pulls alongside and Ruthie walks as though she has no idea. She hears the whir of the passenger window electronically lowering into the door.

"Hey, Barbara?" A man's voice. Barbara is her "stage name." Ruthie turns but keeps walking. The face is maybe vaguely familiar, a middle-aged balding overweight short guy, one of hundreds she has seen through the years. They all blend together.

"It *is* you. We, uh, got together a few years ago but I lost your number."

Ruthie stops because the guy has come to a double-parked car and can no longer follow. She glances into the late-model Lincoln. What is it with short guys and big cars?

"What a coincidence to run into you like this. I'd love to see you again. How 'bout right now?"

Ruthie sees the desperation in the man's face, hears it in his voice. Nothing to fear, just another john.

"I retired today."

"Oh, c'mon. I'll double your price."

Ruthie feels herself waver, always the song of money in her ears. She could use that to buy Dan a nice gift for the boat. She smiles but shakes her head.

The john sees the smile and latches onto it, trying to wear her down. "Look, you name the price and we don't have to go anywhere. A last time. I've always remembered you."

Ruthie feels herself involuntarily leaning toward his window, her breasts resting on the door. After years of being intimate with strangers, Ruthie prides herself on being able to read people, especially men, and when this man glances up and down the street, just the briefest flicker as she leans into the car, she knows to pull back, that she is not going to do this job. But she is too late.

The pain and surprise is so great that she does not scream at first as the man grabs her hair in his fist and pulls her forward into the car. The wig comes off in his hand but he has a clump of her real hair in his fist. His strength for his size is tremendous; he was specifically picked for this job because he is bald and short and would seem nonthreatening. She feels her face slam into the seat, her feet going into the air outside the car window. She flails around with her hands, one finding the man's groin but she is too late. He flinches and groans under her closed hand and the sound of his gasp of pain is the last thing she hears. A sharp prick on her neck fills her body with a tremendously heavy weight and she feels herself fall through the floor of the car into a dream.

Ruthie's body is found by a garbage disposal unit five days later at the back of an alley. When no witnesses are found, when the case is run through the computers and no MO for any current serial killings is established, the case is shunted to the back of the files. Death was by strangulation. Ruthie had a record. Just another prostitute killed doing a dangerous job.

(27)

Salmon leads Mac out an emergency exit at the back of his apartment building. Salmon ignores a large sign that warns a siren will scream when the door is opened.

"I disconnected the wires a long time ago," Salmon says. "Paid the super three hundred bucks for the pass key. It's under that cinder block if you come back here again."

"Where're we going?"

"To see this guy from the list named Henry Pollard who's agreed to talk to me."

Mac follows Salmon through a circuitous collection of connected dingy walkways and alleys to a street behind Salmon's building. He watches Salmon peer around the corner, scanning up and down the street. Mac smiles; it's like Salmon's playing a paranoid the way Dustin Hoffman would in a movie. But just to be safe, he reaches under his jacket and unbuttons his holster and takes off the safety as they step out onto the sidewalk. They walk one block to a garage.

"My car's here."

"You think it's safe."

"It's under a different name. I rarely drive it. Driving scares me."

Mac begins to follow Salmon up the stairs to the fifth floor but after a few stairs Salmon's breathing is ragged.

"You ever have your cholesterol measured?"

"Look, my IQ is fifteen points higher than Einstein's was. I don't need to be in shape."

When they come out onto the fifth floor, Salmon leans against a thick cement pillar and gasps for air. Sweat runs down his face like someone has poured a glass of water over his head.

"Look, if this—" he bends over, puts his hands on his knees, "—if we get this story out, I'll join Jenny Craig."

"If?"

"It can happen. You think Watergate was the biggest presidential conspiracy. *Pleasssse.* Only one in five major stories ever sees the light of day. And that one story is usually structured for consumption."

"And this is what you do with your powerful IQ?"

"Look. On the playground, in the office, in personal relationships, wherever, someone always takes over, someone or some group always rules, whether up front or behind the scenes, whether benevolently or ruthlessly. Why is it so hard for people to extrapolate this basic human interaction to the larger institutions in our lives? State, federal, whatever. People on a basic level understand that the world is not a democracy, people don't get their way based only on merit. And yet, when it comes to their own government we go into a sort of massive psychosis, like we're all on *Leave It to Beaver.* Well, I got news for you. Wally works for the CIA and Eddie's a child molester who will never be caught."

"I can't believe I'm going to get in the same car with you." Mac follows Salmon down a long row of vehicles. "Besides, when it comes to humans, things are rarely as organized as your theories would suggest. People are self-interested, sure. But that doesn't automatically lead to people working together, to the kind of coherent plan you're saying happens behind the scenes. Just look at the lack of organization in any large group—our dreaded federal government being a prime example."

Salmon stops and looks at Mac as though Mac is beyond naive. "First, the people acting in a highly coordinated way don't extend down to the person working behind a Plexiglas window at the DMV. And second, do you remember back in the nineties when the government admitted to doing syphilis research on black men in the South, and radiation testing on civilians since the fifties?"

"Yeah. Reparations were made to those people."

"The ones that survived. They gave radioactive isotopes to pregnant woman, some of whom had children who got leukemia. And there were orphan boys at a state-run orphanage in Buffalo who were fed pills at lunch. This stuff went on into the seventies. Programs were run where toxins were released in subways in New York and San Francisco to test the effectiveness of spreading biological agents through mass transit systems. Not to mention the experimentation by our government on our own armed forces, from marching foot soldiers toward nuclear bomb blasts in the forties and fifties to implanting ID chips in the bodies of new recruits in the nineties. These are just the known examples, the programs that got uncovered or the government has admitted to. There's countless more, truly horrific stuff. This wasn't our grandparents doing this, this wasn't back when the world was black and white. I'm sure those orphan boys who were part of the radiation testing who haven't outright died of cancer are pleased to have some extra money to pay for the checkups to make sure the government hasn't killed them yet, or maybe for an artificial leg because Hodgkin's disease took theirs." Salmon takes a big breath and stops at a light blue beat-up Pinto. Mac looks at a pizza box with tomato stains propped up in the backseat of the small car. He can just imagine the smell inside. Salmon fishes in his pocket for his keys.

"My point is, if the government could do that then, what are they doing now?"

Though grudgingly agreeing, Mac shows no expression. Maybe Salmon isn't as far out there as he sounds. Mac points to the car. "Your basic death trap. Probably engineered by the government to kill people with bad taste."

"This car is a classic, they should have one hanging in the Smithsonian."

Fifty yards away a Chevrolet Caprice with tinted windows pulls down the ramp from the sixth floor. The assignment was to pick up the reporter alone. A dry job, as the target was an out-of-shape guy: just tranq him and take him away. Never to be seen again. The presence of the cop alters the plan. The Caprice waits for orders over the radio, another few moments and the targets might stop talking and climb in the car. The order comes through: it will be wet works, a drug hit, lots of bullets and the drugs are on the way to be planted. Where the design had been for a clean event, the invisible pickup, mess will be a bonus now. In the backseat a briefcase is opened and a cobra machine gun, the kind currently in favor among drug lords, is lifted out. A large silencer is screwed on the end.

Salmon unlocks his door. There is a screech of tires from behind them and Mac turns around as the back windshield of the Pinto and the windshields of adjacent cars shatter. Before his mind even registers the Caprice he is unholstered and ducking against the side of a Peugeot. On the other side of the car, Salmon is not so quick but gravity does the trick as his bulk hits the pavement. The rain of fire is relentless as bullets tear up car metal and parking garage cement. From under the Peugeot, Mac is able to catch a glimpse of the shooter in the backseat, the window half-down.

The Caprice is about to pull alongside for the kill when there is a lull in the firing as the shooter reloads. Mac rolls to the edge of the Peugeot and fires as many electropatches as he can through the open window of the Caprice. He sees a shadow slump forward.

"*Marty,* start the car!!!"

Salmon moves surprisingly fast into the car, the engine of the Pinto roaring to life. Mac climbs into the passenger seat, dropping onto broken glass. Marty guns reverse, backing and turning all in one motion, then floors the gas when the Caprice rams the Pinto from behind, sending Mac half onto the hood, Salmon maintaining control, taking the sharp turn down to the next level at full speed. Mac, holding the dash, pulls himself back into the front seat. The Pinto slams sideways into a parked Saab convertible as Salmon sets up the next ramp turn.

Mac sees ahead on the fourth level the second car, the vehicle bringing the drugs to plant, set up sideways at the end of the driving lane.

"Marty!!!"

Salmon doesn't react; Mac grabs and turns the steering wheel hard to the left just as guns from the second car open fire. The Pinto hits the curb that divides the garage floor in two halves and Mac feels the car go airborne, sideways, one end higher than the other, then a tremendous jolt as the car miraculously lands right side up across the lot. Salmon, who was kept in place wedged behind the steering wheel, peels out, heading down the incoming traffic lane. A minivan veers out of the way and into a Mazda Miata. The Miata doesn't do well. Mac looks behind and sees that the Caprice has jumped the curb. Salmon weaves around a four-by-four backing into a spot. As the Pinto veers onto the second floor Salmon begins pounding the horn.

Down at the entrance/exit gates of the garage, Rodrego, a boy who has just graduated from high school, sits up at the screech of tires and constant beeping echoing down through the garage. He puts his comic book down and watches the long entrance/exit ramps as the sounds get louder and closer. Then a pale blue Pinto, the one the fat guy he calls the Fish, drives, comes skidding around the corner in the wrong lane. Rodrego can't believe his eyes. He can see the Fish waving at him through where the windshield should be and another guy in the passenger seat with a sleeper gun pointed out the back. At first his mind goes blank and he can't remember what to do, but he comes to and dives for the lever that controls the raised spikes that face the Fish's onrushing car. The lever, rarely used, is stuck. Another car skids into the entrance lane and Rodrego sees a man leaning out the passenger window with the biggest gun he has ever seen. Somewhere in the distance he can hear the Fish yelling his name as he pushes the lever with all his might.

The Pinto screams through the entrance just as the lever gives and the spikes drop an instant before the Fish's tires flash past. Rodrego immediately reverses the lever, which gives easily now, and the sharpened spikes raise, awaiting the tires of the second car. Rodrego lies on the floor and hears the ripping sound as the tires are shredded, immediately followed by a sharp screech, a crash, and an explosion. Pressed to the floor, Rodrego reaches up for the phone and calls 911.

Another car passes his hut at high speed out the exit lane and heads up the street. That fat wacko hadn't been lying. Hell, someone offers you a hundred dollars to lower the spikes in case they ever come down the wrong lane in a hurry, you take it. The Fish had given the money to everyone who worked the hut and promised more if it ever happened. Everyone thought he was crazy. Rodrego gets to his knees and looks across the street at the demolished car, flames fifteen feet in the air. Total goners. Rodrego sits back down and waits for the police to take him off hold and get on the line. As sirens begin to sound in the distance he hangs up and thinks of how much the Fish will give him, of all the great things he will buy.

The only people in the lot above the Riverside Drive Park are a family stopped to use the Porta potti and stretch their legs, on their way from one place to another. Mac is out of Salmon's car before it pulls to a stop and running toward a pay phone. He looks at his watch and punches in Eve's number. A creature of routine, she will be just getting her shower. The phone rings and rings. Mac slams down the receiver. It would take at least an hour to get home. By then she might have left. Better to sit tight and call every five minutes.

He walks back to the car against which Salmon is leaning, breathing heavily, sweating profusely, his heart pounding like a drum solo. He needs a few minutes to make sure he isn't going to die.

Mac looks at the bullet holes lining the back and front of the Pinto. A miracle the gas tank wasn't hit, not to mention themselves.

Salmon straightens, calming a little. "They didn't tell me about this kind of thing in reporter school."

Mac walks to the front of the car and pops the hood. A green fluid covering the engine hisses against the hot metal, making a small toxic cloud.

"Well, she'll still get us around."

"After this story I'm never leaving my apartment again."

Mac walks to the phone and punches in his home number

and listens to the phone ring over and over and over; Eve's probably in rinse cycle. He hangs up.

"C'mon." Salmon starts toward the Pinto. "Let's pay this guy from the list a visit. You can call along the way."

Driving down Ninth Avenue into Hell's Kitchen, Mac has a general feeling of unease. He has made Salmon stop twice so he can call Eve. She must have already gone to do errands. A compulsive phone answerer, she has never had the patience to screen calls. He must have just missed her.

Salmon double-parks the Pinto in front of a ten-story white brick building built in the sixties.

"We're here." Salmon pushes his door open with a loud creak. Bullets have damaged the hinge so it opens only partway and he has to squeeze to get out. Mac gets out and Salmon sees him looking up and down the block for a phone. "She's fine. The best thing you can do is help me crack and wrap these bastards. That's how we'll all be safe."

Salmon pushes the buzzer for Pollard's second-floor apartment but there is no response. After three tries Mac walks back to a phone at the corner and calls Eve. No answer.

Mac jogs back down the street.

"I know," Salmon says. "Go ahead. I'll wait for this guy."

"How do we get back in touch?"

Salmon pulls a scrap of paper from his pocket and writes a number on it. "This is my cell phone number but the line isn't secure. You musn't say anything substantive. If I say we should meet at blue, we meet on Riverside Drive and Seventy-third. If I say red, we meet at Third Avenue and Sixty-seventh Street. There are no cameras at those corners."

"Got it. Good luck." Mac waves and turns to go.

Salmon watches Mac run up the sidewalk, then glances hopefully around for a place to wait out of the cold, maybe get fries and a coffee, but there is nothing. He walks over to the Pinto and climbs in to wait. He notices on the floor, smashed to pieces by a single bullet, what is left of his cell phone.

Salmon looks up and down the street, suddenly feeling more exposed, more vulnerable. The breeze rattles the dead leaves on the small trees that line the street.

Eve steps out of the shower, less satisfied than usual. Normally the shower was a place where Eve collected herself, water usage be damned. When she was in college she had taken yoga and found that doing the moves under the showerhead was deeply therapeutic, allowing her to enter the day straight and clear, a daily baptism. But there was no lock on the bathroom door and she kept peering through the steam to make sure it was closed, flashes of Janet Leigh waving her arms filling her mind, a knife jabbing through the flimsy curtain, blood swirling with water toward the drain.

After everything Mac told her last night she had slept badly, lifting awake a few times to see a lurking shadow in the door to the hallway, hovering, coming forward, evaporating. She knows Mac is just being cautious but she also knows that his sense of potential risk and danger is unclouded and razor sharp. He doesn't have the emotional makeup to be foolhardy, to live within the veil of invulnerability that people create when they tell themselves they are not going to die, nor is it possible for him to overhype a situation, to embellish it, the way people do when they make a situa-

GUY HOLMES

tion seem more dangerous, more exciting than it really is so as to glorify themselves. For him to go into the garage and haul out that gun, something big must be up.

She finishes drying and throws the towel on the hook. She pulls on her panties and bra and then a pair of sweats. She reaches for another towel to dry her hair but decides not to use it. It's her day off and no one at the mall is going to care whether she has wet hair or not. That's the best thing about North Jersey, the size of the malls. Maybe she'll visit Victoria's Secret. She feels a flush of heat as the memories of being with Mac the night before fill her blood. She steps into the hall and goes into the bedroom to get her purse.

One floor below in the living room a man listens to her movements through the ceiling. He carefully resumes his task, closing the remaining curtains, so that no one walking by outside will be able to see in. The curtains are heavy and the downstairs turns dark, twilight. The man pulls a cord from his pocket and takes up a position against a wall at the foot of the stairs so he will have surprise.

Eve looks at herself in the large mirror above Mac's chest of drawers. She turns sideways, lifting her shirt, her hand stroking where her stomach would grow. Perhaps, imperceptibly, it already has, perhaps the smallest child, a bit of dream, is already forming inside her. She smiles. She could kiss herself she is so happy as she heads out into the hall and down the stairs.

Perhaps it is the darkness of the first floor, maybe she hears or feels a movement to her side as she steps off the stairs, but when the man lunges forward looping the cord over her neck and pulling back with all his strength, her hand has shot up between the cord and her neck, keeping her esophagus from being instantly crushed. Her bag drops to the floor and the man lifts her off the ground for a moment and she is too stunned to do anything but flail. She feels the cord cutting her hand, her air cut off, her lungs exploding with the need for oxygen, and with one reflexive gesture toward life she jams the heel of her shoe into the man's shin. He grunts behind her and falters momentarily, leaning forward. With her free hand Eve jabs her newly painted pink thumbnail back toward the man's face in search of his eye. If the man's head had been turned half an inch to the side, her thumb would have missed the mark, hitting his temple and Eve Wells would have disappeared without a trace, the case never to be solved. A matter of inches, life and death. But her thumb tears deep into the man's eyelid above his left eye and he screams, moving and tilting farther forward. Eve gets both hands under the cord, drops to a knee and using the man's own weight flips him forward onto her father's collection of decoys, wooden ducks of all different sizes, one of their heads snapping off. The man is on his feet in an instant.

The door is too far to make. The man has the angle. There is a pause, the man and Eve locking eyes, the man's left eye filling with blood. There is a calmness to the man, his breathing even, and Eve knows that this is no rapist, no psycho. He lunges forward but she turns and runs for the stairs. There is no time to think, she is all reaction and as she hears him starting up the stairs she gets to the second floor and runs for the night table next to the bed. The gun is in her hand, the safety flicked off as he comes through the doorway. She turns and fires, the gun impossibly loud, but the man dives, rolling under the shot, springing toward her. She fires again at close range and hears the man grunt as his fist hits her hand and the gun flies from her grasp. He knocks her down and pins her, his knees on her shoulders and then a pillow is over her face, hard. She tries to reach the man's face but he keeps his head tilted back, out of reach. Over and over she digs her fingernails into the man's forearms but he does not let up. A moment most people in the world will never face, the taking of their life, the knowledge that someone is forcing them to die, that one has only moments left and nothing can be done. Her legs are involuntarily moving and she feels the hot rush of water between her legs as she urinates. She swings her arm out, desperately reaching, and her fingers brush the butt of the gun which has fallen under the bed. She stretches for it, trying to pull it with the tips of her fingers, toward her thumb, into her hand. It is almost within reach but she is near the end.

The phone on the night table rings, startling the man, his knee shifting ever so slightly on her arm when he looks up and her fingers pull the gun, her hand grasping around it. She raises the gun with nothing left but the instinct to survive, firing blindly four times, three out of the four bullets hitting the mark, the man tumbling backward off her, dead when the second shot goes through his cheek.

The phone rings a few more times and in some deep recess Eve knows it is Mac but she is unable to move, lying on her back, coughing and gasping for air, swirling black shapes filling her eyes though they are open. She does not know how long she lies there; when she is able to sit up she feels the same tilted perception and lack of balance she has felt before when she smoked pot in school or after riding particularly violent amusement rides. She stands to her feet, her hand bracing against the bed. She looks at the man, holding the gun on him, and drops to her knees to throw up on the floor.

When she has regained enough stability, Eve checks each room on the second floor, the box of bullets from the nightstand in her pocket, the gun reloaded and pointed before her. She walks down the stairs to the first floor, the scattered decoys and some magazines on the floor the only sign of anything amiss. The front door is unlocked. She remembers before her shower stepping out to get the paper and coming back in to answer the phone, what turned out to be a phone solicitation, without ever relocking the door. She quietly turns the key in the lock and slides the bolt.

She checks each room, stepping through every doorway, her whole body shaking, half expecting another man to jump out from under the dining room table, from behind the refrigerator, but no one else is in the house. She climbs the stairs back to the second floor, rushing into the bathroom to wash the blood off, all the while listening for the sound of feet on the stairs, the gun close to her hand on the counter.

Changed into new clothes, she grabs her purse from the bedroom, not looking at the man sprawled backward in a way that one look tells you he is a corpse. She glances but only for a moment at the jagged parabola of brain and blood spray arching up the wall.

Edging forward, waving the gun left and right, she clears the stairs. She makes her way to the front door, unlocks it, then locks it behind her. She immediately sees the minivan across the street, not one she recognizes. Backing out of the driveway she keeps her head low, imagining a shot coming from the minivan, but nothing comes. A neighbor passes and waves but Eve does not wave back. That world, the one of barbecues and neighborhood watch programs, is gone.

She drives until she gets to the mall. She walks up to a pay phone outside a Pizza Hut. She must leave a message for Mac in case he calls in to retrieve messages from their machine. Her hand trembles as she drops in the two quarters and she hangs up the phone. She must be calm. She stares at a black spot on the sidewalk, what was once a pink piece of gum, and slowly, by force of will, she normalizes her breathing. She drops the coins in again and when the machine picks up her voice, though higher than normal, is clear.

"Mac, it's Eve. If you call in for messages don't go to the house. Something happened there. Uh, what we talked about last night. I'm okay, I'm all right though." She pauses and fights to keep her voice from breaking. "Remember where we ate two weeks ago when the tires were changed on my car? I'll wait there for you. I'm okay. Be careful, love." She hangs up the phone and the adrenaline is beginning to wear off; her whole body starts to shake. Before she gets to the car she is sobbing.

(29)

The taxi makes it back uptown to Mac's car in seventeen minutes and he lucks out on traffic, pulling into the driveway of his house in North Jersey forty-four minutes later.

From the outside everything appears normal. He walks around to the back and draws his gun. He takes the key out of the bird feeder and slowly turns it in the lock of the back door that leads into the kitchen. He steps into the kitchen and nothing is out of the ordinary except that it is spotlessly clean; Eve usually leaves the dishes until the evening. Into the hallway, the faint smell of ammonia in the air; into the living room, glancing around, his eyes rest on where the wooden decoys are arranged differently, the ducks and geese in formation instead of the haphazard way Eve prefers. He stands a moment, uncertain, then races up the stairs into the bedroom, the smell of ammonia stronger now, next to the bed two large, pure white blotches in the sea of the off-white carpet, as if the carpet has been bleached. He goes into the bathroom, the faint smell of a shower in the air, and turns in a circle, unsure what to do. He steps into the hall and walks toward the phone on the hall table to call someone, his department? Salmon? He does not know. His hands shaking, he reaches for the receiver and almost doesn't notice the small red light blinking on the answering machine. Numbly, he pushes the button and when he hears her he leans heavily into the table. Though she is trying to hide it, he easily detects the tremendous strain in her voice. He erases the message and checks the bedside table to make sure she has taken the gun. He makes the ten-minute drive to the mall in just under four minutes.

Eve sits in a far corner of the food court, her back to large, plastic plants. A good anonymous spot. From where she is sitting she can see the two main entrances into the semicircle of food stands. People are scattered at hundreds of white tables arranged around a fountain that had held fish when the mall first opened but which now only has coins scattered along the bottom. Children's wishes.

Eve adjusts the sunglasses she bought at the drugstore so they will not press on the abrasion below her eye. The Tylenol had kicked in fast and the bruises don't hurt so much but she hasn't stood in a while and wonders how she'll feel when she has to move. She has magazines but hasn't taken them out of the bag. A Styrofoam bowl of cream of broccoli soup sits in front of her, cold and uneaten.

A medley of innocuous songs engineered to foster a relaxed atmosphere and be entirely inoffensive floats through the air. The CD is programmed to replay and it's the second time she has heard the songs. The evenness of the Muzak, the flow of customers between kiosk and table calms her. Periodically she sees in her mind a picture of the man back at the house and shudders. It was not the mess one would expect in the aftermath of a gunshot wound to a person's head—the arc of blood along the wall was even graceful, almost elegant. And Eve feels no guilt for killing the man. He was, after all, trying to kill her. But the horror of taking another life, the finality of ending another person's existence, comes to her each time the image of the man flashes into her head. I have killed someone. . . .

As if something has been taken away from her, she knows she will never be the same.

Mac doesn't run through the mall; he doesn't want to attract attention, but walks quickly toward the food court, just another shopper on a hurried errand. He sees her before she sees him. She has chosen a spot way in the back and he separates from the crowd and makes his way between tables. He can't help himself and jogs the last few yards to her table and she stands and is in his arms, her face buried in his neck. He does not hear her crying but feels her back under his arms quivering, the skin of his neck becoming wet. He rubs her back slowly and says over and over, "You're safe now, you're safe."

(30)

Henry Pollard looks at his watch and hopes the reporter he agreed to meet at his apartment has given up and won't be waiting for him. When the reporter called it seemed like a good idea to talk to him. People should know the truth. People should know what was really going on. Not that he has the whole picture; he only has small pieces, clues that have been coming to him one by one for the last few months.

He looks up from the back of the downtown bus he is taking and nervously watches as the bus begins to fill, the last load of people crowding into the aisle and standing, leaving little room for movement. An attractive middle-aged woman stands nearby and smiles at him when their eyes meet. Henry Pollard looks away.

The bus pulls to another stop and takes on even more passengers. A messenger wearing black spandex and a silver cross outside his shirt slides in directly behind the middle-aged woman. The bus starts up with a jolt and the woman is thrown a few inches back into the messenger so that they are pressed against each other. The middle-aged woman does not step forward to separate herself from the messenger and Henry Pollard watches her begin to rock her hips backward in a rhythmic motion against the man, her lips parted, her cheeks flushed.

The bus begins to pull over for another stop and Henry leaps up from his seat, reaching across people, getting his hands on the messenger's throat, the messenger falling to the side, Henry ducking behind him, pulling the man's necklace back so that the cross begins to cut into the soft skin below his Adam's apple.

The bus doors open and Henry sees the messenger hopping out, waving to a friend, the middle-aged woman taking an open seat.

Marty Salmon watches each person who turns onto the block. There have been a couple of guys he was sure were Pollard but none of them stopped at Pollard's building. The wind has picked up considerably; the tweed coat just isn't doing it; he keeps thinking of the parka hanging on the hook in the front hallway of his apartment.

Down at the corner a wiry guy with his head down and his hands shoved into his armpits turns onto the street. His black hair stands straight up in the wind. Salmon watches the guy and prays he's the one. The cold has almost defeated him. The guy slows down to take a free newspaper from a receptacle, then begins to climb the stairs of Pollard's building. Salmon opens the Pinto's door and hurries across the street.

"Excuse me."

The guy almost flinches, whipping around, like street crime is still the problem it used to be. He relaxes a bit when he sees Salmon but still tilts away, edgy.

"Excuse me, are you Henry Pollard?"

"Who are you?"

"I'm Marty Salmon. We spoke on the phone. I'm a reporter for the *New York Times*."

Pollard is about to make an excuse to leave but Salmon jumps in.

"Only a few questions. There's money in it if you can tell me why your name is on this list I have."

"How much?"

Salmon looks Henry Pollard up and down, ragged and unshaven. Fifty might do it.

"Two hundred."

"Okay. Ask away."

"No." Salmon scans the street. "I'm freezing my ass off out here. Can we go in to your place or is there a diner nearby?"

Henry looks at the guy. The idea of letting him in the apartment is unpleasant, but on the other hand the thought of being in a diner with a lot of people is unacceptable. Two hundred dollars is worth it.

"C'mon." He turns and slips the plastic key in the lock slot.

The building smells of dead animal. Probably mice, a stack of small skeletons in the walls. Salmon limps up two flights of stairs and follows Pollard into a small dingy apartment with a smell worse than the hallway. Salmon wishes they had stayed outside. Pollard flicks on a light and Salmon sees thousands of newspaper and magazine articles taped to the walls, certain words and headlines circled in red, the only two he can make out, an earthquake in Italy and a line proclaiming the end of the world by an approaching meteor.

Salmon sits on a rickety chair and notices for the first time a nervous twitch in Pollard's left eye. Salmon motions to the walls. "You like reading?"

"What list?"

Salmon pulls a Xerox of the list and tosses it on a coffee table strewn with disemboweled magazines. "Recognize any of these names?"

Henry Pollard studies each sheet and drops them on the table one by one. "No."

"You been visited by any state or federal agencies?"

"I've been getting disability I didn't know I qualified for. They contacted me. Have to fill out a questionnaire each month."

"Disability? You hurt at the job?"

"No." Henry leans forward. "My coworkers couldn't handle the truth. I didn't used to be able to either."

"What federal agency is giving you disability?"

"I don't know the name."

"What questions do you have to answer?"

"Health stuff, some physical, but mostly mental. They wanted me to take some medication and I pretend to."

"Mr. Pollard, do you often have violent thoughts?"

"Doesn't everybody."

Salmon isn't sure what to ask next so he says whatever pops into his head just to keep things going so Pollard won't cut off the interview. "Anything out of the ordinary happen to you in the last year or so?"

Pollard taps his hands together and when he begins to speak Salmon feels the air in his lungs go light, his hand unconsciously copying every word Pollard says, the pieces of the puzzle suddenly slamming into place. Every unrelated event perfectly tied together. Salmon almost forgets to breathe. It is so simple.

31

Mac chooses a motel called the Chateau Amore in Queens not far from La Guardia Airport. Choosing a motel in North Jersey would be a mistake and the Amore is a run-down place with theme rooms for people who are paying by the hour and aren't going there to sleep, probably not the first place someone would look for people lying low for a couple of days.

The Jungle Room and the White House were available but he chose one of the simple rooms, furnished with a heart-shaped vibrating bed and bad acrylics of lovers on the beach. He had told the old man behind the desk they would be there a couple days, then slipped him an extra hundred, no disturbances, no maids, no nothing. The old clerk had thought they were an awfully well-heeled couple to come into the place but figured that "slummin' it" probably turned them on.

Mac pulls the blinds while Eve uses the bathroom. He had told her everything he knows, which isn't much more than what he had told her before. She is holding up remarkably well; that morning she had blown a man's brains out the back of his head but she is calm and clear, wanting to know what the plan is. Often people had an immediate breakdown or a delayed shock but he suspects that like him she has the stomach for it. That doesn't mean she will be able to sleep tonight or won't cry tomorrow, it just means she will be okay.

She comes out of the bathroom and sits on the bed. He sits next to her and takes her hand. He can't tell her that he is in way over his head, that his main hope is a fat out-of-work reporter who may or may not be able to get the job done.

"I've got to go out in the morning, meet the guy who's working on this, get some cash."

Eve reaches into her purse, pulls out two plastic cash chips. "Already did. Cleaned out our accounts, converted our credit cards. It can't be traced."

Mac smiles at the two small rectangles of plastic, instant, untraceable cash. Eve drops one of them into his hand. "I saw Julia Roberts do it in that movie where she's a renegade cop and everybody's after her." Eve gives Mac's hand a squeeze. "We could just leave, we have enough."

"They murdered Sam. And it might never be safe. I'm not sure what we're dealing with."

"Isn't there anyone we can go to?"

"No. We go the wrong way and that's it."

Eve looks at Mac's profile, the strain pulling his cheeks taut. She lightens her tone. "I finally got you into one of these places," she says, jiggling the bed.

"This is the kind of place you like being in? I thought you preferred porno theaters."

"I think I could use some of that."

"Some?"

"We have to stick to our schedule. And besides it'll help me sleep."

Eve turns out the lights and Mac feels her hand and her mouth and the way they are together is reassuring, a unified need to reach for safety, to go to a place they had known before any of this happened.

(32)

Salmon stands a half block up from his building behind a delivery truck. The new doorman, a guy who just started, arrived forty-five minutes earlier but Marv Lupino, the day doorman, hasn't come out yet to head for home.

Salmon, still just in his tweed jacket, shivers, the evening cold. He has a ton of circumstantial evidence to get things started but if he goes to the *Times* too soon, without a "smoking gun" or a known source, he'll just be a catalyst for the bloodhounds at the paper to get on the story and take all the credit.

Marv Lupino finally steps out of the building and hurries toward Salmon's position. When Marv gets a few feet away Salmon motions to him to come to the space between vehicles.

"Marv, c'mere a sec."

"Mr. Salmon, I'm late for my daughter's birthday." Marv steps halfway behind the delivery truck, unsure, anxious to leave.

"I need you to get some stuff from my apartment. I'll give you enough to buy your daughter the nicest present she's ever gotten."

"Mr. Salmon, I can't. My wife already will have my head I'm so late." Marv steps back onto the sidewalk.

"Anyone unusual come to the building today?"

"No. You got a FedEx package and I put it inside your door like always."

"A package. Marv, what was it?"

"Don't know." Marv turns to head up the street.

"The return address?"

Marv thinks for a moment, snaps his fingers. "Oh yeah, struck me as odd, didn't know you were into birds. It was from the Audubon Society."

Salmon cautiously makes his way down the small alleyway behind his building. Probably the gestapo wouldn't expect him to come back to his apartment. And anyway they wouldn't expect him to be able to circumvent the emergency exit alarms. His defenses at the apartment were excellent once he got in.

The red emergency exit door looms in front of him, a dim red bulb over the door lighting a No Admittance sign. Salmon glances around the deserted alley and hurries to the door. He unlocks the door with his pass key, then places it back under the cinder block. The basement is quiet. No one in the laundry and Salmon lets himself into the stairwell and begins to climb the eight flights of stairs more easily than usual. Salmon is excited to get to the package in his apartment. It has to be from Birdie.

At his floor Salmon waits. Two doors down from his apartment a young family is moving in, carrying boxes from the elevator into their new home. When there is a lull in their activity Salmon emerges into the hall and hurries to his door, his hand around his gun in his pocket. He glances into the corner of the door, the toothpick still wedged securely between the door and the door frame where Marv put it back in place. He quickly unlocks

P. E. A. C. E.

the four locks, softly shuts the metal door behind him, and relocks the locks.

He walks through the dark apartment and carefully places large Styrofoam squares into slots over the curtained windows. He flicks on a few halogen lamps but to the outside the apartment stays dark and unoccupied. Salmon plucks the FedEx package from the table and rips it open.

A computer disk. Unlabeled. He grabs his laptop from a desk and hurries into the RF-shielded enclosure. He presses his finger to the hidden heat-sensitive On switch on the laptop and it silently pops to life.

He sits on the floor, inserts the disk into the computer, types a few commands, and waits for a list of the disk's contents to come on screen.

One entry entitled MEMO.

He clicks into MEMO.

He scans the one-page document and his heart begins to pound.

The smoking gun.

He makes a fist and punches the air a few times. He blows out a long breath of air, calming himself, and pulls his notes to his side. No more scrounging for scraps. Filet mignon from now on. He begins to condense his notes and the memo into the article that will make Watergate look small-time.

In the apartment directly above Salmon's a woman lies on her stomach in a deep drug-induced sleep on her bed. An IV pole holds a plastic bag of nutrients and sugar that drip into the woman's arm so the woman will not starve. There are enough bags to last a few days if necessary. Every few hours one of the two men waiting out in the living room comes in, checks the woman's pulse, and flips her. She is someone's sister, otherwise she would be in a body bag, the victim of a sudden aneurysm or a freak case of botulism. The two men watch three monitors attached to pen cameras that have been inserted into holes drilled through the floor down into Salmon's apartment. The cameras are easily turned so that they can follow Salmon's movement in every square inch of the apartment.

The moment Salmon went into the RF-shielded enclosure the order was given and three men were dispatched to take care of him. But a man and a woman helping the family move into the apartment are standing in the hall talking, so the three agents are waiting until the hallway is clear. There can be no witnesses.

The writing for Salmon is easy; a document detailing all the facts of the case from his first contact with Birdie to his recent interview with Henry Pollard. He doesn't lay it on too thick. He knows it will be changed, beautified, and that when he goes to the *Times* the story will no longer be his exclusively. But he needs the *Times*, all the news that's fit to print, all the power that's theirs to wage, to make sure it won't be squelched, to keep him safe. The tabloids break a lot of stuff but can't be trusted. There's TV but he would lose even more control with them; he wants the book rights and a piece of the movie. He stores the article onto the disk.

Salmon hears a noise outside his door and is instantly on his feet. He pulls the disk from the computer, steps out of the enclosure, and hits the lights. The apartment goes dark. He slides the computer disk under the plastic pot of a huge dead fern. He is fumbling for his gun when the front door bursts open. He turns to run down the hall toward the kitchen when he feels as though someone has punched him so hard in the back that it knocks him forward off his feet.

He sees himself getting up and running down the hallway, his legs curiously light, making it into the kitchen, flicking the hook on the metal door that automatically snaps it shut, buying the few seconds he needs to climb out onto the fire escape, the ladder sliding murderously fast under his weight toward the ground, the freedom of the alley stretching before him unobstructed.

The way Salmon has landed in the hallway of his apartment, his head is tilted backward and in the soft-edged disc of light from a flashlight, a pair of black shoes below black trousers is approaching. It is the last thing he ever sees.

In the dark of the apartment three figures move with quick and quiet efficiency. The laptop is put in a box along with a stack of computer disks. Each room is carefully searched. All papers and files are stuffed into nylon bags. One of the men, smaller than the others, sits down with a sheet of Salmon's paper and one of his pens, a Disneyland felt-tip with Mickey and Minnie Mouse waltzing at the top of the cap. He begins to write a suicide note in Salmon's handwriting. The men leave through the front door and leave it unlocked.

In the living room it is quiet except for the sound of a soft rain outside that has just begun to fall. Salmon lies on his back on the floor, a hole in his head from the gun loosely held in his right hand. Forensics will find powder burns from the gun, one Salmon had bought and registered a few years before, on his hand and on his temple. A mysterious square bruise will be found on his back but will be discounted as unrelated to his death.

The position of the body, as is often the case in suicides and murder, will seem to be indicating something, a gesture at meaning from the bridge between life and death, his left hand pointing to a large dead potted fern.

33

Mac slides his skeleton swipe card in the lock of Henry Pollard's apartment when there is no answer. It is 6:00 A.M. Eve had not wanted him to leave but Mac was sure she would be okay at the motel and the only way they'd really be safe was if he found answers. Salmon's cell phone number didn't work and there was no answer at the apartment so he was on his own.

The door opens easily and Mac steps into a dark apartment. He looks in the bedroom, the bathroom, and the kitchen but no one is home. He turns on the lights in the living room and the apartment is eerily spotless, full of stuff but like no one has lived there in a long time. Mac goes into the kitchen and the smell of ammonia is strong. Like at home. Mac looks at the chrome handle of the refrigerator and there is not a single smudge. On the refrigerator door a three-by-five card is taped with the words written in a neat slanted script, *Freedom from the advertising vortex.*

Mac opens all the drawers in the kitchen, then moves to an old file cabinet in the corner and sorts through piles of papers, mostly bills and junk mail. In the bedroom Mac rolls up the futon to look underneath and goes through the closet and dresser.

Slowly, deliberately, unsure what he is looking for, he takes a half hour and searches each room.

Along one wall in the living room a bookcase is tightly packed with books, mostly science fiction and fantasy. Mac runs his fingers along the books, in alphabetical order by author and by title under each author. The bindings of the books run in a perfectly flat line except for the second half of the Heinlein section, where six or seven books protrude slightly as though they have been recently pulled out and put back. Mac pulls them out, nearly bringing down the whole section, they are wedged in so tightly. He flips through *Glory Road* and *Starship Troopers*. Nothing. He opens *Stranger in a Strange Land,* and a page of newspaper neatly folded into a square falls out from between the cover and the first page. Mac unfolds the newsprint, a months-old article from one of the tabloids. Mac scans the page and his eyes go wide. Though he can't be absolutely sure, he thinks he knows why Sam died.

(34)

Julian Sanders sits in traffic in a limo on his way to a television studio to tape a segment for *CNN Reports*. His mother passed away during the night. His brother Charlie is handling the funeral, which will be small; most of his mother's friends have already died. Julian feels his eyes go hot but knows he will not cry. During his mother's downturn, especially in the last few weeks, he could not stop crying, but now that she is gone, eased into what she believed would be heaven by an extra dose of morphine, he does not need to cry.

The limo rolls through an especially jagged pothole and Roderick is jostled awake in the seat across from him. Ben is in the front seat. The anchors on *CNN Reports,* friends of Julian's, will ask the inevitable questions, the same ones he just responded to for ABC's *The Answer:* Isn't he crying wolf when the PEACE system has been so successful curtailing crime? If statistics support the models the computer uses to identify suspects, how can that be racist? Isn't he hurting his own public standing, his future political aspirations, by arguing against a system so overwhelmingly supported by public opinion? The arguments against him are persuasive. And if logic were the guiding rule on this issue he would be hard-pressed to keep the views he has been expounding on any show that would have him. In fact, the instances of racism in arrests are significantly lower in the PEACE Corps than they were with the regular NYPD. Minorities are represented in disproportionately high numbers at every level of the PEACE Corps. So what is he complaining about, anyway? That's what they would be asking, with practiced looks of disbelief at his answers, his buds at CNN.

He is complaining because the PEACE system fundamentally abrogates civil rights; someone should be screaming, because it is a system just waiting to be abused, a luxury car with its door open and the keys in the ignition. He is complaining because of something that was said to him, something he can't talk about.

A few years before at a posh party in Washington, D.C., one of those exclusive affairs for two hundred people where everyone was someone, a guy he had never met before, a well-dressed guy, approached him and shook his hand saying, "Julian Sanders, I've followed your work for years." The man never introduced himself, there was the smell of alcohol on his breath, and his manner was that of a man who has had one too many. "Mr. Sanders," he said with a smile on his face as though they were talking about the weather or the Redskins, "until recently I worked for the government overseeing test runs of a surveillance system. It could be used to fight crime or for a lot of other things. Keep your eye on it. It'll have its eyes on you." And with that the man turned away and wobbled unsteadily, but not too much so, out a side door onto the terrace. Julian followed and watched the man walk, now brisk and straight, without the slightest tipsiness, down the long drive.

At the time of this party the anticrime system was only a farfetched political promise by Bill Harris, a candidate who was trying to make up twelve points on the incumbent, President Raddick. A dream, smoke and mirrors, unimaginably costly and without a chance of becoming reality.

And yet, according to the man, some form of it was already a reality. Julian had played the encounter over many times. Clearly the man was pretending to be drunk, probably his "chance" meeting with the man was not chance. But what was it? How could what the man said not be true, given the PEACE system's astounding start-up time and subsequent success? There had been no bugs, no breakdowns, no mass arrests of innocents identified by an off-kilter computer as many had predicted. Julian had met his fair share of spooks in Washington and he had come to the conclusion that most spy stuff was relatively mundane, bomb counting, technology protection, et cetera, but that behind the known intelligence community, probably grown up out of it, there lurked a deeper force, a deeper understanding and coercion of the country. Julian had no real proof, just a feeling, and a little logic. After all, if President Raddick had known about the surveillance system already developed during his term, why would he, a conservative, with much to gain from an anticrime system, have attacked anticrime technology as unworkable? Clearly he didn't know—or, he did know and this surveillance system was never supposed to have been revealed except for President Harris's initiative and public acceptance. Either way it led to the same conclusion. The system was developed in secret, not to spy on criminals, but to spy on us.

(35)

Lisa idly flips through channels in her mother's TV room. Though it is noon outside, the room is entirely dark except for the light of the TV. Lisa has a box of tissues next to her but isn't using them. If it is possible to run out of tears, she has. She can no longer cry. It has been five days since Sam died but Lisa has no sense of time. The days blend together and the only thing she can do other than sleep is watch TV. In an odd way the game shows are comforting; she does not really follow them, just watches the screen, people jumping up and down, winning prizes and money.

Lisa switches the channel and comes to rest on CNN. Julian Sanders is sitting at a long desk with three men who are asking him questions.

Julian leans forward and responds forcefully, "PEACE *has* worked so far. But we need to be careful here. Just because something works doesn't make it right. Just because something appears to have no problems doesn't make it perfect. Just because—"

"Julian," one of his inquisitors cuts in, "just because you're speaking doesn't mean you're answering my question." There is laughter around the table.

The door opens and Lisa's mother stands in the doorway bathed in light. Lisa shades her eyes.

"We need a load of groceries, Lisa. I made up a list for you," Valerie says.

Lisa doesn't respond. Valerie pays no attention and makes her way to the curtains covering the front bay window. She pulls the cord and the curtains slide open, flooding the room in light. Lisa puts a pillow over her face. Valerie makes her way to the couch and lowers herself from her walker to sit next to Lisa. She strokes the back of Lisa's neck, then takes Lisa's hands in hers.

They sit this way for a long time. When Valerie gets up to go she leaves the list of food on the table.

Lisa walks down the street toward the corner grocer. She knows that there is plenty of food in the freezer, that her mother is only trying to get her to do an errand to help her.

Lisa hears the faint squawk of a two-way radio, two voices then static. She looks around but there is no one except for a woman she doesn't recognize sitting on a stoop across the street. The sound stops. Lisa continues on. For a couple of days she has had the eerie feeling she is being watched—in the house, at the funeral, a sense that someone is peering in on her, examining her.

She is almost at the grocery when she turns to look back up the street. The woman on the stoop is gone.

36

Mac sits in his car outside the PEACE precinct, watching officers go in and out. Just a week before he would have felt so comfortable there, as though it were a second home. Now HQ seems menacing, something unknown. He had called in to see if Potesky was on duty and the operator had told him about the "accident."

Mac grips and ungrips the steering wheel, something for his hands to do, somewhere for the anger to go. Codd will arrive soon and, one way or another, give him some answers. There is every chance that Codd is out of the loop, but if so, Mac will tell him everything. Either way, he will gain an advantage over what he has now, a missing reporter, two deaths, and a hazy picture of what is going on.

When Codd shows up Mac's plan is to grab him before he gets inside, but Codd doesn't arrive in his car. Instead he steps out of a limo right in front of the HQ entrance. By the time Mac is out of his car Codd is already inside the doors. Mac has no choice but to follow him inside. The limo makes up Mac's mind which tack to take: charge hard at Codd as though he knows.

Mac enters the HQ building. Probably knowledge of what is going on is limited to a few people at higher levels of power, so Mac does not search each face that passes in the halls, does not read into each comment or condolences offered about Sam by other officers. Tom Martinez actually gives him a hug as he makes his way toward Codd's office. Dimpter comes up with a surprised look on his face.

"Wells, didn't expect to see you here."

"Just gotta take care of something."

"I'm sorry about Mullane."

"Thanks."

Mac continues on and doesn't turn back to see Dimpter watch him and then pick up a hall phone.

The glass of the door to Codd's office is fogged so Mac can't see in. He knocks and enters. Codd looks up from a small cabinet, where he is pouring a drink.

"Come on in, Wells."

Mac closes the door behind him. Codd hands him the shot glass with whiskey in it and pours himself another.

"You heard about Dan?" Codd seems genuinely sad, shaken even. Mac nods, and decides to go slow, feel things out.

Codd sniffs, then lifts his glass. "To Dan. At least he died doing what he loved most." Mac downs his shot, his eyes watering briefly from the sting and heat in his throat. Codd sits behind his desk and motions Mac into a seat.

"So it was on his boat?"

"We're still going over it, but it's pretty clear-cut. We found an empty bottle on deck. Toxicology tests will come back later this morning. Probably drinking, fell off the boat and hit his head. What an awful week."

Codd seems genuinely crestfallen but Mac decides to lay it on the line.

"I know there are side effects from the electropatches."

"What?" Codd looks up like Mac has just said there is a spaceship on the roof.

"Look, Captain, I don't know what you know but Sam's death was no accident. He was killed because I shot him with my sleeper gun and someone was afraid the side effects in a PEACE officer would attract too much attention."

"What are you talking about? This is crazy."

Mac pulls out his sleeper gun and points it at Codd's chest.

"If I'm crazy I'll be relieved of duty after I put you out and that's all that will happen . . . but if I'm right, you'll be the one who has to undergo psychiatric tests, know what I mean?"

Codd looks at the gun then at Mac. "You're just under stress."

Mac braces his arm to fire. "You have three seconds. One, two—"

"Stop this!"

Mac hesitates.

"Wells, what's wrong with you? The only thing that's going to happen if you shoot is I'm going to have a nice nap in this chair and your career will be over!"

Codd is convincing but Mac notices a coldness slipping into his expression, like an actor watching to see if his performance has worked. Mac fires, the electropatch whizzing by Codd's temple and hitting a framed photograph on the back wall of Codd shaking the mayor's hand.

"*Wait!*" Codd's hands are up in front of his face like he is trying to halt traffic. "We have had problems."

Mac relaxes his trigger finger. "I'm listening."

Codd changes his expression, no longer a man grieving the loss of a compatriot, no longer a man who is afraid of the tranq-gun pointed at him. His face becomes conspiratorial, desperate, a man who wants to control what will happen next. "Some of the people shot with electropatches have developed complications, subtle behavioral changes to advanced states of mental disorder, paranoia, self-aggrandizement, it runs the gamut."

"The government knew this the whole time?"

"As far as I know, it caught everyone by surprise when it first showed in the jails in prisoners who had been tranqued when they were apprehended. The guns will be phased out when the Grid is fully operational."

"In the meantime people lose their minds? And Sam is killed."

"Sam fell down the stairs. We can talk about this, right?"

"Keep talking."

Someone knocks on the door. Codd doesn't answer. The figure floats away. "What do you want to hear?"

"Why'd Sam react to my shot?"

"Alcohol level in the blood."

Mac looks at his empty shot glass. Codd smiles slightly.

"Of course, it's not exact. If you're an alcoholic and are zapped, you have no chance. Something to do with the amount of acetyldehyde produced in the liver. You have alcohol in your system and get put down by a tranq-gun and, more than likely, the floodgates in your brain open, a tidal wave of hormones, cholecystokinin, lipotropin, dynorphin . . . the stuff that controls fear, rage, suicide, all the best emotions, pours through your neurotransmitters. It's like walking around in a constant fight-or-flight response increased ten times. At least that's the way I understand it. They don't really know what's going on. No one knows what one drink in your system will do. I wouldn't chance it, though."

"You mean I could have an 'accident' like Sam and Dan."

Codd leans forward on his elbows. "You know how hard it was to get PEACE implemented? Wells, I want you to understand how much is riding on its success. More than you understand."

"What is it? Money? Prestige? When did you stop being a cop?"

Codd tilts back in his seat, looking Mac up and down like he's measuring him for a suit. "I always liked you, Wells. You have a talent that can't be taught. A certain . . . lack of feeling under pressure. You could have been something special. Still could."

"Tell me who you work for."

"I'm just a team player who appreciates that over two thousand lives have been saved in the last six months because of this system . . ."

"But cold-blooded murder is okay."

A spot in Codd's upper cheek twitches. "Look, I'm not the one who got a little girl and her mother killed because he likes to play with señoritas."

Mac is on his feet, his gun poised.

"It doesn't matter what happens here," Codd says. "That fat lump of shit you're counting on so heavily isn't going to be able to run the story anyway. Not anymore."

Mac aims between Codd's eyes. It would be justice to shoot him.

Codd sees Mac's expression, the certain lack of feeling he was just complimenting. "I didn't know they were going to kill anyone! You have my word! Dan was my friend. I have a wife and two boys. I'm just trying not be next. You have to understand."

Mac pauses, lowers his gun. Codd's pleading is pathetic, but Mac doesn't want every PEACE officer in the city after him. Mac backs toward the door. "This never was about crime, about saving lives, was it?"

"Mac, don't be naive. We live in the most prosperous country in the history of the world. It didn't get that way playing nice."

Mac holsters his gun, opens the door, and heads down the hall.

•

Codd picks up the phone the moment Mac is out of the room. He dials a number and the middle-aged man who arrived in town that morning and introduced himself as William picks up on the other line. Codd's hands are sweating.

"Yes?"

"He was just here. He drank the remote."

"Good. We've already got people on it." William hangs up and Codd lays the phone down on the desk. He knows the reason they're still leaving Wells in play is so they can find his wife, tying up all loose ends. He did not mention to William that he had just told Wells everything at gunpoint. That would be unacceptable. Probably if everything came apart they couldn't trace it to him. It was only, after all, confirmation at best; Wells already knew a lot. But what if they had his office bugged? Then it was already too late.

Codd sits back in his chair and wipes the sweat from his forehead. He thinks for a moment; he has never done anything like what he is about to do, but he pushes a button on the communication console and makes a call within the department.

37

Mac times the sweep of the camera outside PEACE HQ so that it is pointed away from him when he steps down to the sidewalk. He walks past his car without stopping, hurries to the corner, and heads down a cameraless side street. Mac looks back toward HQ but the street is empty and he steps into a clothes shop halfway down the block, a hip place with mostly retro eighties clothes. He picks out a black baseball cap, a pair of wraparound sunglasses, and a black jacket.

At the next block he crosses the street in a crowd of people. He can feel the blaze of a camera's eye above. Probably, at that moment, DADD is scanning everyone in the precinct's vicinity looking for a match. Mac pulls his cap lower. What they aren't counting on is that he knows the system, that for the next few days he will not again look like himself.

What Mac isn't counting on is that half a block behind him a gray van pulls along slowly. Inside the van are two men watching a small hand-held tracking monitor, which receives an exceptionally strong signal sent by a radioactive microtransmitter he swallowed in Codd's office.

Mac walks to a row of cabs waiting for fares. His head feels light from the alcohol. He opens the door to the first cab but it is too clean inside, too new-looking, the backseat covered in plastic. He walks back to the next cab in line, this one beaten up, the dashboard full of books. The cab driver is an immigrant from China and smiles a lot as Mac gets in. Mac points up the street. "Just head toward the Upper West Side." The cell phone in the front rings and the cabbie picks it up and begins to speak in rapid Chinese.

Mac looks out the back window, a rental truck, a van, a Mercedes with tinted windows, and countless cabs; he sinks lower in his seat. Codd's words, " . . . that fat lump of shit isn't going to be able to run the story anymore," had the sound of fact, of inevitability. Codd wasn't bluffing. Probably Salmon was gone. Mac could go to the media himself, to the *Times,* to TV, but what if they wouldn't go with the story; Salmon had said that that was a possibility. And what if they believed him but had to have confirmation and confirmation was no longer available? The story was pretty fantastic and he had no proof. If someone had come up to him a couple days before Sam died and told him what was going on he would have never believed it. And the media couldn't be trusted to do the right thing. He was always surprised when people actually used media as a reference source, relaying something they had just read on their computer as if it were fact. All the gossip that's fit to pass on.

He looks out the cab's back window and all the cars behind have changed except for jostling cabs and the gray van. Ahead the flashing lights of police cars strobe the air; Broadway is blocked off and cars are being diverted. Behind police barriers a large crowd of people is gathered. Mac taps the Plexiglas and points for the cabbie to pull in close to the crowd. Mac slides his cash card through the pay slot and the doors automatically unlock. Pulling his cap down tight over his forehead he darts from the cab into the crowd. A voice he recognizes pours out over loudspeakers but Mac can't see.

" . . . If you seem suspicious," the voice echoes forcefully, "if you are poor, happen to be born a certain color, in this country, now, today, you are guilty until proven innocent. You can be shot, electrified, and put to sleep without having committed a crime. All the so-called PEACE officers need is probable cause. Probable from what? Probable from clichés and entrenched bigoted perspectives. Probable from some computer that has already made mistakes, causing hundreds upon hundreds of decent hard-working Americans to be hunted down . . ."

Mac looks behind him, the gray van parked at the edge of the police barriers, and he begins to move forward through the crowd. Overhead the PEACE cameras silently pan back and forth in their protective Plexiglas shields. The speaker comes into view on a small stage at the front of the crowd and Mac recognizes him, Julian Sanders from CNN. Behind Sanders a large sign proclaims the gathering A REAL PEACE RALLY. Mac bends his knees so he will be low in the crowd and keeps making his way forward. To the side he catches glimpses of another crowd, a smaller crowd behind another row of police barriers, carrying printed signs that say PEACE WORKS and GIVE PEACE A CHANCE. Pro-PEACE people still fighting the battle though they've already won the war.

Sanders reaches a fevered pitch, the rhythm and force of his words transfixing the anti-PEACE crowd, a few calling out "amen," Sanders throwing his hands in the air. "Hidden cameras watch our every move in public now. How long will it be until they are in our homes? How long until they are in our bedrooms? How long until our most private moments will be scrutinized? Crime is bad in our country. It has reached into our homes and shook us all to the very bone." Sanders pauses dramatically. "But when you give up one iota of the freedom our forefathers so wisely wrote into the Constitution and the Bill of Rights, you open the floodgates, we all move closer to a police state. . . . Democracy is fragile. It is unruly. But it is right. We are a free people. We must not let those afraid of democracy extinguish the light. We must not let their fear put us all in a jailed society. We must show them the way."

Wild applause erupts as Mac gets to the front. Mac looks back and sees three men in suits scanning the demonstration, totally immune to the people's enthusiasm. Mac looks to Sanders, his hands in the air above his head, palms toward the crowd, and suddenly sees behind the podium a face he recognizes. Tim Dimpter is standing there staring back at Mac. Dimpter does not smile or wave.

Mac ducks down and quickly moves away from Dimpter in a crouch. In an orchestrated move, five men dressed in black, wearing Frankenstein masks and carrying large REAL Peace stickers begin climbing the three poles in the area that have mounted cameras. The police move in and there is a scream from somewhere in the crowd as a bottle thrown at the REAL Peace climbers from somewhere in the pro-PEACE crowd smashes to the ground. Both crowds surge toward each other. The police barriers are quickly breached and total pandemonium breaks out, with people pushing and shoving one another and the rest of the crowd hurrying for cover.

Mac hears Sanders appeal for calm before he is hurried off the back of the stage by two large black bodyguards, one of them holding a ball gun in his hand, a device that fires a bean ball designed to knock a target unconscious without permanent damage. Mac ducks behind the stage, heads across a twenty-by-twenty-foot square section of road that has been cordoned off, the pavement ripped up to put in a new section of water pipe. Sanders is on the other side of the construction site, walking quickly between the two bodyguards toward a limousine. Dimpter steps out of a shadow only a few feet away, his sleeper gun aimed.

"If this is for that stuff with Barb," Mac says, "I made that up." Mac keeps his gaze directly on Dimpter and quickly analyzes his diminishing options.

"Take out your gun and lay it on the ground."

Reaching for the gun, Mac briefly considers diving and firing, but against someone trained like Dimpter it won't work. Dimpter is set in his stance and would likely squeeze the trigger before Mac was unholstered. Mac slowly lowers the gun to the dirt and cups a handful of gravel.

Sanders watches the two men through his tinted window, both with tranq-guns. Definitely odd. A tranq-gun can only be fired by the PEACE officer it is assigned to; the palm print recognition handle ended the problem of cops being shot with their own guns. He rolls down the window a crack. He motions to Roderick.

"Put your hands on your head." Dimpter motions with his gun.

Mac, on his knees, puts his hands on his head, acting as submissive as possible, trying to draw Dimpter as close as possible.

Dimpter steps forward and kicks Mac's gun away, out of reach.

"Codd send you to take me out, Tim? That's too bad. I always thought you were a good cop."

Dimpter pauses for a moment. "The captain did send me but I'm going to enjoy this. You've always been too arrogant, Wells."

Sanders watches the PEACE officer aim his gun at the kneeling man's head, execution style. Sanders nods toward Roderick.

Dimpter has moved close with Mac's defeated pose, let his guard down just a fraction. Mac is about to fling the gravel in his hand into Dimpter's face when a bean ball glances off the top of Dimpter's head, dropping him to the ground. Mac catches sight of one of Sanders's large bodyguards folding the ball gun under his jacket and stepping into a limo, which speeds away.

Mac scoops up his gun and heads north on Broadway, toward Salmon's place, no time to question why Sanders helped him. He glances behind him, sirens filling the air as more police arrive at the rally. All around people are jogging or walking quickly to get away. Mac glances at each face. The men in suits are nowhere to be seen.

A half a block behind Mac a young couple, dressed like college kids, the nylon pants, the vinyl jackets, walk hurriedly as though leaving the scene. Without ever having a direct gaze they keep Mac in their sights. Across the street a lone balding man in his fifties keeps pace. Another half block back the three men in suits have switched to a car that looks like a cab. It will never pick up any fares. Their faces in the dark car are softly lit by the red glow from the tracking device.

Mac crosses the street and heads into the Barnes & Noble through the electronic revolving door that shows movies, images of falling leaves, on its glass panels. The largest book/music/movie store in the world, Barnes & Noble rises five floors covering two full city blocks, the two mammoth buildings connected with an enclosed moving sidewalk bridge through a three-hundred-and-sixty-degree movie tube. Mac hurries to the nearest section, the electronic magazine racks, and steps behind a row of magazines devoted to home technology. After a few seconds, a bald man who was on the other side of the street enters. He looks at a stack of disk books, then looks around the store before walking toward the fiction section. Next the young couple who were twenty yards behind Mac on the street enter the store and look around. The young man picks up a paper magazine and takes a seat near the door. The girl wanders forward toward the music section.

Mac watches the door but no one else comes in. The young man moves his lips slightly, an innocuous gesture to anyone watching, the young man just reading the article aloud to himself, but to Mac it is the clincher. He makes his way across the room until he comes to the wall at the front of the store. He walks along the wall until he is near the entrance to the store. His gun in hand under his jacket, he begins to walk along the wall toward the young man. Every few seconds or so the young man glances up but never looks sideways toward Mac's approach. Mac raises the gun and fires. The young man slumps in his chair and no one even notices, just another person dozed off in one of the cushy reading chairs. Mac walks up to the man and unbuttons the top button of his shirt just to make sure. Adhered to the man's neck is the small paper-thin voice communicator. Mac reaches down and pulls the young man's skin-colored receiver, slightly larger than a pea, from his ear. He puts it to his ear and hears radio communication. *Lost com with surv one. Lost com with surv one.* Another voice immediately answers, *Move in, repeat, move in.* Mac steps back into the stacks and a moment later the massive electronic revolving door whirs to life. The three men in suits enter. They glance down at the man in the chair and begin to scan the store. One of them looks down at a small black box in his hand. "A Man and a Woman" is playing over the store's music system, people are waiting in line to pay for books. The man with the black box gestures toward Mac's area of the store. Mac realizes they have some sort of tracking device. Mac looks down at his clothes, feels his backside, maybe an adhesive on the chair in Codd's office? He checks the soles of his shoes but they are clean.

The men split up to come at Mac's position from three directions. The one with the box in his hand is coming front and center across a small open atrium area stocked with chairs and small tables. Mac takes out his PEACE identification card and hangs it around his neck. He steps out in the open and, before the suit can pull a weapon, shoots an electropatch into the man's forehead. Mac grabs the tracking device from the man's hand.

"Wow, you PEACE officers are getting cuter and cuter."

Mac looks up and it's the young girl, one of his trackers,

with the biggest smile you ever saw, like she's awestruck. He punches her in the face, probably harder than he needed to, and as she hits the floor the holster under her jacket reveals the butt of a huge black gun, the kind that makes a softball-size hole in a body from thirty yards. She should have pulled it. Why didn't she? Mac moves across the atrium toward the revolving door. Spinning toward the outside he takes a last look into the store but sees none of his pursuers.

He jogs east across Broadway toward Columbus Avenue. Perhaps the undercover female did not know the surveillance was busted and the orders were to follow him, maybe to Eve. Mac steps into a small, dark alley two blocks away. Behind a Dumpster he takes off all his clothes so that he is totally naked. His whole body is shivering but he doesn't think about it. With the tracking device in his hand he jogs down the alley away from the street. The red blinking light moves too. Mac stops, thinks back to Codd's office. The only thing he took with him . . . *the drink.* Something was in the drink. He takes two fingers and shoves them down his throat and at first it doesn't work; he only gags. But the second time the contents of his stomach roar up his throat, over his hand and onto the ground. Steam rises off his hand and off the pool of vomit. If he is too late, if whatever they fed him is already in his intestine, he will have to keep moving, his chances will not be good. He jogs back to his clothes, checking the tracking device, and the red blinking light stays motionless. He wipes his mouth and hands off on his undershirt and discards it. He puts the rest of his clothes on, the smell on his hands making him involuntarily gag.

He steps back into the street and turns east for Columbus to catch a cab. He gets half a block when Tim Dimpter steps out from behind a parked pickup truck, his sleeper gun leveled at Mac's chest.

"Didn't know you had friends in the resistance."

"Neither did I."

Mac dives and rolls as Dimpter fires, the patch whizzing past Mac's ear. Mac's momentum carries him over the edge of a stairway and he tumbles head over heels down the stairs, banging all the way down into a pile of cardboard boxes and bags of garbage. He draws his gun in the moment Dimpter's silhouette steps into view above. Mac pulls the trigger a hair of an instant after Dimpter, Dimpter's shot grazing Mac's temple, Mac's shot hitting Dimpter square in the chest. The moment of the patch's chemical reaction on Mac's skin, the release of the voltage, seems to go on forever, a screaming spark through his arteries, the world going white.

Mac wakes up, his shoulder, his hip, and the back of his head sore from the tumble down the stairs. Dimpter is lying on the wet cardboard next to him, out cold. Mac pushes away a piece of trash and the sidewalk above is full of morning pedestrians. Most glance down at him as they pass with hurried disapproving looks. He stands to his feet and leans heavily into a wall, his head light. He unsteadily climbs the stairs and looks for a phone. He walks toward Columbus Avenue and stops when he sees the little girl in the floral, multicolored beret who was gunned down his rookie year. She is standing at a store window. He squints his eyes but it is definitely her. An uneasy feeling, a kind of heat, rises into his chest as he walks over to her. She is looking at the Halloween display of a TV store, animated 3-D pumpkins and witches leaping from one flat-screen wall TV to the next, fake spiderwebs draped between the sets.

Mac stops a few feet away from the girl and she looks up and smiles. Mac feels a lightness, a huge weight evaporating from him in seeing the girl alive. But the lightness is dispersed by the screech of the gray van from the night before coming to a halt on the curb behind him. Mac reaches for his gun but he has left it back on the stairs. He must get the girl to safety. He looks back to her but she has her fingers over a small ear piece in her ear and in her other hand is a gun. He begins to back away, something like a smile and anger crossing her face. She shoots the gun over and over even after he has fallen to the ground.

Mac snaps awake, the backfire of a garbage truck echoing up the street. Dimpter is next to him, out cold. The air is dark and chilly, the street perfectly still, not a single person out. Mac struggles to his feet and there is pain at the back of his head. He reaches there and it feels rough, black dried flakes of blood on his fingertips. He starts up the stairs and there is pain in his left hip and right shoulder. His head throbs as though it is the morning after a month-long alcohol binge. He steps onto the sidewalk of the cross street, leaning against the railing in front of a brownstone. At least he is alive. A pay phone dome glows ahead at the corner of Columbus. He walks toward it, pausing under a tree at the corner to scan for cameras. With no crowds DADD would quickly pick him out if it was looking for him. It is a low-crime area, cameras only every few blocks. The nearest is two blocks away.

Eve sits in a chair next to the bed. Her face is puffy and streaked. For the longest time as the day grew late she didn't cry, but as the early morning came and there was no word from Mac she finally let go. She does not think he is dead. It does not feel like he is dead. But when she sees on the news the report of Dan Potesky's "accidental drowning" she begins to grow unsure. Mac would definitely have called. He had said not to contact anyone unless he didn't come back for two days. Then she was to call Lisa Washington or just leave, go to her parents. But she would never leave without him. She didn't want to die but if they took him from her

she would call a press conference or go to the news services—
something, anything, she would fight no matter what.

During the day she had gone out and rented a car under a
false name, her old name before she was married, Evelyn Frank-
ford, using her old ID and paying with a cash chip, saying she had
lost her new ID. The rest of the day there hadn't been much to do
but wait for Mac and worry. She fingers the note he left, the bottom edge shredded from her tears, Lisa's number circled in black
ink. She reaches for the phone and it rings.

"Eve," Mac's voice sounds strained and weak.

"Where are you?!"

"Corner of Columbus and Seventy-eighth. I need you to
come get me."

"I'm coming now. Don't move."

"Eve . . ."

"Yes . . ." There is a long pause and she can hear Mac
breathing. Tears flow down her cheeks again. She speaks before he
can. "I know," she says. "Me too."

If he had the energy Mac would have waited in the shadows of a
store's doorway. But after hanging up, his legs gave out and he collapsed against the base of the phone. Two PEACE cars went by,
but luckily bus stop billboards of naked models hid him from
view. For a long time Mac fights it but he can't keep his eyes open
and drifts into sleep.

A gang of six teenagers walks down the street. They aren't
wearing their colors. To be caught wearing colors puts you in jail.
Night is the only time they can roam and even here where cameras
are less frequent it's still dangerous, not anywhere near as good as
it used to be in broad daylight everywhere in the city. To walk
down into this part of the city as a group they've had to follow a

hand-drawn map, zigzagging to avoid camera placements. They are looking for a good car to lift, take a ride over into Jersey, rob a house, get some money. They stop and look down at Mac.

"That ain't no homeless person. Look at his shoes," the tallest one says, the leader. He pushes the smallest of the group forward. "Go through his pockets, man."

"You. Could be a plant, sleepers do that shit."

"You a fuckin' faggot, you know that?"

Eve comes skidding up in the rental car. She is out of the car, Mac's father's gun aimed at the gang members before they can react. They back up but aren't scared. Eve walks over to Mac and is shocked by how bad he looks, as though he's lived on the street for weeks. He smells of equal parts garbage and puke. One of the gang whistles at Eve. The leader, showing that he is unafraid to the rest of the pack, calls out as Eve helps Mac to his feet. "Got what you need right here. . . ." Eve puts Mac in the car and takes off.

The gang turns and continues their search for a car, something with a real sweet audio system.

William Kane watches the water of the Hudson River flow brown and cold. The sun is just rising and he sits on a large cement bench in Giuliani Park. If someone enters the park they will not be able to see him sitting there. He has chosen the spot because of this. Across the water he can see the edge of New Jersey, skyscrapers and tall apartment buildings crowding, it seems, to the edge of the water. A pretty penny to live over there with a view from the kitchen of the most famous skyline on earth. Kane turns up his collar. The older he gets the more he feels the cold. When he was little he could barely stand to wear a shirt. Now he piles on the layers. The day is a typical October day, gray, a low blanket of dark-tinged clouds threatening rain. It was supposed to be sunny. Clouds were good. Fewer people on the street, easier for the cameras to locate someone, if someone was still around to be located.

When the old man's people had contacted him that morning he had been surprised. He knew the old man traveled, seemed to spend a lot of his time in Europe; there were moments when they were talking and the faintest hint of an accent, maybe Danish, slipped into the old man's words. But Angelson had never come on location on one of his projects before, to meet in person no less. Angelson had said he had other business in town, another meeting, but Kane didn't know whether to believe that or not. For a moment after he had hung up the phone he had been scared. But the project wasn't going badly. It had been one week since the PEACE officer was shot with a tranq-gun and nothing had gotten out.

He hears the steps approaching, hard-soled business shoes against cement, but doesn't turn around until Angelson sits down next to him, the barest whiff of some expensive cologne filling the air.

"All the birds taken care of but one?"

"One and his mate."

"Maybe these two have flown the coop."

"We've worked up a psych file . . ."

Angelson turns and looks at Kane and Kane is struck, even more than usual, by the sudden youth of the old man's face, skin unmarred and unlined, as though he has dropped twenty years since the last time he saw him. A face to go with his hands. He didn't know that plastic surgery could work a miracle in such a short time. He glances at the old man's ears, at his mouth, and there is none of the telltale stretched skin that always gives a face-lift away. It is literally as though he is sitting with a younger man.

"He'll stay and fight." Kane turns away and looks across the water. "He'll stash his wife somewhere and fight. He'll never run. His partner was also his best friend."

"A hero then." Angelson looks back out to the water where gulls swarm and dive at something that has floated to the surface. "What about the wife?"

"Highly educated. Definitely a problem. We're watching acquaintances. He's a bit of a loner but she has a lot of contacts. We've accessed all hotel/motel registers hooked into computers and we're covering the rest by foot. I'm using the FBI for manpower. A cover story is in place."

Out in the water two gulls fight midair over a hunk of rotted flesh. The bigger gull wins and flies away.

"The other target, the partner, still not a problem?"

"She barely leaves the house."

"Good." Angelson stands. "Bring in the independent if we don't have success soon with the first two."

"Sir. He can't be in good shape. He's been hit with an electropatch, he had alcohol in his system."

"It's not just for him."

Angelson's footsteps recede and Kane waits before leaving. He knows what Angelson meant. The zoo must be kept clean. But maybe Angelson was implying more than that. Kane had always assumed that the other agents who disappeared from a project were simply reposted, went back to their old agency with a promotion. But maybe the "zoo" was always cleaned.

Out across upper New York Bay the sea of smog and heavy air is separating, a large swath of sun pouring down, the Statue of Liberty's crown reflecting the light like stars. William Kane reaches in his jacket and takes the safety off his gun.

The Paramount Hotel. Midmorning.

Scott Joyce has been awake since shortly after dawn. The Cartoon Network is showing *Looney Tunes* and Joyce smiles as Bugs Bunny chases Elmer Fudd around a tree. Years of life in the military have left him unable to sleep late. In general he hardly sleeps at all. A few hours of light dozing is enough, a handgun always nearby.

Two and a half days in the hotel room and no go signal has come. There was one call to let him know there were only two firm targets left but that one or two targets might be added. He prefers to be able to prepare, to plan, but as jobs go this is easy. If the targets keep dropping he will get to keep the money without having lifted a finger. Not a bad deal.

He pulls the food cart close and plucks a banana from a bowl. He has arranged to have no maid service and to have room service leave all deliveries outside his door.

He throws the banana peel on the tray, swallowing the banana, and walks to the edge of the room. He does a handstand against the wall and effortlessly begins to do vertical push-ups. Other than to exercise there is no other preparation to do. He has memorized the faces of the married couple. It will be an easy job.

39

Mac wakes in the motel room. Eve is talking quietly on the phone. "Yes, yes okay . . ."

"Who's on the phone?"

Eve hangs up and turns around, surprised. "Oh, just a wrong number. They wouldn't get off. How're you feeling?"

Mac looks at Eve and doesn't answer. He sits up, his hand brushing his empty holster. "Where's my gun?"

"You didn't have a gun." Eve approaches. "Boy, when I picked you up you looked like shit. What happened out there?"

"I'm lucky to even be here."

"Well, I got some pills for you. Take one of these. It'll make you feel better."

Mac sees the label on the bottle. Thermadom, a tranquilizer. He pushes the bottle away. "Eve, what's wrong with you?"

Eve looks at the label on the pill bottle and laughs. "Oops. Wait a minute." She walks over to her purse and fishes inside. Mac looks at her, this woman he has known for almost ten years, bending over her purse, and suddenly he knows that somehow this woman is different from Eve. Like it is Eve, but it is a different

Eve, an Eve raised under totally opposite circumstances, different parents, an alternate path.

She turns and holds the new bottle of pills. "Here it is. These will help you get back to your old self."

"I don't need any pills, just some aspirin."

Eve sits on the edge of the bed and close up Mac can see the differences of this Eve's face, the way the lines have formed around her eyes and mouth, the hint of eye shadow.

"Mac, you have to take these. You were shot with an electropatch!"

"Wait. How do you know I was shot?"

"You're not in your right mind, Mac." Eve's voice is terribly calm. "You're hallucinating now, experiencing paranoia . . ."

Mac comes to, hitting the floor of the motel room, the sheets and blankets gripped tightly in his fists, his entire body drenched in sweat. He gets up, his head and back sore, and looks around. Eve isn't in the room.

The water from the shower beats on Mac's skin like metal pellets, the water spray from the nozzle screaming in his ears. All of his senses have been heightened. His thoughts rise and fall like voices in a stream, flowing and tumbling, increasing and decreasing in volume, the thoughts normally unheard in a day rising to the surface, fighting for space inside his consciousness. Occasionally one sounds so loud, his mother's voice calling his name, Sam screaming to watch out, that he quickly whips around looking for the source. As clear as day it came from the room, someone nearby, but there is no one. Mac breathes deeply and fights for control. He punches the plastic shower wall and the pain flaring in the side of his hand sharpens his focus. The volume of voices lowers, the stream recedes, and Mac is able to think again. Pain helps him focus but he can't keep punching things.

Eve's note is taped to the bathroom mirror. She has gone to buy some fresh clothes and some medicine for his scrapes and cuts. Mac feels the wound on the back of his head and it has closed itself. No time for proper stitches. In the mirror his face is different than he remembers, skewed, hard. He has been looking for proof that something was bad in the PEACE system, that Sam's death was no accident, and he has found it: himself. He is living proof. He towels off and walks into the room. He lays out his handgun, tranq-gun, ammo, and money chip in a row on the heart-shaped bed.

At the sound of a key card being swiped through the lock Mac is behind the door, tranq-gun in hand. Eve opens the door, her arms full of bags. Mac shuts the door behind her. She turns, drops the bags and is in his arms. She hugs him so hard that a bruise on his back throbs with pain but he doesn't mind.

She lifts her face from his neck and looks up into his eyes. "Mac, what's going to happen?"

"Dan's dead. They killed him."

"I saw it on TV."

Mac leads Eve over to the edge of the heart. They sit and he tells her everything, from Henry Pollard's apartment to his talk with Codd. Eve takes it all well until the shootout with Dimpter.

"Are you noticing perceptual shifts in your thinking? Voices, paranoia?"

Mac nods. "What time is it?"

"Just before noon." Eve looks for a moment as if she might begin crying but takes a long breath, gathering herself. "We'll just get you excellent medicine. Remember I told you about that cousin of mine, went away to college, dropped one hit of acid and had a psychotic break?"

Mac nods. Eve is recovering. Becoming a psychologist, troubleshooting.

"Well, none of the drugs they tried worked on him—lithium,

orthidim, nothing made a dent. So they tried a new designer drug and he's home again, resuming his life, supposed to be free of side effects."

"He still on the drug?"

"He has to take it every day."

"God."

"I won't lose you, Mac."

"I seem to be able to control it somewhat. It comes in waves. Right now I feel relatively clear."

"It's just the beginning. We won't know how bad it is until there's been enough time to see patterns in your behavior. Why don't we leave, Mac? Like Dan said. Just go lose ourselves in Maine."

"It's too late to leave." Mac reaches in a few of the bags. "Did you get papers?"

"There's nothing in them."

Mac drops the papers out of a bag and scans each front page.

"Maybe Mr. Salmon got the story in after the deadline. Maybe he went to TV."

Mac grabs the remote and turns on the TV, the local twelve o'clock news just coming on, the square-jawed anchor looking up and smiling.

"Our top story as of noontime today. The drowning death of Lieutenant Daniel Potesky, a senior member of the elite PEACE force, has taken a new twist. Initially thought to be accidental, his death has now been ruled a homicide. Police and PEACE force officials are searching for Mac Wells . . ."

A picture of Mac flashes onscreen over the shoulder of the anchor.

" . . . a decorated hero in both the police department and PEACE Force, for questioning in connection with this murder."

Mac hears Eve's intake of breath, feels her hand on his arm.

"A police spokesman confirmed that the incident was drug-related. Any information or tips to Mac Wells's whereabouts can be phoned into the PEACE crime stopper's phone number shown below. . . ."

At that moment in the third floor cafeteria at PEACE HQ in the heart of Manhattan, there is total silence among the sixty PEACE officers as the same news program switches to a story about the mayor unveiling a new learning center for kids. A few mumbles, then the dam breaks and everyone is talking, disbelief flowing across the room in waves. At the back of the room, Tom Martinez, a watch room supervisor, stands near the packaged cupcakes alone, the cream he was about to pour into his coffee still poised in his hand. Most of the officers around the room are top-flight people, confident and honest, but young. They will toe the company line. They will each overcome the sheer lunacy of the scenario that has Mac Wells and Dan Potesky involved in some sort of drug scheme and participate in the hunt. It's their job and they're well-trained. But Martinez has known Mac since back in the NYPD and if there were any chance he was crooked, Martinez would have sniffed it out. Something else is going on. But what? Martinez pops a lid on his coffee and leaves the room, avoiding conversations. He decides to skip lunch. He hurries down the hall toward the bunker.

Lisa Washington sits in front of the TV at her mother's, stunned. The young Hispanic woman anchor is just finishing her report.

"Authorities are also exploring possible links between Lieutenant Potesky's death and the death of PEACE force member Sam Mullane at First Memorial Hospital seven days ago. Though officially ruled an accident, investigators are leaving no stone unturned in their search for the truth and for hero turned fugitive, Mac Wells."

Lisa feels the words on the news pulling her out of a fog, lifting her out of the thick gloom that has been her life since Sam's death. Suddenly she is sharp and focused. None of what she has just seen makes sense.

"Lisa!" Lisa's mother's voice comes from her upstairs bedroom. Her mind racing, Lisa doesn't answer. She must find Mac.

"Lisa, honey, the garbage men are coming up the street."

The hydraulics from the approaching truck grow louder each time it pauses at a driveway.

"Lisa! You there?"

"Yeah, Momma."

Lisa stands and looks at the TV, a commercial for diapers on as if the news report didn't just happen. Lisa walks into the kitchen and out the back door. She rolls the can down to the curb as the garbage truck pulls in. A young Dominican man easily hoists the trash can and gives her the eye.

Walking up the drive, she doesn't stop until she has heard the elderly neighbor's voice for the third time.

"I said, livin' the good life, huh, Lisa?"

"Excuse me?" Lisa turns to see a shadowy figure on the screened-in porch next door, Mrs. Dallow.

"All those gentleman callers you had. Clean-shaven and well-dressed. White fellas to boot. You doin' all right for yoursel'."

"Mrs. Dallow, you're saying I had visitors?"

"You are a pretty girl but Lordy, three at a time, just the other night."

Lisa suddenly has a flash, figures in the dark, movements in the corner of her vision, something over her mouth.

Through the door away from Mrs. Dallow, who is still talking, Lisa grips the back of a chair at the kitchen table, a longer flash, of hands, a glimpse of gloved fingers coming around the side of her head. She looks up at the naked bulb coming out of the center of the ceiling, voices rising and falling, asking her questions. She walks to a light switch and flicks it on, the bulb glowing to life. She opens the medicine cupboard where the soup cans had inexplicably been stacked. One voice deep in her mind grows louder, asking questions about Sam, about Mac. Lisa walks to the sink where she was nauseous and runs her hand along the faucet, her face distorted in the chrome, another face, vague and blurry, forming in her mind, coming together with the deep voice. A man, tall like the sheriff from her childhood, leaning forward, commanding her to answer. But this is no sheriff. He is not there to help her. He is telling her what to remember and what to forget.

40

FBI Special Agent Dale Weintraub steps out of the car in front of his twenty-eighth motel of the day, the first in a strip that meanders down the highway toward the airport. He looks down the row of neon signs and the only one that stands out is the last in the line, a place, announced by a huge flashing neon heart, called the Chateau Amore.

Weintraub walks toward the front door of the dive in front of him, a place called Benny's, the constant sound of planes taking off and landing shearing the air. His partner pulls ahead and slowly begins to case the parking lot, snapping wide-angle photos every five cars or so, the images instantly sent to the FBI computer for analysis, rental cars run for names, privately owned cars cross-referenced with known friends and acquaintances of the suspects.

Dale hasn't been told what this guy and his wife did. The entire New York office was suddenly put on alert. The scuttlebutt is that it's drugs. And because the guy is a PEACE officer all stops are being pulled out to avoid bad publicity. The orders are to approach the suspects with extreme prejudice. If they resist arrest, kill them. Dale has never shot a woman. He has killed two men in his career and wounded two more. The guys he tagged, every one of them, were scum, and were shooting back or about to. He did not feel bad. But extreme prejudice is an order to shoot, even an unarmed suspect, even in the back, if he or she is trying to get away. The male is supposed to be extremely dangerous. Extreme prejudice or not, Dale has decided he will not shoot these people unless he has to. Probably he doesn't even have to worry about it; they're in Tahiti or something.

He enters the motel lobby, all worn red velvet and sad prints of landscape paintings on the walls. Not spending the profits on renovations, that's for sure. A pretty Indian woman in modern western clothes stands behind the counter. She smiles, the lipstick on her lips just the right shade of pink against her tan skin.

"May I help you, sir?"

Dale Weintraub slowly reaches into his breast pocket, the moment he loves, the instant before the FBI ID is shown, the moment before the recognition that will come, the extra sparkle in the eyes of women, the gray suit's not quite a uniform but it'll do, the slight stammer in the men, the ancient rolling on the back, or the puffing of the chest, before authority. Dale's seen it all, innocent people acting guilty, guilty people acting innocent. He holds the badge for the Indian woman whose name tag welcomes him and announces her as HOSTESS DARA. He glances down at Dara's hands as he pops the badge back into his breast pocket and is disappointed to see the ring on her finger, gleaming gold and cubic zirconium. The pretty ones are always married.

"Just a few questions, ma'am." He pulls the laminated Xeroxes from his breast pocket. "Seen either of these people?"

Dara examines the photos studiously. "No. They have not come here, I am sure. I remember faces. She is very pretty."

"If you see them, would you mind calling this number."

Dale flips Dara one of the cards from his pocket. "There's a good reward."

He looks for the sparkle in Dara's eyes and, as she smiles and nods, it is there, but maybe it is the thought of a reward or the flickering of the fluorescent lights.

Julian Sanders has taken a suite at the Plaza Hotel. Being back at his mother's is too much. His brothers are there packing up her stuff but he just couldn't bring himself to help out. Roderick is in the room next door, asleep. Ben is sitting by the door watching a small hand-held TV. The death threats have increased with his stance on PEACE. An unpopular stand and by a black man too, the double whammy. The FBI had cautioned him about one letter in particular in the most recent batch. Not only was the guy prolific, sending Julian letters every other month or so, he was getting angrier and angrier, and according to the profilers at Quantico his letters, the tone, the words he used indicated that he was highly intelligent and probably capable of murder. This guy was not just talk. Julian is surprised that after all these years no one has ever tried. It only takes desire and a gun. The irony of it is that he's safer here in New York with the PEACE system in operation than he would be in any other major city.

Julian had seen the news reports on the murder of the PEACE lieutenant, had seen the picture of the PEACE officer he helped escape at the rally and it is bothering him. Had he helped someone involved in murder? If that is true it will upset him a great deal. But his gut tells him there is more to it.

"Ben, what do you make of that whole business with the sleeper after the speech, the guy on the news they're hunting for now?"

Ben switches off his TV and looks up, serious. "The shooter smelled like PEACE Corps all the way. Maybe the officer on the ground is in this drug thing they're saying he is. The PEACE force is so conscious about image I have no trouble imagining them putting down one of their own in public. But what struck me, what was weird, was the execution style the shooter took. It seemed personal. It makes no sense."

"My thoughts exactly."

"He was being chased. The question is why."

Julian looks away. Maybe it's something, maybe not. Julian thinks of the man at the cocktail party years before. He picks up the phone and makes a call.

Jason Barber sits in an eight-thousand-dollar leather chair in his fiftieth floor corner office of the Trump Emperor building. He stares through the floor-to-ceiling windows at the sky. The phone rings with a soft reassuring beep every thirty seconds or so. But he doesn't pick up. Because of Julian Sanders's phone call a few minutes before, he's decided not to take calls the rest of the day.

Julian Sanders had given Jason Barber his first job out of law school, had taken a chance on a kid with average grades but ambition to burn. With Julian's help he moved into corporate law at Smith, Tressen and Bolt, then became active in city politics on both sides, establishing a vast network of contacts in real estate, city government, and on Wall Street, the three areas that made a perfect base for setting up shop as a high-priced consultant.

The essence of his job is bringing people together for business transactions and occasionally finding information that isn't supposed to be found. A hired gun, he gets things done and, in New York, is one of the most sought after at what he does. The child of a white mother and a black father, Barber easily straddles the different worlds of the city. Everyone thinks of him as one of their own.

When Julian Sanders had called and asked for his help he knew something must be up, for Julian had plenty of his own contacts. Barber had seen the news reports and Julian had told him that the man now being sought by authorities across the city, Mac Wells, was the man he had seen at the rally. Julian had described the execution-style hit, which made no sense, especially between two sleepers. And why all the hoopla, Julian had asked. If Wells was bad wouldn't they have found him quietly, closed the case down without press? Barber realized that Julian had an excellent point. He knew the way PR worked inside and out. The only reason the powers that be would air their dirty laundry and launch an all-out manhunt, plastering Wells's face everywhere would be a) it is the right thing to do and, bad press or no, justice is all that matters; b) it is a mistake, just a bad PR decision; or c) there's more to the story than meets the eye, they must find Wells at all costs, and plastering his face everywhere limits his movement, the cover story discredits him, everyone who sees the news flashes will assume he's guilty, just another cop turned bad. It smells like a cover story.

A layperson who looked at what Barber has before him would never reach that conclusion without a healthy dose of paranoia. But Barber knows how things work, how people can be set up, how the media runs with the story so that for all the world a person appears guilty, is convicted in the minds of the average citizen, a kind of mass hypnosis, except they aren't guilty, or at least not in the way they are portrayed.

Barber is apolitical. He likes having the PEACE system. It

has transformed the city. But he owes Julian more than he can ever repay and Julian is a good guy to do a favor for, a man who will be at the top of his game for a while and maybe even president some day. Plus, the thought that something he doesn't know about might be going on in the city spurs Barber on. At heart he is a voyeur.

Jason Barber picks up the phone. He has joked over cocktails with every major player in the city, but what has come in most handy over the years are the smaller contacts, the people who do the legwork, the privates, or the wannabes, the captains and majors, not the generals. He punches three letters into his palmtop. John Codd comes on screen.

"John, how's it goin'?"

"Jason, good. What's a hotshot like you slumming down my way for?"

"Well, I've got people, you know, who are betting heavily that PEACE is here to stay. Was just trying to get an angle on this Wells thing."

Codd doesn't respond for a moment, as if he's been asked to do a complicated math problem. "We're upside down here with this thing," he says finally, leaning forward, a confessional tone. "I've known him for years, never saw it coming."

"Yeah, that's tough. Sometimes you just don't know people like you think you do. Any new checks being instituted to make sure the corruption isn't a widespread thing?"

"I'll have to get back to you on that. Uh," Codd pauses, takes a drink of water. "I'm sure this is just the case of one bad apple. Confidence in the original screening program remains sky high. We're not commenting on this until it's wrapped up, you understand."

"Got everything I need, John." Barber punches a button on his palmtop and the names of Codd's family scroll past. "If I remember correctly you have two teenage boys, Jason and Nick, totally rabid Knicks fans. I'm packaging over four courtside, to the season opener."

"Jason, you don't need to do that."

"It's my pleasure, John."

Codd smiles. "Thanks." Codd's voice is overly jocular, relieved. "You just made me a hero."

Codd signs off and Barber pops the disc from his palmtop, a visual and audio recording of the call. Barber presses a button and his assistant comes into the room, the points of her three-inch heels silent on the Persian rug.

"Sarah, I need voice analysis on this, the whole profile workup, asap." Barber has only met John Codd a few times, slime factor of ten but a cool customer, never at a loss for words. He turns to look out the window and already knows what the results of the voice-stress test, the fluctuations of Codd's voice, the emphasis and use of certain words will be.

Codd is lying.

(42)

Mac dries his hair with the towel and the towel gets smudged with hair dye, no time to do it right. He knows they are closing in. Perhaps they are days away, perhaps it is only hours. Eve had rented the car under her old name and they would be on to that, would have video tape of her picking up the car, would be combing every parking lot of every motel in the metropolitan area. The best thing to do is leave the car, to go on foot, take the chances with the cameras. The only way he and Eve are going to be safe is to get the story out, so that is what they will do. Eve will not let him go alone now and he knows it is useless to argue with her. He is sick and they have a better chance if she comes. Besides, she is in it as much as he is; they tried to kill her, she has the right.

He washes the hair dye down the drain and rinses out the sink so no stains will be left behind. He carefully drops the towel and the hair dye bottle in a plastic bag. No traces. He puts on a white T-shirt and a black jacket and looks at himself in the mirror; the short jet-black hair makes him look younger, more innocent. He lifts the last piece of the puzzle he is constructing from the paper bag, a studious-looking pair of clear glasses. He puts them on and is instantly smarter, more thoughtful.

Eve knocks on the door and when she opens it he forgets for a moment why they are doing this. She laughs and he laughs. She reaches forward and adjusts the lapel on his jacket and he looks for a seam between her forehead and the black wig she is wearing but there is none. A tight pair of blue jeans that look like Eve painted them on, a beat-up jean jacket, heavy makeup, and the wraparound sunglasses he bought complete the picture. If she walked past him on the street he would not know.

"This new hair of yours really turns me on," he says.

Eve walks away from the bathroom in character, an exaggerated swing of her hips. "Maybe when this is over we can keep the wig."

"And get a maid's uniform."

Eve laughs but just then a car screeches outside and Mac grabs a gun off the bed and is at the window, peering out a crack in the blinds. It is just a kid showing off for his girlfriend in his souped-up car, but the lighthearted mood is gone. Mac and Eve look at each other and without a word finish packing.

Mark Figaro sits behind the main desk at the Chateau Amore, watching Saturday morning cartoons and trying to stay awake. The show on, *The Adventures of Nice Man,* about a superhero who always gets dumped on when he's out of costume because he's such a nice guy, is Mark's favorite. Normally Mark would watch at home but is pulling a double shift because Mel, the moron owner of the place, called in and isn't coming until the afternoon. But Mark can't really complain, he's only seventeen and Mel took his word about being twenty-two with a wink and a nod, because Mark looks twenty-five and is big, six-five and two-sixty. It's good to have a big person behind the desk for the occasional out-of-control guests. Mark has only been there a month and already had to call a cab for a sobbing woman who came out of her room with torn clothes. This pip-squeak guy tried to get the woman back in the room, tried to tell Mark to mind his own business, so Mark demonstrated to the guy why exactly he was hired and the guy left immediately. One slap was all it took. There were perks to the job.

Mark's head drops onto his forearm and he gives up all pretense of looking alert, the dreams coming immediately, Mark as Nice Man, saving gorgeous women from dark motel rooms and getting their numbers instead of being dumped on. He is just punching out yet another pip-squeak when a siren goes off and Mark whips around in the dream, looking for the cause of the sound.

Dale Weintraub stares down at the big guy behind the reservation desk and taps the bell a few more times. The guy sits up with a start, wiping his mouth, a garbled "May I help you" spilling out.

Dale flashes his badge and watches the boy sit up at attention, make a poor attempt at parting his hair with his hand; obviously he's never seen an FBI badge before.

"I'm Special Agent Weintraub with the Federal Bureau of Investigation." Dale pulls out his two photographs of Mac and Eve Wells but holds the one of Eve Wells forward. The kid is good-looking, probably thinks of himself as a ladies' man. "You seen this woman in the last few days?"

Mark instantly recognizes Eve. He pauses before answering, a touch of chivalry overriding the impressiveness of the sunglasses and dark suit in front of him. "What'd she do?"

Dale sees Mark's hesitation, so he lies, uses an almost jovial tone. "Oh, we just want her for questioning, nothing to do with her."

"She checked in here a coupla days ago."

"What room?" Dale can't hide the rise in his voice, his body leaning forward across the desk.

Mark sits back and reaches for the phone, like Mel would give a shit if he gave up some chick to a Fed. "I'm not supposed to give that out. My boss never told me what to do if the FBI came. Aren't you supposed to have a warrant or somethin'?"

"There's a reward."

"How much?"

"Substantial, more than you make here in a few months."

Visions of Nice Man saving the damsel in distress disappear from Mark's head. "She's in fourteen B."

"Give me the key."

"I have to come with you."

"Not on this one, son."

Mark shrugs and hands over the key.

"Stay here. If she's there I'll be back to get information from you for the reward."

Weintraub heads out the front door, trying not to hurry, scanning the length of the hotel for the door that says 14B. It's at the end. He walks up to the car where his partner, Ted Marker, has just taken a picture of yet another row of cars. Dale points to the end of the building. "They're in fourteen B."

Marker drives ahead to park the car and Dale crosses over to the building, unholstering his gun, walking slowly toward the door to the room. As Dale gets close, Marker appears at the other side of the door from around the corner of the building. Dale tosses Marker the key. As he nods and shows three fingers to Marker, Marker quietly slips the key into the lock and nods back. Dale begins the countdown, his fingers counting one, two, three, and the lock is turned and Marker is in the room first, pointing his gun low and to the left, Dale taking the straight-ahead shot. But there is no one.

The bathroom is empty and spotless. When Dale comes out Marker is already on his walkie-talkie. Dale looks around the room, nothing left behind but a half-full coffee cup. With the back of his hand he touches the Styrofoam. He turns to Marker.

"It's still warm."

Marker pushes the button on his walkie-talkie. "Control, premises have been recently vacated, I repeat, recently vacated."

Dale is out the door scanning the horizon. Probably they've switched cars and the rental is in the parking lot. He looks for two figures but there is no one. A few hundred yards away the drone of traffic continues endlessly. The Brooklyn-Queens Expressway, heading north and south, virtually anywhere. He turns back into the room to await the forensics team and does not see along the highway a bus pulling over and stopping to pick up two passengers on their way into the city.

When the bus pulls in Mac and Eve get on and sit separately, Mac in the front and Eve in the back. If Salmon can't be located Mac will drop off the story at a few different news services, everything he put onto paper back in the motel, and he and Eve will be gone. Mac allows himself a glance up at the mounted camera at the front of the bus. They are watching. It is watching. But Mac knows the way DADD works. He knows what it looks for. Face type is important, but if it is skimming it will look for other surface cues—clothes, behavioral clues, a man and a woman together. It won't be looking for a hip young guy with jet-black hair and glasses.

The bus lurches back onto the expressway toward Manhattan, where a thousand cameras, where many thousands of beat cops, FBI agents, and highly trained PEACE officers are all scouring the city, looking for one rogue officer.

Zoo HQ.

The call has just come in, two FBI agents locating a room in

Queens, recently vacated. They are checking the parking lot for the car. In a few seconds William Kane will know whether Wells has switched transportation or not. They can't be far. After almost a day of no leads the chase is on again, the net closing in and Kane smiles a bit to Tom Schorr but Schorr just looks back blankly. Kane knows a nerve in Schorr's cheek doesn't work, marring him with a perpetually expressionless face, but it gives Kane pause. It makes Schorr seem soulless.

Kane absently reaches into his pocket to feel the pager there. A simple three-digit code tapped into it and Martha would get the message, would remove the bags always packed with a second set of clothes from the closet, would gather Elizabeth together, and be out the door in less than ten minutes. Shortly after Kane first got into working with Angelson and he started to realize the reach of the programs he was part of, of the power that must exist to order these programs into existence, he had come up with a plan to disappear.

On a hike with Martha up in the Appalachian Mountains he had told her what she needed to know, which wasn't much. The pager would never go off unless it was time to move; he had alternate identities, contacts, and plenty of cash set up, but really it would never come to that, he was just being extra cautious. He had always been extremely cautious, it was like going down to his State Farm agent and making sure he had enough insurance. Except it wasn't.

He remembers the look on Martha's face. There they were, sitting halfway up a mountain on a large rock with a view of a long, wide valley leading to a range of lower hills, no one around for miles, the silence unbroken except for birds in the pine trees, and he had just told her there was a chance, albeit slim, that one day she might have to give up everything in her life at a moment's notice, disappear without a trace, and she had smiled. She had always been an exceptionally even-tempered person but her expression took him aback. She looked at him a long time and he knew she was looking into him, reading him to make sure he was giving her the whole story, searching him with the question, *You really don't think this is going to happen?* So he told her it wasn't. And that had been enough.

The call comes in from the contact in the FBI HQ that the agents have located the car. Wells has switched transportation and Kane snaps to, issuing orders to Schorr.

"I want the tolls covered yesterday."

"We already have people there."

"High-powered lenses?"

"Yep. Nothing too close. We can read every car."

"No face gets through without being scanned."

"It's rush hour."

"Put a slowdown in. And cover the highway all the way up into Connecticut. Maybe they're cutting loose."

Schorr turns away to talk into a phone. Kane leans forward to look over the shoulder of one of the console operators. On a few of the screens city buses turn their way slowly through town. Kane taps the operator on the arm.

"There a bus line near the Chateau Amore?"

The operator punches a few keys and the information pops up on the screen. "Yes, sir."

"We have any cameras on that line?"

The operator scans his screen. "On about sixty percent of the buses, sir."

"Punch up and scan whatever buses you can access that have passed the motel in the last forty minutes or so."

Seven screens fill with the interiors of buses. The operator types in a command and DADD begins working its way though each bus, every face, even the smallest child, outlined in red, scanned and analyzed. On one of the screens the camera pauses on a young black-haired man, his head tilted down and to the side, his mouth open, the rhythmic rocking of the bus lulling him into sleep. DADD focuses on him, tries to get a scan of the face but cannot get a good angle and moves the camera on to the next passenger.

The bus lurches to a stop in front of a Plexiglas waiting station. Mac, his head tilted down, listens to the motor of the camera, focusing and zooming, incessant. A middle-aged nanny gets on with a two-year-old boy in her arms. The boy, in blue denim overalls and a baseball cap that says Dexter, is crying inconsolably. Eve watches the nanny make her way to the seat just in front of her. She looks at Dexter's little fists pummeling the air at some unseen injustice, then looks at the back of Mac's head at the front of the bus and smiles. The boy turns so that he is standing in his nanny's lap and looking over her shoulders at Eve. His crying lessens a bit as he takes in the new view. But something about Eve is off-putting and the reprieve from the crying is short-lived. He bursts again into uncontrolled sobs.

Eve waves her hand and softly shushes him but Dexter is having none of it, twisting away from her as though she is wearing a mask. And she is. Eve touches her glasses and takes them off so Dexter can see her eyes and the decibels of his crying instantly diminish. She twirls the glasses in front of him, the dark lenses catching sunlight, the sparkle catching his eyes. He reaches for them, totally entranced, and the nanny turns in her seat.

"Thanks so much, dear. I hope he's not being a bother."

"It's good practice."

"Well, if practice makes perfect, then this fellow has made me about perfect." With a smile, the nanny turns back forward, pleased to have Dexter silent for the bus ride, totally unaware that at that moment she and the back of Dexter's head are being scanned.

•

On one of the monitors Eve leans forward making baby faces, touching Dexter's nose then pulling away. Dexter reaches forward to pull her hair and a few blonde strands fall out beneath the black wig. Kane has stepped away from the monitors and is on the phone with his people, pulling them toward Queens. The FBI is already moving unilaterally, tightening the net. Schorr's phone rings just as Kane gets off. He steps a few feet away but Kane hears, "Yes, sir, I understand, sir . . ." and it tells Kane all he needs to know. Schorr is working directly for the old man. Two lines of communication. Schorr is not to be trusted. Not that he didn't already expect that, just a good confirmation. Schorr hangs up and Kane walks back to the monitors.

Suddenly a soft tone sounds and the operator pulls one of the images onto his central screen. There is Eve outlined in red in a commuter bus seat playing with a baby and laughing. The image, a beautiful woman at ease and happy with a baby, has a visible impact on William Kane and the console operators, takes away their edge for a moment. This "fugitive" is no criminal, just a woman that any of them would have been happy to win a date with. Schorr clears his throat and whatever he feels, it doesn't show.

The operator points out the obvious. "We have a match, sir."

"Yes, I recognize her. What's that bus's location?"

The operator calls up the information. "Manhattan, approaching Fifth on Sixtieth."

"Our closest unit?"

Schorr steps forward. "Two blocks away."

Kane turns to Schorr, fully aware that his management of the situation is being noted by the man he is giving orders to. "Send them in to trail. Bring anyone you have close by in for the pickup."

•

Scott Joyce slides on his second running shoe, not too new, not too old, and ties the shoelace. The small runner's knapsack is already packed with everything he will need. On a table at one end of the hotel room a radio communicator squawks with a flurry of calls between units closing in on Fifth Avenue. Perhaps they will get there and the targets will be swooped up and his job will already be done. Easy money. He stands and quickly glances in the large wall mirror. The heartbeat wrist monitor, the sports headphones, the wraparound sport sunglasses, everything to suggest a serious runner.

When the call comes he is ready to go.

As the bus turns onto Fifth Avenue, Mac catches sight of a dark green four-door Dodge Intrepid with two men in the front seat idling along the park. He casually glances back and watches the car edge out into traffic behind the bus. He sees Eve, her glasses off, playing with the baby, and instantly knows what has happened. He stands and heads to the back exit doors, lightly brushing her arm. Eve puts on her glasses and stands, leaving Dexter behind. She grabs onto a pole by her seat while Mac waits at the door. When the bus gets toward the end of the park, Mac pushes the strip that signals the bus to stop and the driver pulls over.

Mac begins to walk down Fifth toward the end of the park and Eve trails ten feet behind. Mac bends to tie his shoe as the bus roars past, Eve walking ahead, totally unconnected to him, Mac glancing back up Fifth, the Intrepid parking, one of the men, a big guy in a suit, stepping out of the car, brushing himself off, as though he is not following them. Mac stands and begins to pick up speed. He comes alongside Eve at the entrance to the park and grabs her hand, running full speed into Central Park.

•

Kane wanted it to be quiet, a car swooping in, maybe one or two startled witness who wouldn't know what they had seen. Central Park on a Saturday is not quiet.

"I want every unit at Central Park now."

"The feds too?" If Schorr could change his facial expression he might look surprised.

"Just limited. Whatever they have along the exterior of the park. We'll take care of the interior. Use NYPD as support." A reasonable plan. Kane turns to the console operator. "Any coverage in the park?"

"None, sir. That's Central Park PD. We're blind."

Kane thinks of the day, turned warm and sunny since morning. The park would be packed. Kane steps back from the operator, turns to Schorr. "We should bring in the independent."

Schorr nods and Kane, like a captain of a ship who suddenly knows for sure he no longer controls the crew, immediately understands that the decision has already been made, the independent is already on the job.

(44)

As soon as Tom Martinez saw Mac Wells on the local news as a fugitive, he asked the commander on duty if he could pull a double shift in the bunker—his car needed work and money was tight, et cetera. It's about his eleventh straight hour of work, he is paired with Jim Lincoln again. In another five hours he'll have to go off-duty. Maybe Mac has skipped town, that would be the smart thing. But also the guilty thing. Why would Mac run if there were no reason? It just didn't make sense. Even if he was being framed he could just turn himself in and fight it.

Earlier, taking a break out at the food machines, Martinez had overheard Tim Dimpter's partner Robert Chow say that Dimpter hadn't shown up for work that day, hadn't called in, and his wife hadn't seen him, totally AWOL. Martinez has never liked Dimpter. An ambitious guy, excellent cop in all the surface ways, but something impossible to put a finger on always bothered him about Dimpter, as if you couldn't quite trust him. Maybe his disappearance is connected to Mac, maybe not. Martinez is about to get up to make another trip to the vending machines when the first code light goes off and DADD transfers the replay down onto the central screen.

"Just some movement into Central Park. Doesn't look like criminals," Jim Lincoln says.

Though the image is from a distance and not of the best quality, something about the way the man runs makes Tom Martinez lean toward the screen.

"Jim, play that back for me, slowmo."

Again the two figures, a man and a woman, holding hands, run and disappear into the park.

"Now regular speed."

For a moment there is just the normal coming and going, people turning to watch a man and a woman sprinting into the park, then two men in suits enter the frame, running full speed after the couple.

"What do ya make of that?"

Tom Martinez doesn't say what he makes of it, Mac being chased by two men in suits. FBI? Something else?

"Put a call into the park police. Let them handle it."

Martinez tilts back in his chair, unsure what to think. He had thought if the moment came and Mac was ID'd on screen he would know what to do, would be able to tell whether Mac was guilty or not, would be able, perhaps, to help him in some way, convince him to turn himself in. He glances sideways at Lincoln on the line to the Central Park Police Department and Lincoln has no clue it was Mac on the screen. Martinez leans forward and punches up the exits in the lower half of the park. Nothing to do but watch and wait.

The door opens and Lisa Washington stands there. She motions to Martinez.

"Tom, can I see you for a moment?"

•

The park is overflowing with tourists and people taking advantage of the Indian summer day. Mac and Eve run one hundred yards along a cement path, weaving between the crowds, then cut left into a small woods. The men behind have lost them in all the people and Mac slows down to a hurried walk through the trees. Eve is breathing heavily as much from the surprise as the run. She trusts him and does not ask questions. He looks down at their hands clasped together since they entered the park. On another day this would have been a nice time, next to Eve, the sun streaming through the branches.

"They made us on the bus. There were two men following. There will be more soon but we have a better chance here in the park than out on the streets. The park police use patrols, it's off camera." Mac feels Eve's hand tighten on his. "Soon we'll be coming to the Sheep Meadow. There'll be a lot of people there on a day like this and we'll cross there over to Central Park West and make our way to Marty's."

"Okay."

Mac looks behind him. There is no one else in the woods. He and Eve begin to climb a small hill amid the pleasant smell of wet dirt and leaves. It is richer, more pungent, than it would normally be, and Mac is suddenly aware of the birds singing back and forth to one another as though they are right by his ear. The cracking of a twig beneath Eve's foot bursts into the air like a miniature thunderclap. But then it is gone. As if some great hand has turned the volume of the world back down to normal. On the bus Mac had noticed nothing unusual in his thought patterns, but now there is a constant hiss of static in his ears as though the great hand has turned down the volume but left the dial between radio stations. The hiss occasionally pops and crackles, startling Mac, but he tries not to let it show.

The fence that marks the large boundary of the Sheep Meadow comes into view. The meadow is full for a fall day, people throwing Frisbees and stretched out on the grass and blankets spread all the way across the vast circle of grass. Enough people are milling about, coming and going, that it is effective cover and Mac leads Eve into the crowd. They make their way among the coolers and the tossed footballs. The low hum of voices, occasionally disturbed by a sudden cackle of someone's laugh, all mixes with the hiss in Mac's ears, rising and falling in waves of volume. Mac ignores it, keeping his eyes on the fence's perimeter for any sign of pursuit. At halfway across the field it shows: two men jogging up to the fence, dressed casually to blend in but their faces serious, scanning the crowd. Mac pulls Eve's hand down as he drops to the ground. He looks ahead to the gate at the other end of the field and three men and a woman looking like four typical New Yorkers out to enjoy the day are just arriving.

"How bad is it?" Eve lies on her side, looking at Mac.

"Bad enough."

"How's your brain?"

"I'm hearing God's Muzak."

"We've got to get medicine."

"After Marty's. On our way out of town."

A few feet away from Mac and Eve, a large group of high school–age people sit around drinking and passing a joint. A boom box with a tattered sticker that says No Boom Boxes Allowed across its top blares "Under My Thumb" by the Rolling Stones. A few of the kids stand up and begin to toss a Nerf. Supersoaker water guns suddenly appear, the boys against the girls, the battle going hand-to-hand, partners choosing each other with unspoken words, the air between them thick with the understanding that this is not a battle of the sexes but a joining of them. One member of the group, a boy with a premature goatee, sits apart from the struggle, nursing a half-smoked joint. Suddenly a misfired spout of water splashes his face as he is about to take a puff.

"Aw, man. You got the weed wet."

"You smoke too much anyway, Ethan," one of the girls taunts back, a little too loudly, wishing Ethan was taking part in the battle of the sexes. Ethan looks around to see if anyone has heard that he smokes too much and his eyes rest on Mac and Eve. Eve's black wig is crooked. Ethan rubs his premature goatee thoughtfully.

Mac watches the woman and three men on the western side of the park enter through the gate and fan out through the crowd like brush beaters, flushing out the game. They move slowly, methodically, checking each person's face, immune to any self-consciousness at the intrusion into people's space. Mac watches them, their movement somehow affecting the hiss in his ears, cutting through it, shaping it. And then it is gone. The sound of the world is again as he has heard it for thirty-two years, the tone of grass growing no longer fills his thoughts. He looks at Eve and she is watching the three men and the woman making their way closer. Mac reaches for the knapsack and slips his hand inside, then turns toward the approach of their pursuers, still a good distance to go.

From a few feet away Ethan watches Mac, follows Mac's gaze toward the woman and three men searching the crowd, PEACE types, maybe DEA, definitely not civilians looking for a spot to sit. Ethan looks back to the couple, the man with a dye job and the woman in a wig, and maybe it's the pot, Ethan has been smoking strong for an hour, but normally if he saw people running from the cops and the guy had his hand in his bag like there was a gun in there, Ethan would walk as quickly in the other direction as he could. But instead he calls softly over.

"Hey. You being chased, man?"

The man turns his head sharply toward Ethan and the aggression is obvious though the man's expression is blank, an unspoken, unseen acknowledgment between two men, one man communicating to the other, watch your next move, buddy, it could be your last. Ethan is vastly regretting his decision to speak up, the whole world going into slow motion. Near him his classmates are still jumping around, totally oblivious to the fact that the next moment, a culminating instant in lives of ease and comfort, may explode with a weapon thrust into their faces from a small gym bag.

The woman in the wig leans into the slow-motion picture, staring at Ethan, sizing him up from behind thick black glasses. She doesn't smile when she speaks but there is something of pleading in her words and her voice slices through the man's aggression, turns the situation on its head so that the action snaps back to regular speed. "Yes, we are, and we haven't done anything wrong."

Seeing that he is not going to be shot Ethan regains a bit of his swagger. "Hawaii Five-O, man," his comment coming out suitably flippant but his shaky voice betraying him. Ethan looks to the search party closing in, still far enough away but it's only a matter of time. Probably DEA thugs. In which case the joint still in his hand and the massive bag of weed in his knapsack won't bode well for his future at Harvard. He looks at Eve. Definite superbabe material. Out of his age bracket maybe, but close enough to stir the chivalry adrenaline.

"Location change!" Ethan's voice booms over the rest of the group, and they all stop, looking to him, for he is the unacknowledged and unchallenged leader of the group.

The girl who wanted Ethan to join the Supersoaker struggles goes into a pout. "C'mon, Ethan. It's the third time."

Appearing casual, Ethan carefully dangles the bag of pot in front of his chest. "It's my party and I can cry if I want to." He turns and nods to the approaching authorities. "Besides, yonder fuzz."

The group casually looks to the three men and the woman as if they are looking at nothing in particular. They begin to collect their stuff.

At the southern end of the meadow a jogger runs up to the fence where a stand of trees hangs over the border and provides good cover. Only a few feet away but out of sight a small class of six year olds on a field trip are sprawled out in the grass, eating their lunches. The teacher is just telling them that when they are finished eating she will take them across the park to the zoo. The kids all cheer. Scott Joyce slips off his knapsack in a practiced way and pulls from the outer pocket a small, powerful rifle scope. He focuses in on the three men and the woman working their way through the crowds, and then begins to scan people they haven't gotten to yet. The three men and the woman walking through the meadow are highly trained and have memorized the photographs of the two targets, but Joyce, even from the distance of a hundred yards, outpaces them easily. He does not need to rely on his memorization of photographs. When he gets to the targets he will know.

Ethan points past Mac and Eve to an open area at the northern side of the meadow. "Thataway." As the teenagers start toward the chosen spot Ethan nods to Eve and she and Mac stand up in their midst and begin walking too. Eve slides over toward Ethan so she and Mac will not be walking together. The boys of the group are slightly ahead but two of the girls of the group wearing flannel shirts and black plastic pants keep looking at Mac and Eve. Ethan catches their expressions. "All the way to the fence. We are leading my new friends here, Betty Crocker and Father Brown, to freedom from the Mod Squad."

One of the flannel shirts, the one with the crush on Ethan, frowns while the other flannel shirt smiles shyly at Eve and Eve smiles back. The drugs aside, Eve can tell that these are children of the affluent, kids going Ivy League or traveling the world after high school. They can afford to take risks. The number of seated people thins closer to the edge of the meadow and the path to the fence becomes clear. The fence, only fifty yards away, is covered in shade from overhanging trees.

At the other end of the meadow one of the four agents glances at the faraway group of kids moving to the edge of the park, but they aren't moving toward an exit so the agent resumes the search.

The frowning flannel shirt keeps looking at Mac. Something about his face . . . she is sure she recognizes him but can't think from where. She looks at Ethan, totally oblivious to her all day, and turns to Mac as they're walking.

"Have I met you somewhere before?"

The man turns toward her and she is sure she has seen him. "No, no I don't think so."

The other flannel shirt looks at Mac more closely and recognizes him too. Somewhere deep in her memory Mac's face registers, it was on TV somewhere.

At the southern end of the meadow Scott Joyce scans back and forth close to the group of teenagers. In another few moments he will have them in his scope. Nearby, on the other side of the trees, the teacher of the six year olds has begun to strum a guitar and the children are gustily singing "Itsy Bitsy Spider." A Kodak moment. Actually the singing is relaxing in an odd way, the dichotomy between what Joyce is hoping to do in a moment and the innocence of the children gives Joyce pleasure. He doesn't smile, he's not a sicko, this is a job, nothing more. He just appreciates irony.

The second flannel shirt, a sweet girl, often passive and made a little anxious by the things her friends decide to do, suddenly realizes who Mac is, his picture on TV rising up from her memory banks in a flash, the story, the commentator's words coming back though she has no time for the news, the TV was only on in the background and barely catching her attention. She hears herself audibly gasp and her legs are no longer moving. She is not like Ethan or Adam, able to be glib about something serious. She can no longer walk and can only hear her parents telling her how proud they are of her, voices in her head like a chorus casting judgment on her decisions to smoke pot and help fugitives that day. She looks up and everyone has stopped and is looking at her like she has a giant bird on her head. From somewhere ahead she hears Ethan asking her what's wrong but she can't keep her eyes from staring at the cop. The cop who's looking back at her in a way so that they both know what she is thinking, that she has recognized him. When the words come out of her mouth they come of themselves and sound odd, high-pitched, and removed, as though her mouth is moving but someone else is throwing the words there. "You're the cop on TV everyone is looking for, the drug thing where your boss was murdered." Everyone turns and looks at the cop now.

Scott Joyce hesitates at a group, eight or so kids standing still, because in his scope a girl is taking a step back from the group, pointing; there seems to be a disagreement. Joyce carefully watches and the group, as if in answer to his prayers, separates, stepping backward, revealing his male and female targets. He pulls the folded rifle from his pack, one of only two exactly like it in the world, built for a small fortune to his exact specifications, collapsible into a lightweight rectangle less than one foot and a half long but able to fire an armor-piercing Teflon-coated bullet to a target at extreme distance, the span limited only by the length of the chosen shaft and the talent of the shooter. He firmly holds the middle section, the trigger, and caliber load and folds the barrel and the shoulder brace up and snapped into place. He slides the scope in and quickly resights the group.

"Oh, c'mon, Thea, take a 'lude," Ethan is saying, his voice shaky because he has recognized the cop too, but still acting calm to save face; one must never lose it, even if the ship is going down.

Mac takes Eve's hand, no point in the charade anymore. The fence is only ten yards away. The flunkies haven't looked up. There's still a chance to get away.

Joyce lines up the crosshairs on Mac's head. The children are launching into "Old MacDonald." He blows out a breath of air, settling his body, making the shot perfect. One moment Mac Wells will be a fugitive, the next moment he'll be . . .

"Mister?" A child's voice.

Joyce flinches, the crosshairs jarred up into a tree. He looks down at the little boy, chocolate smeared around his mouth, his hand clutching the arm of a sleeper action figure.

"Whad'ya doin'?"

Joyce looks back to the group of high schoolers still there, then down to the little boy. A little too much irony. He begins to fold his gun. "Just taking measurements of the meadow, little fella." In seconds he has the gun back in the knapsack. "Hey, you better get back to class," he says, waving, backing up along the fence before jogging away.

Mac pulls Eve toward the fence. In a few moments they are in the shadows of trees overhanging from outside and their pursuers haven't noticed. Eve begins climbing the enclosure with Mac giving her a boost. The group of kids watches them, motionless. For the first time of the day none of them, not even Ethan, has a word to say.

Mac is quickly over the fence and leading Eve down a slight wooded slope to a wide, paved walkway called the Mall, which runs north and south and is lined with trees and busts of famous writers. A large crowd of people move up and down the walkway, some stopping to look at the busts, and Mac and Eve step into the flow heading north.

It is almost a serene, safe feeling in the thickness of the crowd, which is moving to and from some kind of gathering, a festival at an area one hundred yards ahead called the Bandshell.

The sound of a single pair of running feet emerges suddenly from behind and Mac turns but it is only a portly middle-aged jogger trudging by. Mac lets go of Eve's hand and she drifts a little away. She looks pale, tense; he can't believe he has involved her, that he has allowed her life to be in danger. He had hoped to check out Salmon's apartment and get the truth into the right hands without ever being detected. Slip into Manhattan and slip back out, maybe up into Maine, maybe head west. But they had been spotted right away, foxes desperately weaving through the woods, the number of hounds overwhelming. And his perceptual shifts seem to be increasing, probably his time as a functional person is decreasing every hour. His only thought now, the drive in every part of his body, is to get Eve out of the park and to safety.

Ahead Mac reads the banner stretched across the end of the walkway: THE PEACE AUTUMN CARNIVAL/CONCERT *Celebrating Safe Streets.*

The chatter of people suddenly rushes overly loud into Mac's ears then just as suddenly diminishes back again to the regular din of a crowd. But it is different somehow, heightened and echoey, as if it is fake, being pumped in from unseen speakers. A woman walking toward Mac, coming closer, looks up into his face and he is sure she is staring. Then she is gone. For all he knows the hounds are nearby. That very moment they might be watching, waiting for an opportune moment.

Fifteen yards back Scott Joyce walks at an easy pace, just another New Yorker enjoying the day, his eyes hidden by tinted lenses never leaving the targets. The pistol under his sweatshirt, silencer tipped, is ready to go, but crowds are unpredictable. Probably in the confusion they would run, hit the ground, or stand numb unable to react. But one never knew. Perhaps they might turn heroic. Perhaps the one person to see him pull the trigger would be an off-duty cop or some fearless guy waiting his whole life to be a hero. It takes only one individual to get the ball rolling, to give a crowd courage, the next thing you know they would be attacking you en masse, heroes all. No, better to wait. Perhaps take the man out first then track the woman some more, take her out separately. Joyce can see a celebration up ahead, balloons and a crowd, can hear band music, people milling in all directions, a good place to drop someone at close range, then disappear.

The chatter in Mac's head has increased again, a child crying, a teenage boy and girl having an argument. For an instant, he is even sure he heard his name on the lips of a six-year-old girl. *Mac Wells. . . .* Mac glances over at Eve and she smiles a little but he can't let her know it is getting worse. He nods to her as though everything is going to be okay. Up ahead the carnival is loud and packed, a good place to get lost. But then suddenly Mac feels as though he is being watched, an age-old feeling where one turns around and finds another staring, except that now it is heightened and Mac knows someone is there.

He turns, glances backward, and amidst the crowd his eyes fall on a man in a jogging outfit, listening to headphones. The man's eyes are hidden by sunglasses but Mac has no doubt and lets himself drift sideways away from Eve. A PEACE officer? Probably not. Not their turf. The man, just forty feet away, with only a few people between them stops walking and looks straight at Mac, dropping the cover. There is a long moment of recognition before either of them moves, the jogger even smiles slightly. No time to look over to Eve, to see if she is a safe distance away.

Mac draws his tranq-gun first, Joyce pulling out his gun only a moment later, the firing almost simultaneous, people scattering, dropping to the ground, neither man feeling the rush of adrenaline that accompanies confrontation, neither man's aim inhibited by anything other than the civilians that dodge in and out of the shot. Two of Mac's electropatches just miss over Joyce's right shoulder as Joyce crouches into a firing position, a bullet tearing through the cloth of Mac's jacket, grazing his arm without breaking the skin. Mac's gun clicks empty. Joyce releases a barrage of pinpoint shots as Mac dives, rolling behind a bust of Balzac. Mac looks back toward the carnival and sees Eve crouched behind Edgar Allan Poe. Mac pops out the tranq-gun's cartridge, reverses it, and slides it back in.

Joyce calmly walks forward, assuming Mac is out of ammo, his aim trained at Mac's position for the slightest movement.

The gun in her hand out of the knapsack, Eve steps out from behind Poe and pretends she is just shooting a paper target. Her hand shaking badly, she gets off two shots, the first shot lucky, hitting Joyce in the left shoulder, swinging him around and knocking the gun from his hand. Surprised, he looks over at her.

A police cruiser, its lights and sirens going, barrels down the Mall toward them. A group of Rollerbladers wearing headphones skate past Joyce unaware and Mac jumps in front of them, running, Eve joining him, keeping the bladeheads between themselves and Joyce. Joyce scoops up his gun in his right hand and sprints after them.

One by one the skaters pass Mac and Eve, leaving them without cover but they are able to get to the carnival just as Joyce has a clear shot. Music is coming from a live band playing hits of the eighties—Culture Club's "Karma Chameleon," blaring into the air. A huge cardboard cutout of a smiling idealized PEACE officer shaking hands with President Harris towers over the crowd. As Mac and Eve work their way closer to the Bandshell, Mac pushes Eve in front of him so she will not be shot from behind. The crowd changes from families to teenagers, kids surging and dancing, making it difficult to get through.

Joyce gets to the carnival's edge just as the police cruiser comes skidding up. Though no blood shows through his sweatshirt, it drips steadily down his hand.

One of the park police officers is out of the car, his gun aimed before the car stops completely. "Freeze! *Drop the weapon!!*" he screams.

Joyce doesn't even turn or acknowledge the police, just slips into the crowd, melting away. Both cops race forward.

Keeping their heads low, Mac and Eve push through the throngs of young people. Only ten yards back Joyce shoves people out of the way. He squeezes by a drunk woman who wraps her arms around him and won't let him pass. "C'mon, given me a kiss," she slurs. "It's Mardi Gras."

Joyce punches her in the stomach and she tumbles off him, dropping to her knees. A huge muscular man in a cowboy hat standing nearby grabs Joyce by the shoulder, spinning him around. But Joyce hits the man once in the throat with his index finger and the man's eyes roll back into his head. He stumbles, falling against one of the support posts holding President Harris and the PEACE officer aloft. A two-by-four and another horizontal bar snap under the man's bulk. The enormous cutout tilts precariously forward, rocking back and forth over the crowd. In the pandemonium Joyce resumes his push forward, the targets nowhere in sight.

Mac and Eve have cleared the main crowd and are moving toward Bethesda Fountain, a large shallow pool on Seventy-second Street, emptied for winter. Eve is breathing heavily. Mac quickly scans the area and sees a man and a woman in helmets getting ice-cream cones at a stand, two electric mopeds parked nearby. He pulls Eve toward them, the keys still in the ignition.

Mac pulls the key from one of the mopeds and tosses it into a bush. Mac hops on the other moped, feeling Eve's weight behind him, her arms wrapped around his chest. Before the man and the woman, newlyweds from Kentucky on a dream trip to New York, even notice, he has sped away. The man turns and drops his cone.

Back at the carnival Joyce breaks free from the crowd in time to see Mac and Eve disappearing up a paved path under tree cover. He runs up to the second moped, the man standing there.

"Where's the key?" he asks the newlywed.

"I don't know," the newlywed says, still too stunned to react.

Joyce climbs on the moped and smashes the plastic casing around the starter with his fist. The newlywed finally responds, grabbing Joyce's arm. Joyce swings the butt of his gun to the guy's temple, dropping him as the wife screams and everyone turns. Joyce trips the starter switch and the moped comes to life. He guns the throttle and heads up the paved path after the targets. The job has become a total mess. Not that he can't handle it, he has been in worse, much worse. Their being on the run complicates things, probably makes this his only chance. The moped hits a gully and bounces up, the engine groaning, not used to being driven all out. He sees them ahead, weaving between people along the path. He would have preferred the rifle from a distance. That would have been nice.

45

Two Central Park PD officers stand on duty at the Bow Bridge. Before PEACE was developed crime was so prevalent in Central Park that the park was given its own police force, a massive number of street cops were dispatched to stamp out crime. An officer behind every tree, the mayor liked to say. And the plan had worked so well that when PEACE came the park police vehemently resisted having cameras, protecting their turf, fearing their jobs would be lost. You don't fix what's not broken. They had their own HQ, their own radio communications, and were fiercely independent.

At that moment the radios of the numerous officers stationed around the park are crackling with all kinds of reports and commands. All hell is breaking loose in the park. Jerry Fulgenzi, the younger cop on Bow Bridge, jumps when his number is called.

"Yeah, four-oh-two here."

The dispatcher speaks in a calm, dispassionate voice as though reading a grocery list. "Two stolen mopeds, one with white male, possible injured and armed, considered dangerous, coming your way."

The two cops instinctively reach for their guns but there are no mopeds in sight. The crowd is thick and for half a minute there is no sound, then gradually a distant whine like the buzz of a fly can be heard. The drone of the engine, though quiet, grows and grows, the two officers unable to tell from which direction it is originating. Then suddenly from behind a cluster of people a moped explodes into view and speeds toward them. Jerry fumbles with his gun and steps out of the path of the moped as it streaks past. He looks at his partner, Luwanda Perez. "I thought she said a single male." Another moped with a single male breaks free from the throng and zooms between them. She and Jerry sprint after it toward the large woods called the Ramble.

Walton Smith, an NYPD traffic cop, sits in his three-wheel ticket cruiser on the sidewalk of the Seventy-ninth Street transverse. The steering wheel pushes into his huge stomach and he sees three white kids stuck in traffic in a station wagon point at him. "Well, you can kiss my fat black ass," he says under his breath, for all his bravado feeling suddenly self-conscious and hoping the car will move forward quickly. All police forces in the city have been put on alert and a Traffic Division dispatcher, Charlene Tillman, a woman Walton has had a crush on for six months, comes on the radio.

"Smith."

He loves that she ignores protocol and uses his name. "Yeah, Charlene."

"We got a white male suspect, armed and dangerous, might come your way through the Ramble."

Walton lets his voice go as deep as it will go. Barry White, the cop. "Got it."

"Be careful, Walton."

"Will do." He clicks off, absorbing the information for a

moment. Five years of sitting in a glorified golf cart handing out tickets to knuckleheads and he was finally going to get his chance. And Charlene had used his first name, concern in her tone. No mistake about it. If the bad guy came his way he would collar him and then go ask Charlene for a date. So what if he was a big man and she was all of five foot. He was agile. He throws his ticket booklet on the dash and pops the glove, getting out his gun, unfired since a test range in the summer. "It's showtime, baby," he says to it and slides out of the ticket cruiser. He lumbers up an old set of crumbling steps into the Ramble.

Mac weaves in and out of people strolling around the periphery of the Ramble, children dodging him, mothers covering their mouths, fathers waving angrily. If he can get through the Ramble to the Seventy-ninth Street transverse they can catch a cab, which often cut through the park on their way between fares. The feds or whoever they were would probably be looking for them to walk out of the park. They probably wouldn't have stopped traffic, that would draw too much attention. The park police, as far as he could tell, hadn't been brought into it which meant they were trying to do this quietly. It meant the guy on their tails wasn't an aberration, the guy trying to kill them was the hunter the agents were beating the brushes for, he was the plan.

Mac almost clips a young girl and lets off the throttle a little as he climbs deeper into the Ramble, given its name for the myriad of paths wandering and twisting through its hills.

The asphalt of the path is broken in places and Mac has to come to an almost complete stop so as not to bounce Eve off the bike. For the first time he becomes aware of the tightness of her arms around his midsection. She is holding on for dear life, literally.

Cresting a hill, almost halfway to the transverse, Mac looks down the wooded slope and sees the gunman on the other moped racing ahead on a parallel path. With the weight of only one rider the gunman easily pulls in front. Mac looks ahead and the trails merge; the gunman is looking to cut them off. He will get there first. Mac turns off-road up the gentle wooded slope. He crests the hill and heads down the other side. The grade of the hill changes suddenly, becoming steep and it is all Mac can do to keep his balance, rocks and downed trees appearing out of nowhere, an endless plunge toward the moment when he knows that he will lose control, the steering wheel jerking around in his hand like a jackhammer, Eve's forehead pressed into his back as if she is trying to burrow into him. In an instant they will be flying through the air but then there is a loud pop, the front tire of the moped tearing on a stump, Mac able to bring the bike under control, skidding sideways to a stop. He hears Eve moan something behind him.

He swivels. "You okay?"

"A little nauseous."

Mac hops off, helping Eve who is taking deep breaths. Ten feet ahead of them is the path. He turns off the moped and can hear the drone of the jogger's moped approaching. Mac puts down the kickstand and Eve leans against the moped. Mac runs toward the path, lifting a broken branch off the ground and stepping behind a tree at the edge of the pavement. The jogger comes around a corner, full speed, his gun drawn. Mac times the swing perfectly, a homerun or at least a double off the wall, the gunman taking the impact on his chest, flying backward, his moped skidding forward on its side, throwing an arc of sparks. The gunman lies perfectly still. Mac walks toward him, his breath going from calm to ragged. This is the man who is trying to kill his wife. This is the man who . . .

Eve sees the violence in Mac's body, what is about to happen. Mac raises the stick above his head.

"Mac, *no!* He's hurt enough."

There is movement up the hill in the woods. The jogger shifts, not quite out cold. Mac pauses, looks up at Eve.

"The police are coming. They'll take him."

Mac looks toward the crest of the hill, two park police there, hands on their knees, another two officers one hundred yards away jogging along the valley. The cops on the hill start down the slope. Mac drops the stick and takes Eve's hand. They run northeast across the path up another hill, toward the sound of traffic.

Jerry Fulgenzi and Luwanda Perez make their way carefully down the slope. No need to turn an ankle; their target is motionless on the ground and the other two have fled. Let someone up ahead chase them. Jerry and Luwanda disappear into a small grove of birch near the bottom of the hill. Jerry takes the lead, unholstering his gun. The leaves underfoot smell of decomposition, still wet from the earlier rain. For a minute Jerry's view of the path is obscured. He picks up speed near the edge of the trees and emerges to check out the downed suspect, but there is only the empty path and the two mopeds.

Mac lowers Eve down the eight-foot wall to a little sidewalk that runs along the southern side of Seventy-ninth Street. Traffic is moving slowly, cars honking. Mac hangs down and drops to the ground. In the eastward lane an empty cab sits in traffic. Mac leads Eve to it and the cabbie waves them in, unsure of where they came from.

"Stop and go, stop and go, mon, dis city is a big pile of shit." The cabbie, a large dark-skinned man with an islands accent, turns around and smiles pleasantly. "Where would you like not to go?"

"Broadway up in the eighties." Mac leans closer to the Plexiglas. "What's the holdup, you think?"

"De cops, mon, lookin' for someone to hassle."

Mac feels Eve sit lower in her seat. The traffic has completely stopped.

Scott Joyce runs through the woods toward Seventy-ninth Street. Two cracked ribs, probably a concussion, cuts and bruises everywhere—not too bad for taking a dive off a moped at full speed. He does not feel the pain from the gunshot or from the new injuries, rather, he lowers it, turns down the knob, something he will deal with later. The best military training in the world prepared him for far worse than this. He sees the top of the wall that borders Seventy-ninth Street ahead and kneels at its edge.

Just twenty feet away down on the street, Mac and Eve sit in an idling cab. Mac looks forward, only traffic, then turns in his seat back toward the East Side. Four more men in plain clothes, still a distance away, two on either side of the road, are slowly making their way up Seventy-ninth, checking each car as they go. Mac swipes his cash card and grabs Eve's hand.

"Okay, you gonna hoof it, mon, God be wi' you," the cabbie says as they step out and begin to make their way along the sidewalk.

Scott Joyce sees his targets. From his knapsack he pulls his rifle, collapsed and folded, and easily swings it open, from smaller than a loaf of bread to a perfect weapon in three seconds. He slides the scope in place. Take the man first, those are the orders, the woman will be easy after the man goes down. From this distance it will be impossible to miss. As Joyce adjusts the scope he does not think of the targets as people. They are like moving sacks of flour, a job to be done. He does not question what they have done. Back at the Mall, though, after the shoot-out, a momentary thought had crossed his mind. The male target was so eerily calm, an utter lack of panic during the shooting, it reminded Joyce of himself. But now he sets himself into firing position, one leg folded under, elbow braced on knee, the crosshairs following the male target's bobbing head. He lets the breath go from his lungs and . . .

"Freeze, motherfucker!"

Joyce feels the pressure of the gun barrel against the back of his head. He glances sideways, only moving his eyes, in his peripheral vision a tremendously overweight cop standing there, sweat pouring down his black face like someone has sprayed him with a hose.

"Put that rifle down slowly and don't even twitch."

"Man," Joyce says, "restrictions sure have changed since I was a cop."

"Put the fuckin' gun down."

Joyce begins to lower the rifle to the ground, his other hand drifting down to the handgun in his belt holster. "I bet you never even fired that gun on duty."

Joyce's hand flashes for his gun and Walton steps back, his arm flinching, his shot missing Joyce's head by inches and Joyce's two silenced bullets hitting Walton just to the left of his badge.

Mac has Eve down and covered behind a car at the sound of the gunshot. He looks back and sees a large cop standing at the top of the wall back in the Ramble, immobile, just staring forward, as if he has seen something in front of him that he can't take his eyes off. Then he falls forward over the wall and, landing headfirst, crushes the hood of a limousine. The limo's horn is jammed on and people climb out of their cars to see what has happened. Soon cops will be swarming into the area.

Ahead to the left off of Seventy-ninth Street, a gated service entrance leads back into the park. Staying low, Mac pulls Eve between cars to the entrance. They step over a locked chain and jog up the weed-filled road back into the park.

Five minutes later at the edge of the park Mac jumps down from the wall that borders the park to the sidewalk between Seventy-seventh and Seventy-eighth Streets. He helps Eve down.

There are no pursuers in sight. Police cruisers are screaming up Central Park West toward Seventy-ninth, all hell breaking loose the moment a cop was confirmed down.

Less than one block away, stuck in traffic on her third time around the exterior of the park, Lisa Washington anxiously searches for any sign of Mac and Eve past the phalanx of ambulances and police and PEACE vehicles. A traffic officer waves her through and she drives away.

46

Julian Sanders steps out of the cab at Eighth Avenue and Fifty-eighth Street and walks to the subway stairs, following the directions. He takes the escalator down to the trains, walks across the platform, and gets on another escalator heading up to the street. He knows Roderick is somewhere just behind him, watching carefully but keeping a distance. One black man is passable but two's a crowd.

For all his fame Julian is usually able to move through the city with ease. Today, in a Yankees cap and a pair of sunglasses, no one is bothering him. And that's the plan. Not to be followed. The note had given explicit instructions and Julian is following them to the letter. Julian steps into another cab and gives the address. His fourth cab in ten minutes. As the taxi swerves out into traffic Julian fights the urge to turn around. Instead he takes a small hand mirror from his knapsack, and checking his reflection, looks over his shoulder at nearby cars. The car hits a pothole and the mirror shakes in his hand, making it impossible to get a fix on any of the cars. For all he knows hundreds of men are on his tail at that moment. Not to mention the cameras. The spy stuff just isn't his game.

He takes the slip of paper with the directions on it from his breast pocket and tells the driver to pull over. The directions had been couriered personally to Julian by a firm that handled the movement of packages like diamonds or sensitive documents. Two burly men in suits had arrived at the hotel and insisted on seeing his identification and crosschecking his photo against one they had brought with them before they would turn over the business-size envelope that contained Jason Barber's directions for a meeting.

Julian steps out onto the curb at Times Square and enters the five-story World Gap store. He walks past all the impossibly young salespeople standing near massive rows of jeans and shirts, toward the entrance at the other end of the block. He exits there and immediately enters the Barnes & Noble bookstore across the street. Out of the corner of his vision he sees Roderick coming up the street and knows Jason Barber will already be inside waiting for him. Julian takes the escalator all the way to the top floor. Not one for crowds, he normally avoids these vast bookstores packed to the gills with people using computer terminals, reading magazines, and drinking free ultracaffeinated coffee. People used to go to the public library to hang out and actually bought books at bookstores.

Julian walks through the children's department and takes up a place in the travel section where he can watch the escalator. He pulls a book on Bermuda from the shelves and pretends to leaf through it. He knows Barber is around somewhere, probably watching that very moment. All this backtracking is probably totally unnecessary, but if it isn't, Julian isn't taking any chances with security. Julian checks his watch; time for things to start.

"Julian."

Julian turns and Jason Barber, big-time consultant, is standing a few feet away wearing a pair of old jeans, a baseball cap, and large Serengeti sunglasses. Julian almost laughs. He has never seen

Jason Barber out of a suit. Jason pages through a travelogue on tropical islands like it's the most interesting book he's ever seen.

"Jace, this really necessary?"

"I think so. You follow the directions?"

"Yeah, those glasses are a bit—"

"It's serious, Julian. You have people here?"

"Yes."

"How do they know to come?"

"Panic button in my pocket."

"Good. Ever been to the islands?"

"Bermuda, Jamaica, the usual stuff."

"There's some small islands down there, off the beaten track, great fishing, great people. I'm gonna go down and check it out. Haven't had a real vacation in years."

"What's going on, Jace?"

"The day I started checking things out for you, my townhouse was searched. You know how I feel about security. I've got the best technology money can buy guarding that house. I can't begin to tell you how improbable it is they didn't trip something. Every system has a backup, every backup has a backup, but they got in and out like they were never there. Then when I got home they went into my office and accessed my computer—something I was assured was impossible by one of the most expensive information security firms in the world. I'm used to being checked out, it's part of my business. But this is *way, way* beyond anything I thought was possible. It scares me."

"Gotta be the government."

"Above anything I ever heard of."

"I'm sorry I got you into this, Jace."

"Hey, remember me when you're president. I wanted to warn you in person, make sure you understood how serious this might be. You've done so much for me. It's the least I can do for you."

"Thanks. We're obviously looking at something far larger than a PEACE drug scandal."

"Definitely."

"Any ideas?"

Jason Barber glances back down toward the escalators. "I don't know, but I bet that cop everyone's looking so hard for knows." He pulls out a slip of paper. "Got the number and address of a freelance reporter who may also be looking into this. I was unable to get in touch with him."

A woman, middle-aged and overweight, walks toward the two men. She is clearly just a shopper but Jason Barber watches her closely as she passes.

"Time for me to get on first class."

"It can't be that bad, Jace. There are still laws."

Barber smiles as though Julian is a child. "That's the thing about you guys drawn to be in the press, Julian. Everyone thinks you're all cynical, scandal-seeking people who want the truth. But in reality you're all idealistic." Jason looks around. "My advice, Julian—you ought to take a vacation too." He does not offer his hand, maintaining the pose of separateness.

Julian watches him walk down a row of books, just a man at ease, browsing through the shelves. Then he is gone.

(47)

William Kane stands back from the monitors at Zoo HQ and wonders how much longer he has. There is always a time frame to fix things. In his pocket the pager is warm in his hand and he realizes he has been holding it tightly for a while. He takes his hand out of his pocket. In front of him Schorr stands near the monitor operators and talks on a secured phone. Damage control, saving his own ass probably. In the last few years Kane has experienced setbacks on a few projects, leaks, loose ends that needed to be tied up and such, but never anything like this, with a program of this magnitude. Hell, a cop dead, a shoot-out in broad daylight in Central Park—it was all spinning out of control. Probably the targets weren't even in the park anymore. All he could hope for was that the targets had nothing, or not enough, and would run, disappear. To be dug up and silenced later.

If they had the whole story they would already have contacted the media, and his contacts at CNN or the networks would already have called. Then the operation would go into a different mode. Kill the story. It would be difficult, but bigger ones had been killed. Obviously Wells had been hanging around, maybe trying to find more, but Central Park was just a first dose. They stayed and they were dead.

Schorr clicks off his phone and Kane walks over to him.

"So what happened?" Kane watches Schorr's face and realizes the man hardly ever blinks.

"Most likely they're out of the park, on the West Side."

"I mean with the independent."

Schorr shrugs as though they're talking about the weather. "Crowd interference, and the female target can shoot. There was no paper on that."

"So the blood trail was ours? Great."

"Only a shoulder wound. Next time we locate them, he'll finish it."

Kane turns away from Schorr to the monitors. "Concentrate on the West Side. Have the parameters been changed?"

The young monitor operator, probably Special Ops communications then a brief stint at NSA before being recruited, answers over his shoulder without turning. "Yes, sir. Even if the targets change their appearance again we'll pick them up. Anyone matching height to weight will be crossreferenced for identification."

Kane lets his eyes drift over the multitude of screens, honking traffic and people obliviously scurrying about their business. Somewhere in those swirling images, a few specks in a sea of movement, a man and a woman are hiding.

The diner, located across the street and a few storefronts up from Salmon's building, offers an excellent view of the front doors and of the alley to the backdoor entrance, everyone who comes and goes. To get to the diner Mac had picked a cab that had been idling in front of a deli on Amsterdam driven by an Afghani who looked like he did not watch the news, let alone speak English.

Their plates long ago cleared away by the young disinterested waitress, they sit quietly and watch, hoping that any moment Salmon will waddle down the sidewalk and duck into the alley.

They had talked about leaving, but Eve was adamant about at least making an attempt to find Salmon; she repeated Mac's own words back that it was the only way they would be safe, and he knew she was right. But the idea of her vulnerability now makes him sick. He has already accepted in his mind that he may not make it. And that will be worth it if he can get her to a place where she will be protected. Mac wipes his forehead with a crumpled napkin. For some reason he can't stop sweating.

Eve looks at him. She can tell it is getting harder for him to hold it together. They have to get medicine. Soon. She shifts in her seat, the bruise on her hip sore, a reminder that the chase through the park, which was beginning to seem distant, isn't, that the safety they have could at any moment evaporate. A single drop of sweat falls from Mac's eyebrow to the table. He has told her that he can make it. She has faith in him. He is good at what he does, but what effect would sudden psychosis have on him? She leans forward, not wanting to draw attention.

"How do you feel?"

"Not bad. A little high." Mac smiles. He must put the best spin on the way his brain feels, alternating between relatively normal, the steady background buzz since the park, like a faucet constantly running, to moments where the falling water takes the shape of voices.

"What if Salmon's dead?"

"Then we phone in what we have and head up to Maine, maybe Nova Scotia. Towns and islands up there where it's cheap, where people are private. We stay for a year until the money runs out, then . . ."

"We can definitely get money from my parents." Eve takes Mac's hands.

Mac focuses on a little kid sitting a few booths away with

his mom. The kid's staring. "Probably we won't have to hit up your folks. We can start again, new identities. We'll both be able to get work as new people."

"Can I pick any name I want?" Eve tries to be light.

"No. Your name will probably be Esther or Tallulah. We'll have to work up identities from obituaries. Can shave a few years off your age if you want." Mac checks out the kid, still staring, now smirking, like he knows something.

"So we'll be dead people?"

"We use the obits from thirty years ago. Find a child who died real young, then write to the state government as that person, saying we misplaced our birth certificate, requesting another copy. We get a new driver's license with the birth certificate, then credit cards, a passport, the sky's the limit."

"Sounds too easy."

"It is easy."

"Doesn't the state crossreference deaths with births?"

"Not in Maine."

"So we become new people."

"New people, Tallulah." Mac looks over and the kid is still at it. Time to go.

"Mac, what is it?" Eve turns in her seat.

"That kid's made me. Won't stop staring."

Eve looks and the kid is just a typical six year old, bored while his mother eats a large bowl of tapioca.

"Mac."

Mac feels Eve squeeze his hands. He looks at her.

"Mac, he's not looking at you. I think maybe it just feels like he is."

Mac looks and the kid is smiling, like he's gotten away with something.

A limousine pulls in front of Salmon's building, double-parking. Mac looks out the window and sees a large black man get out and hold the door for Julian Sanders, who pauses for a moment then enters the building. It has to be more than coincidence. But even if it isn't, it's time to check Marty's apartment. The longer they wait the more likely someone might recognize him.

"Mac, what—"

"C'mon, time to go." Mac is up and pulling Eve by the hand.

They hurry across the street to the alley, which leads to the back of Salmon's building.

Julian Sanders enters Salmon's building with a touch of apprehension. Salmon hadn't answered his phone but Julian thought he would stop by, knock on his door.

"What can I do for you?" Recognition shows in the doorman's face. "Mr. Sanders . . . really enjoy your show, sir."

The doorman is a middle-aged man whose name tag says Marv Lupino.

"Well, Marv. I'm here to see Mr. Martin Salmon."

"Go on up, sir. It's Seven E."

It occurs to Julian, not for the first time, that fame is like a skeleton key; it gets you access to all kinds of things. People let you do things because they feel they already know you.

He gets on the elevator and it slowly creaks to life. In the limousine he had pored over the details of his meeting with Jason. Why would a man like Jason Barber be so scared? They *had* searched his house and got into his computer, but this was a man recently featured on the cover of *New York* magazine. A man whom all presidential hopefuls paid a visit to if they were serious about winning New York. Julian knew Jason was a careful man, not given to overly excited responses to anything, and here he was leaving the country.

The elevator doors open on the seventh floor and Julian suddenly regrets telling Roderick to stay with the car. No one is in the hallway. He'll just go to the door and won't stay long whether Salmon is there or not.

He pushes the doorbell, an ugly-sounding buzzer, but there is no response. There is a bad smell coming from the apartment and Julian tries the doorknob. It turns. He looks around then gently pushes open the door, tripping a tiny transmitter inserted into the doorjamb. The smell in the air is thick, overpowering. Julian pulls a handkerchief from his pocket and covers his mouth.

Julian doesn't realize that someone is behind him until he feels the gun in his back.

Mac pushes him forward. "Move now!" They are hurrying across the apartment, Eve shutting and locking the apartment door, all of them gasping for air and stepping around Salmon's body lying in the unmistakable pose of the dead, a stillness beyond sleeping. They get to the kitchen, the air fresh through windows that have been left open, and Mac shuts the kitchen door.

"Sit down." He motions Julian into a chair. Eve is standing over the sink as if she might throw up.

Mac sits across from Julian. He turns slightly toward Eve. "You okay, honey?"

Julian glances toward the woman, composing herself. Honey? A couple.

"What're you doing in this apartment, Mr. Sanders?"

"I'm looking into this story. Heard Martin Salmon was as well."

"Why'd you help me at the rally?"

"Instinct. Do you know why Mr. Salmon's been killed."

"They killed him because they didn't want the story to come out."

"Who's they?"

"People in PEACE, people who developed it, who are backing it."

"So what's the story?"

"Front-page news across the country."

"It would have to be a hell of a—"

"Across the world—" Mac says.

"What's the story?"

Mac ignores Julian. "Marty had ideas about how the flow of information to the public is manipulated, how some news organizations, even yours, are heavily influenced. What I want to know is what your criteria is. If I bring you this story, will you put it on the air?"

"For TV you just need to tell what you know, that doesn't mean you'll get on the air. For print you probably need two sources, or a source and documentation of some kind. The sources can be anonymous, but they'd have to be ironclad. I don't actually usually break stories, but if it's valid, I'd be glad to hand you to the right people."

There is a sound from outside the front door, someone fumbling with keys. Mac freezes, listening, but after a few moments realizes it is the apartment next door.

"Honey," Eve says.

Mac turns to Eve, who has recovered.

"We shouldn't stay here."

"You're right." Mac stands, pulls out the .45, and hands it to her. "I'll be right back."

Eve takes the gun and holds it at her side.

Mac pours water on a dishrag, covers his mouth, and heads back into the hallway to the rest of the apartment. He turns on a light. The apartment looks clean, too clean. Mac notices things he hadn't the few times he was in the apartment before; on the wall a photo of Salmon shaking hands with Jimmy Carter, a framed diploma from Harvard.

Mac looks at the body, and, flat on the floor, Salmon's immense weight shows more than when he was standing. Sprawled like someone who has fallen midstep, he has the appearance of a heart attack victim. His one hand is folded under his body; Mac rolls Salmon onto his shoulder but there is nothing. Salmon's other hand is stretched forward above his head, his index finger extended like he is pointing. Mac follows the finger but it points to a blank wall. The only other thing in the path between Salmon's hand and the blank wall is the large potted dead fern a few feet to the right. Mac stands and looks around the apartment, the computer gone, everything probably carefully searched. It's time to hit the road. Mac turns to get Eve.

"It's under the plant," Salmon's voice as clear as day in the room. Mac whips around but Salmon's body lies stiff on the floor. Mac waits for him to say more but his face is frozen.

Mac edges around the body toward the plant and lifts the pot. Underneath is a computer disk with the word *Pulitzer* in Salmon's messy handwriting scrawled across the front. Mac stops at Salmon's body, looks down. He slides the disk in his pocket and thinks about speaking back aloud, but instead says the words in his mind.

Thank you, Marty.

He heads back to the kitchen.

"Time to go."

"Wait!" Julian starts to get to his feet. "If you know what this is all about, I can help you."

"Give me a number."

Julian pulls out a card and writes his hotel and room number on it.

Mac remembers Marty's communication code. "If I call to set up a meeting we'll meet at One hundred tenth Street and West End Avenue."

"Okay."

"Exactly one minute after us I would leave if I were you."

Mac pockets the card and turns for the door.

"Shouldn't we call the police about Mr. Salmon?"

"You talk to the cops and you're compromised. We won't call you."

Exactly one minute later Julian Sanders walks out Salmon's door, leaving it ajar for someone to return home after a long day at work to a hallway that smells unimaginably bad. Julian steps into the elevator and punches the button for the lobby. What could possibly make the front page across the world? Certainly not some drug scandal involving the PEACE Corps. It would have to be bigger. . . . The elevator door opens to the lobby and three men in suits wait for Julian to step out before they get in. He forces the typical perfunctory half smile one uses exiting elevators, and they make note of him but do not respond and enter the elevator as one. As he makes his way across the lobby he sees through the front doors one car double-parked at an angle and another pulling in and stopping sharply behind his limousine. Four athletic-looking men, in normal clothes but with the same short hair as the three men who got on the elevator, step out of the car and take positions at the front of the building.

Julian pushes through the doors as though he has lived in Salmon's building all his life. The four men examine Julian as he walks to the limousine. The hair on Julian's forearms and on the back of his neck bristles, the invisible primal cues a man receives from other men flooding him. He notices, as Roderick holds the door for him, that Roderick's jacket is unbuttoned, that Roderick leaves his shooting hand free.

【48】

The computer kiosk at Fourteenth Street near NYU is small by the standards of the city, only three help desks and fifty computer stations. Mac picked a cab with an old Asian driver who wouldn't have recognized them if they were President Harris and the First Lady. Eve chose the kiosk because it was a place she had hung out when she was a grad student and remembered that it didn't do much business. It was a place they could do what they needed to do and probably escape notice.

The stream of people, mostly students, through the door to the help desks is sporadic; they are ordering plane tickets, flowers, anything that one can buy through a computer. Mac and Eve have taken over a computer at the back of the shop, a convenient partition of potted trees between them and the rest of the store.

It's taking a while to get Salmon's disk to run—the software used, already over two years old, is not recognized by the computer's pre-existing software. Eve is waiting in line at a library on the Net. Only a few people are left ahead of her, displayed on her screen as pigs dancing toward a cliff. Another pig shimmies to the edge then jitterbugs out into midair. Only a few more minutes.

Through the leaves of the potted trees Mac watches the front doors and sips a Punch, the nuclear bomb of hypercaffeinated colas. It seems to calm his mind. Eve was afraid it would do the exact opposite, speed him up into an unimaginable state, but somehow he had known it was the right thing. Food, too, seems to help.

He looks at Eve, so intent on the computer screen, so strong under such incredible circumstances and it is all he can do to keep from leaping onto the table and declaring his love for her. Eve turns.

"You okay?"

"I love you."

"I know."

"No, I love you. The tranq-gun's changed me. I feel it differently, in every part of me. No matter what happens, I'm glad to have this, to have you."

A tone sounds and the computer begins to upload Salmon's disk. Mac pulls his chair in as Salmon's article comes on screen.

Reading the first few pages, Mac allows himself to smile. The article is excellent. Concise and well-written, like something one would expect to see on the front page of the best newspaper. Marty was very talented.

Eve scrolls to the fifth and last page and Mac blows out a breath of air—it's all he can do to keep from yelling in relief. There, after Salmon's article, is a scanned memo from Rhine Corporation to the National PEACE Command, a panel of twelve people handpicked by the president to coordinate and oversee the development of the program, predating the New York PEACE start-up date. It warns the National PEACE Command, dubbed the Apostles by the press, to implement all necessary measures during the Manhattan PEACE test to avoid civilian casualties, due to possible serious side effects. Mac glances at the door. The memo wasn't acted on; extra measures to avoid civilian hits didn't come into effect until months into the anticrime initiative.

Mac looks at the words on the screen, floating, ephemeral, and yet he knows the weight they carry, the wide net they cast, the powerful people they implicate. Probably even President Harris. With the election a little more than a month away Mac suddenly understands the magnitude of the forces he and Eve are up against. In their hands they hold the balance of power for the leadership of the country.

"They knew all along." Eve turns.

"Yep."

"Potesky give this to him?"

"Must have."

"We have enough now?"

"Enough for me."

Mac and Eve step out onto the sidewalk. The New York Times Building is just a cab ride away.

Perhaps because the disk is in his pocket and an end is in sight, or perhaps because he is feeling progressively worse, Mac doesn't notice the Plexiglas globe high on the corner of a building sweeping the street, doesn't take the usual precautionary steps to walk down the sidewalk separately from Eve.

At the same moment downtown in the PEACE bunker and uptown in Zoo HQ, a soft tone goes off and DADD throws a large image of Mac and Eve onto central screens.

Kane turns to Schorr. "Dispatch everything we have." Schorr is already on the phone, walking out the door.

In the bunker Tom Martinez sits up. Jim Lincoln leans forward too. "Hey, that's Mac Wells." Lincoln looks over at Martinez. "Alert our crews?"

"Uh." Martinez shifts in his seat; there's nothing he can do.

"Yeah, give the order." Martinez sits back. "You okay to watch this for a minute? Gotta hit the can."

"No prob." Lincoln doesn't even look up.

Tom Martinez heads out into the hall and walks up two flights to a bank of pay phones. He dials Lisa Washington's number.

Mac sees Kane's men from a block away, both in front and behind, but doesn't see the PEACE undercover team coming forward only twenty feet away. Before the PEACE team can move, though, Mac grabs Eve's arm and they are plunging down a subway stairway into the Fourteenth Street station. The station is a network of long interconnecting tunnels leading east and west to various train lines and is packed with afterwork commuters. Leading Eve, Mac dodges people down another set of stairs to a platform. At the edge of a train track a fight has broken out and DADD's cameras behind the TV's are focused on the disturbance. Mac pulls Eve through the thick crowds to the side of a newspaper stand.

Mac steps to the window of the newsstand and flashes his PEACE badge at the turban-wearing man inside.

"Need to come inside the kiosk for a moment."

The Indian man doesn't comply right away, as if he can't understand what Mac has said.

"Open the door, *now!*"

The man disappears to the side and Mac goes around to the door. The man opens up and Mac steps in and pulls Eve behind him. Mac and Eve sit on the floor in a space underneath the counter. Mac pulls the tranq-gun and points it at the surprised man's face.

"But you are a PEACE officer."

"Just keep selling papers for a while and then we'll leave."

Someone comes to the window above Mac and Eve's head and buys a bodybuilding magazine.

Mac feels Eve's hands wrapped tight around his arm. Over

and over people come to the window and buy papers; trains pull in and out. A steady rhythm of crowds. Mac suddenly feels his body floating, a frightening disorientation, the world is going out of focus. He desperately tries to fight it but a tremendous need to sleep overtakes him.

Eve watches Mac close his eyes, his hair and shirt drenched with sweat. She looks up and the turbaned store owner is frowning down at her, at the gun drooping in Mac's hand, the fluorescent lights reflecting off his wire-rimmed glasses.

"I do not want trouble, young lady."

"We just need a place for a while. Please, it's life or death."

"So he is not a PEACE officer?"

"He is—" Eve is cut off as someone comes up to the kiosk. Eve doesn't hear what is said but she watches the Indian gentleman pause, then gesture down to her.

"No, just my cat. Keeps me company. If I see them I let you know."

Eve sees the shadow of the person grow on the floor as they peer over the counter. The shadow withdraws. The Indian man glances down to Eve, then frowns. He gestures toward Mac.

"What's wrong with him?"

"He's sick. He just needs to sleep a little."

The kiosk owner doesn't answer but grunts as if the world is on his shoulders. He turns, pausing, standing perfectly still except for his lips which move as though he is having a conversation with himself. He turns back, looks at Eve, then reaches into a soda container and hands her an iced tea.

"Thank you."

The kiosk owner doesn't answer but turns away and begins to cut open bundles of magazines, his lips moving again.

Eve takes a sip of the iced tea. If she and Mac are found, if someone points a gun over the counter, she doesn't know what she will do. Before the park she would have imagined herself fighting back, she would do anything to save Mac. But she has made no effort to dig the .45 out of the knapsack, to be vigilant. Mac is getting sicker. If a cop came, maybe the best thing would be to turn themselves in, maybe they would get lucky, land in the hands of the good guys. She does not know what she thinks about whether they will make it. She is no longer thinking in those terms. Amidst the smell of newsprint and perfume samplers from magazines she no longer feels the desperate need to survive she felt at the house or the terror she felt in the park. Just an unreasonable calm. She wonders if she is in some kind of shock, similar to what new recruits feel after surviving the first week of combat. An invincibility, the mind closing to reality, sculpting it to an acceptable form; one could take only so much stress.

She sips her iced tea. The liquid is cool in her throat and she feels better, more focused. She looks at Mac, his face dead still, and it occurs to her how much she relies on him, how much of her strength derives from her belief in his excellence as a tactical thinker. If he was awake she would be alert, helping in whatever way she could, not even thinking of giving up. Courage was in a large part peer pressure. Sometimes people did extraordinary things because they were too busy or too embarrassed not to. She lifts her hand to her neck, gently touching the tender skin. It was a good thing she hadn't been able to see when she shot the man at FarQuar. Being out of it on the floor after the shooting had given her a nice little built-in separation between cause and effect. She knows if she had actually seen him flipping backward, the back of his head exploding, whether or not to get the gun out of the bag might be the least of her worries.

She looks up and the kiosk owner's lips continue to move. She hears his voice faintly and realizes for the first time that he is saying a prayer.

(49)

One hour later the crowd out on the platform has been reduced by two-thirds and Mac wakes, suddenly clutching for the gun that is no longer in his hand.

"Mac, you fell asleep."

Mac sits up. "How long?"

"About an hour."

The kiosk owner looks down at Mac from his perch on a stool. "There are no police. You can leave now."

Mac looks up to the man and notices for the first time a handgun in a holster attached under the counter. Mac looks down to his tranq-gun on the floor next to Eve's leg with an empty iced tea bottle. The kiosk owner could have turned them in but didn't. The owner turns away like they aren't there. Eve helps Mac to his feet but he is already alert.

"Thanks," Mac says to the man, who doesn't turn around or act like he's heard. Mac lifts the tranq-gun off the ground and sticks it in his shoulder holster. No pursuers in sight. The stairs up to the street are about a hundred yards away.

•

Leaning against a large pillar directly in their path, Tim Dimpter wipes the sweat from his forehead with the back of his hand and smiles. His shirt is soaked through. He knows he is not well, can feel that his mind is wrong. And it is Wells's fault. After he kills Wells he will go after Captain Codd. Codd had assured him that with no alcohol in his system he would be safe. But here he was sick, and getting sicker. It had to be the cold medicine he was taking when Mac tranqed him; Codd hadn't said anything about cold medicines. For twenty-four hours Dimpter has been fighting the urge to stick the gun in his own mouth. The thought that one momentary flinch of his finger, one reflexive twitch in a few nerves, could explode oblivion out the back of his head gives him solace. But the end can't come until he has dealt with Wells and Codd.

As soon as Wells was ID'd in the station he had come, but everyone else had left after the initial search. They assumed Wells had slipped through and gotten off at another station, but Dimpter knew there was no way Wells would ever take a train unless he absolutely had to. Every station would be swarming with PEACE officers the rest of the way up the train line. The best bet was to hide, then make it back up to the street. Dimpter looks up and can't believe his luck. He draws his .45 and begins to walk down the center of the platform toward Mac and Eve.

In the PEACE bunker the two new watch guards, an old friend of Tom Martinez's from NYPD days named Jeff Rector, and a rookie, Marge Heilbron, sit up in their chairs as the warning tone sounds. Tom Martinez comes forward from behind them where he has camped out in a chair along the wall.

"All teams in Fourteenth Street vicinity, DADD's got a man

on the Queens-bound L platform armed with a handgun. Respond immediately."

"Geez, that's Tim Dimpter," Martinez says.

Dimpter raises the gun, his hand shaking. He feels as though he is about to start crying, and though Mac is still out of range he pumps off five shots. The explosion of the gun sends everyone nearby flat to the platform. Farther away people jump into the tracks or push toward the stairs, screams and shrieks echoing up into the vaulted ceiling. All of the shots but one speed harmlessly over the heads of the crowd. One shot ricochets off a pillar into the floor at the feet of a Muslim family in traditional North African garb, specifically at the feet of their four-year-old girl. The father, a large bald man, runs toward Dimpter and though Dimpter has dropped the gun and is crying, his hands raised in the air like he is trying to reach something, the man is no match for a trained PEACE officer. Dimpter drops the father with one punch to his jaw.

Mac has Eve press behind a pillar as commuters run by. Through the rushing crowd Mac catches glimpses of Dimpter's face, his expression so contorted he barely looks human. Is that what awaits him? A monster firing into a crowd? Eve had not seen it was Dimpter. Better to keep it that way. This drug she wants to get him—who knows if it works. Perhaps the condition only gets worse. Dimpter has regained his composure and has picked up his gun and is staring at it in his hand. Behind Dimpter Mac sees four people trying to get in against the crush trying to get out. He recognizes one of them, a guy dressed like a Rastafarian, dreadlocks and a knit cap, and Mac knows it is an undercover PEACE UC unit. He takes Eve's hand and they blend into the crowd exiting the other side of the platform.

•

At one of the many stairways that lead down into the subway from the street, a van pulls onto the curb. The side door opens and seven men get out and head down the stairway. One block away, two more vans pull up to another subway entrance and eight men and two women head down into the train station.

"Tim!" one of the PEACE officers, the Rastafarian, is only twenty feet away, his tranq-gun aimed. "Tim. Put the weapon back on the floor."

Dimpter was about to put the gun into his mouth but the sound of a PEACE officer behind him stops that thought. Wells is somewhere ahead. He wants to kill Wells first. Dimpter runs forward. He hears two electropatches whiz by close to his ear. He weaves in and out of the pillars and is soon part of the last of the crowd making its way up the stairs.

Tunnels head off in four directions and Mac heads west on a crowded walkway. He and Eve walk quickly until the passage opens into a large area, another hub with newspaper stands and various tunnels continuing west or turning north. Mac pulls Eve to a newspaper stand out in the center of the room. He looks back the way they came. No Dimpter. No agents. No faces he recognizes.

"What is it? You okay?" Eve's pretending to browse through the latest issue of *Vanity Fair.*

"Yeah." Mac rubs his temple. "The weirdest thing, all my senses have gotten so much stronger."

Eve puts her hand on Mac's head.

"I can feel the blood rushing through your hand."

"We have to get some medicine to arrest this. If you have a pyschotic break, you might never come back."

"*Shhhhhh!*" Mac pulls Eve behind him. "Someone's running this way. More than one person."

Dimpter comes out of the tunnel at full sprint. He stops and turns in a circle. He begins to walk past the newsstand toward the other side of the room but stops twenty feet away, Mac's crouching image reflected from behind in the gray screen of a large dormant ceiling TV. Dimpter whirls around and begins firing, the magazine and newspaper stacks exploding around Mac and Eve's heads, small bits of newsprint thrown into the air like confetti. Mac fires back but Dimpter doesn't duck for cover, even turns his body, facing Mac full front so he will be more of a target. From the same corridor that Dimpter entered the PEACE UC unit arrives. Dimpter pumps off a couple of rounds in their direction and they dive behind a trash can and two pillars. At that moment, from two corridors on the other side of the room the seventeen agents dispatched by Tom Schorr pour into the room, guns drawn.

Dimpter whirls around to face the men. The agents are looking for Mac and Eve, not a deranged guy with a gun, so at first they don't react. In some deep recess of Dimpter's mind he understands that he is on the same side with these men but what he sees are seventeen people with various handguns pointed in his direction. He lifts his gun and fires. The return fusillade of bullets is immediate and deafening, the impacts on Dimpter's body knocking him backward and to the ground behind a cement trash can.

The Rasta PEACE officer presses his body as hard as he can to a pillar as chips of concrete fly off a nearby wall. The bullets suddenly stop and he looks over to his team, everyone safe. He hears footsteps running up the tunnel. Another PEACE UC unit slides into place.

The Rasta PEACE officer sneaks a peek around the pillar

and sees Dimpter on his back, covered in blood, his chest rising up and down in a ragged way. The men with the guns approach Dimpter's spot, weapons out in front like it's a war zone.

The Rasta motions to the rest of the PEACE officers and as one they direct their tranq-guns toward the approaching agents.

Dimpter, unable to move his legs, struggles to load another clip into his gun. His hands feel weak and it is hard to grasp the gun, which is covered in blood. The sounds in the room—someone screaming from faraway, Beethoven's Fifth drifting out of nearby speakers—seem to come to him down a long passageway that is growing smaller. Then suddenly the gun in his hand is no longer so heavy, his whole body becomes light, and without pain he feels himself rising, floating up into the air so that he is looking down on himself, the men with the guns only a few feet away.

"Peace officers! Freeze! *Lower your weapons! ! !*" The Rasta holds out an ID badge from behind the pillar and the agents stop in their tracks.

Dimpter watches from above as his body rolls onto its side, swinging the gun along the floor to the edge of the trash can. Suddenly he drops from his hovering perch back into his body, into the numbness and pain, blood pouring out of his mouth and dripping down into his lungs, gagging him. As he aims the gun he feels as though he is laughing but he can't be sure.

The shots, though wildly off the mark, are enough to draw fire from the agents and the room ignites with an explosion of electropatches and bullets.

Back at the PEACE bunker Tom Martinez watches in disbelief with Rector and Heilbron. Martinez grabs the microphone from Heilbron, who is staring at the gunfight on the screens with her mouth open.

"All units proceed to Fourteenth Street tunnel between the L and number one trains. Gunfight in progress with officers down. I repeat, proceed to Fourteenth Street tunnel. Use extreme prejudice. Officers are down." Martinez pushes Heilbron to the side.

"Call ambulances, Marge."

Heilbron slides her chair down the counter to a bank of phones and punches a button.

A tone sounds and DADD pulls up a picture of Mac and Eve crawling across a floor in the subway.

Martinez grabs the microphone again. "Mac Wells. This is Tom. Come in, Mac."

"What are you doing?" Marge rolls her chair over from the phones.

Rector leans toward Heilbron. "Kid, if you don't want to see this, now's a good time to hit the can."

"I can't . . . Sergeant Martinez isn't even clocked in."

Rector leans closer to Heilbron. "I'm ordering you to go."

Marge Heilbron pushes her chair back uncertainly, then heads for the door.

Mac lifts Eve to her feet at the edge of a corridor. Inside his knapsack Tom Martinez's voice calls faintly from Mac's PEACE earphone. Mac stops.

Eve has her hands over her ears, the roar of the gunfight deafening. Mac leads her around a bend in the corridor and the sound diminishes.

"Hear that?" Mac looks at Eve.

"It's like thunder."

"No. I'm hearing a voice."

The voice from the knapsack suddenly gets louder as Tom Martinez shouts into the microphone. "Mac, you jerk. *Pick up!*"

"I hear it too." Eve pulls the knapsack from her back.

Eve digs through the bottom of the backpack, finding Mac's PEACE earphone and throat communicator.

Mac reaches for it. "Forgot we had that."

"Mac, come in *dammit!*"

Mac attaches the communicator to his throat and slides in the earphone.

"That you, Martinez?"

"I'm watching you on our monitors right now. I'm gonna guide you outta there. Continue the way you're headed."

Mac hesitates.

"*Now!*"

Mac removes the communicator. "Eve, it could be a trap." The guns suddenly go silent.

"*Mac!*" Martinez is so loud in Mac's ear it hurts. "The feds are coming. You gotta move now! "

"We could call nine-one-one," Eve says.

Mac slaps the communicator back on his throat. "Okay, we're moving."

Far down the corridor five agents spill into view. Mac pulls Eve into a side corridor, a ramp leading down to another level. "Is that the way you're saving us, Tom?!"

Martinez doesn't reply. He is calling up cameras in the path ahead of Mac and Eve. On one of the screens he sees what he wants and leans to the microphone. "They're everywhere, Mac! You're just gonna have to trust me. Keep the way you're goin' and get your ass to the F train!"

Tile from the wall next to Eve's head explodes from the impact of bullets. Mac and Eve duck and run, the corridor curving in a constant arc so they are able to stay just out of shot.

Tom Martinez watches the screens, the tension so desperate, a kind of horrified smile is frozen on his face, his left hand shaking a little, poised above a button on a side console. "Just a little farther. Almost got you now."

Mac sees the Grid area ahead, the Grid devices newly installed, blinking primed and ready, but doesn't have time to stop. He and Eve run through it and nothing happens. When he hears the electric hum of the Grid and then the unmistakable sizzling discharge, a sound not unlike when a bug flies into the electric current of a bug zapper, he does not look back. The first of the agents, a woman, is stopped cold, frozen in the electronic field as the rest of the pursuers are trapped on the other side of the Grid zone.

Mac and Eve turn the corner onto the platform for the F train. Passages from Tchaikovsky's *Swan Lake* are playing from the TVs. Few people are waiting near the tracks; most are instead clustered around the TVs twenty yards away. Mac and Eve mingle into the crowd. Nearby, a teenage girl is pulling away from her mother and the bag held between them dumps food onto the platform. Mac looks back through the crowd to the two entrances into the room but there is no one. Mac realizes that he and Eve are breathing loudly from their run and suddenly he can feel the eyes of people on him. The entire crowd knows who he is.

He looks back to the two entrances but only a few people are trickling in. A lone boy standing against the wall catches his eye and suddenly Mac knows that that boy is beaten by his father. There are no visible marks, Mac just knows, can tell by the way the boy is standing, passing time. He looks around and suddenly is aware of seeing not so much people but stories, each face flashing an image, a feeling into his brain as though he is hardwired into each individual on the platform: a well-dressed man is an alcoholic, a college-age girl is scared of men, a man in his fifties is ready to die, a child . . . Mac looks at the small boy and has an unmistakable feeling, waves pouring through his consciousness. The boy is four or five years old, his appearance normal, but Mac is overwhelmed. He feels that the boy is, for lack of a better word, evil. Entirely evil. The boy turns toward Mac and stares back, seeming to know what Mac is thinking. The boy smiles a little and

Mac is thrown by the boy's bizarrely large, tear-shaped eyes, the interiors hard and black with pupils the size of dimes.

The sound of the approaching train fills the room and people move toward the tracks. Suddenly out of one entrance Tom Schorr and five men burst onto the platform and Mac sprints ahead of the crowd, pulling Eve toward the arriving train. It is too crowded for Schorr's men to open fire. All but one man run for the train doors which have just opened. This one man, a pistol marksman, an alternate at the Olympics before he was recruited, lifts his pistol and aims, a difficult shot, the target moving laterally to his field of vision, in and out of obstacles and people. But as he lets the air go from his lungs, about to pull the trigger, he is confident of the shot. Intent on the target, he ignores the figure stepping into the corner of his vision, the electropatch hitting him in the cheek with a stinging sensation, stealing the shot that would have made him a hero. He slides to the ground unconscious and Lisa Washington whirls around the other side of the pillar to cut off the agents closing in on the train.

Mac and Eve run past her and she is only able to tranq the first man as Tom Schorr and the others duck behind a line of people waiting to board.

Mac and Eve leap into the middle car and Lisa backs toward the doors, then steps on. Mac sees Lisa, unaware of what she has just done, seeing her tranq-gun at her side, and tenses his hand on his own gun. He watches Eve step forward and hug Lisa as she approaches.

"Mac, did these men kill Sam?"

"Yes."

All the grief that Lisa has been carrying, for the loss of a lifetime of shared love, for the little babies that she will never know, rises inside her, an immense anger that spins her around at the sound of the door between cars sliding open, that raises her hand to fire, that keeps her finger pulling the trigger long after the two agents lay in a pile at the end of the car. She does not hear her own scream, the unbelievable anguish of it, until she feels Mac's hand on her arm, gently pulling her gun hand down.

Mac sees Schorr peering through the Plexiglas of the door at him and instantly recognizes the peculiar expressionless face from the meeting in Potesky's office. A cacophony of voices rises in Mac's head and he is unable to move.

"We gotta keep goin'," Lisa says, pushing Mac and Eve ahead, going last, backing up slowly, her tranq-gun aimed at the door. The expressionless man makes no move to enter until after Lisa steps into the next car.

Lights from inside the tunnel flicker on the scratched Plexiglas of the windows, making shadows, and over and over Mac's gun hand flinches at the monsterish figures who are about to shoot through the windows. The car is silent except for Eve's hushed voice and Mac turns a moment to see her whispering to Lisa, glancing at him and shaking her head. Mac wipes his eyes and looks back through the window but no one is moving. An Hispanic woman hugging a small child and gazing up fearfully shakes her head as if he is about to turn his gun at her. He can hear her words, some sort of prayer she says over and over in Spanish, and notices that the child's hair is extremely curly, tight swirls that seem to form letters. . . . He feels a hand on his shoulder but can't turn away from the small child until he suddenly realizes he is leaning over the little girl, running his hand through the girl's hair. He turns and Lisa pulls him away.

Mac looks down at Lisa's hand pushing him. He is vaguely aware of people's faces passing on the side and as they get to the door between trains, there is something he wants to tell Lisa, something he remembers that is important, but his head is so heavy, his senses so askew, all he can do is struggle at the door into the next car, struggle not to go inside. He breaks free from Lisa and tries to pull her back out onto the bouncing platform.

"Mac! *No!* We have to get to the front of the train!" The tunnel is loud, suddenly opening into a platform, a station at which the express train doesn't stop, the train plunging forward. The train hits a switch and lurches, Eve and Lisa stumbling forward into the first car. The electronic hiss of the Grid is immediate, Eve and Lisa and all the people of the car freeze, then fall to the ground. Mac steps farther to the side of the little platform between trains, pressing against the safety chains.

Martinez points at the monitors in disbelief. "Did you see that, Rec? Someone just lit up a Grid zone without authorization. That's impossible."

Sergeant Jeff Rector turns a switch back and forth. "I can't get it to disengage, Tom. And the cameras on the train aren't responding either. Either the system's haywire or somebody's overriding us."

One car back, Tom Schorr peers ahead through a pair of small binoculars, unable to see Lisa, Eve, or Mac. They must have fallen out of sight. Schorr starts forward, cautious but excited; hundreds, even thousands, are looking for this man and he has bagged him. He gets a few steps away from the door between trains and motions his last agent to the lead. The agent slides the door open and steps onto the rocking platform. He carefully slides the Grid car door open and looks in, Wells nowhere to be seen. He knows something is wrong and begins to turn but Mac has swung back onto the platform and tranqed him before he can react, the agent falling forward into Mac's arms, Mac swinging him around like a shield, the man taking four bullets in the back from Schorr's gun.

An old heavy man with a cane swings his cane down on Schorr's hand, knocking away his gun. Mac drops the agent and

steps toward Schorr, pulling the trigger but the gun is out of electropatches. Schorr looks up, holding his hand, unaware that
Mac's gun is out.

"You know what this does?! !" Mac motions with his gun.

Schorr nods.

"Then don't move a muscle." Mac carefully retrieves
Schorr's gun from the feet of a small girl. Mac glances around and
suddenly sees that the train car is mostly full of children. Two
teachers halfway down the car are trying to comfort the ones that
are crying. The sound of the train seems to get louder by the instant, the children all watching, their faces pressing forward, staring into Mac, and for a flashing moment Mac sees them all as
small corpses, one by one sitting lifeless in their seats.

Schorr sees the look in Mac's face and is careful not to make
any sudden movements.

"Not feeling so good, are you, Wells?"

Mac focuses on Schorr.

"You know we can save you if you come in. We've found
drugs that work, that end the psychotic episodes."

Mac steps toward Schorr and points Schorr's gun at his
head. "I have nothing to lose. What's the drug?"

Schorr seems so eerily calm, almost unworldly. Mac blinks
and suddenly Sam is standing in front of him instead of Schorr.

"Masic. It's an antidepressant, not on the market yet," Sam
says.

"Sam, I'm sorry I didn't believe you. I fucked up. I'm so
sorry."

"It's okay. Just give me my gun back."

"Okay." Mac hands over the gun.

A small dark girl sitting nearby next to the old man with the
cane suddenly gets to her feet and Schorr turns at the movement,
swinging the gun in her direction. Mac glances from the gun to the
girl, the girl from the Bronx Courthouse. Her looks have changed

since she died but somewhere deep in Mac, further than conscious thought can go, he knows that this girl and the girl who died because of him are the same person. She will not be murdered this time. Mac looks up and Schorr is again in front of him. In one movement Mac grabs Schorr's gun hand, thrusting it toward the ceiling and headbutts Schorr, a direct hit from the hardest part of Mac's forehead to Schorr's temple. A hit that is so hard that Mac's eyes go black for an instant. Schorr does not drop right away. Some force keeps him standing until blood trickles out of one of his ears and he collapses to the train floor.

Mac turns and slides open the two doors to the first car. He aims Schorr's gun across the train car, a tricky shot between the heads of two seated civilians. Mac feels the up and down of the two train platforms and lets his legs go loose so that his torso is almost still. The world goes slow, time stretching out, the target the only thing he can see. He squeezes off the shot and the bullet hits one of the Grid apparatuses square, breaking the triangulated signal and sending everyone out of suspended animation. Lisa grabs a pole and climbs to her feet. She pulls the emergency brake.

Moments after the train skids to a stop a few hundred yards short of a station, Mac, Eve, and Lisa step to the tracks. Ahead they can already hear the squawk of PEACE radios, can see the searching beams of flashlights. They hurry the other way.

50

Zoo HQ.

William Kane has the phone pressed to his ear as though it will help him hear better, will somehow change the news.

"But who helped them? . . . Uh huh, uh huh, so that's at least two. Yeah, put out the cover right away. I'll get right back to you."

Kane looks around at the room, the two operators bent over their computer screens. It would take exactly one hour to bring in the cleaners and break everything down. It had been designed to be mobile, to leave no trace.

He dials the old man's number. Angelson picks up at once.

"What's your assessment?" The old man as usual already knows the situation. He wants predictions, wants to control the future.

"The virus is definitely spreading. We have contamination in at least two—"

"Civvies or—"

"Or."

"You're on the ground. Is containment still an option?"

"Yes. The target is hanging around to make a splash."

"You've cordoned off information zones?"

"Yes."

"I want the zoo able to disengage at any moment. Call in the cleaners and have them on standby."

"Yes, sir."

"William?"

"Yes, sir?"

"Hold tight. We can ride this one through."

"Of course, sir."

Angelson hangs up the phone. The mobile of black and white birds swirls slowly in a circle on his desk. Kane would come through, probably. But something had seemed different in his voice. It was time to put some plans in place. Some alternatives in case the story blew and the covers weren't good enough.

He gives the mobile a push and the birds swoop and dip toward one another, appearing as though they will crash, but they never do.

(51)

Bryant Park, behind the New York Public Library.

Eve sits at a table in sunglasses and a hat. Though it is getting dark people are still around, a group of kids plays with a hacky sack. Mac is next to her, slumped forward asleep, his forehead resting against the back of his hands on the tabletop. Every so often he mumbles a few incomprehensible words, his whole body flinching.

Across the park another woman, older and well-dressed, steps out of a cab. She walks over the grass to an empty table.

Eve watches the entrances to the park to see if anyone comes in shortly after the older woman. No one does. Eve strokes Mac's cheek and gets to her feet. She does not walk directly to the older woman's table but walks around the perimeter of the park so as to approach from a different direction than from where Mac is sleeping. When she sits down at the table the older woman doesn't look up.

The older woman slides a bottle of pills from her bag onto the table. Eve cups them in her hand and drops them into her lap.

"Can you tell me anything at all, Eve?" The older woman talks without looking up.

"No, I'm sorry."

"Are you going to be okay?"

"We're working on it."

"You know these pills are experimental. I only have them for the trials I'm running . . ."

"Bev, I can't thank—"

"Just take care of yourself. Get out of this, whatever it is. I want my favorite student back."

"I've got to go."

"You can always call me."

"Thanks so much, Bev."

Eve gets up and walks away.

Professor Beverly Epstein sneaks a peek at the receding back of Eve Wells and feels as if she might cry. With no children of her own she has always secretly thought of Eve as more than a favorite former student, as more than a protégée. She gets up and heads for the street to catch a cab back down to NYU. She does not know what any of it is about; all Eve had said on the phone was that what was on the news was untrue and that her life was in danger. Beverly Epstein throws her hand in the air to flag a taxi and wonders if she has just seen Eve for the last time.

Mac feels himself traveling backward, not so much through time as with time. As though time is a pool of water though which he can head in any direction, as though time is what he is made of. He can still feel a part of himself sitting at the table but he is also falling through the table, falling into other worlds, one after another. For a moment it occurs to Mac that he is dreaming, but it doesn't have the texture of a dream. Aside from its inherent strangeness everything about it feels real. Is real. Mac feels himself stop in a place where a blindingly white light shines on all sides but he doesn't have to shield his eyes. Suddenly a black figure rises into the light. It has no features and Mac instinctively reaches for his tranq-gun but it is gone. Around the figure small bits of darkness scuttle about and Mac knows not to let them touch him. The figure does not reach out toward Mac but he can feel it examining him. Mac is not scared and senses that this is why the figure keeps its distance. Mac feels as though he could turn right or left and just plunge into the light away from this figure, that every direction is a doorway, a continuation, but Mac wants to return to Eve. And somehow he knows the way.

He walks toward the figure and the figure shivers like water, then comes right at him, unbelievably fast, swooping toward him so all he can do is throw up his hands. The figure bursts into a thousand pieces of darkness that fly into the air and slowly turn to leaves falling. The blinding light is the sky and the leaves are dropping all around his backyard as a boy, his father raking nearby. Mac is so tired, deep red grooves in his hands from the rake, his arms hurting so that he just wants to lie down in one of the huge piles and go to sleep. His father makes his way over.

"C'mon, boy, we have to finish. We have more work to do." Mac feels his father's hand on his shoulder. He looks into his father's face and it is so calm, so free of stress that it almost seems to be the face of a different man. It is not as he remembers his father but it is as real as any time he ever spent with him. His father smiles, squeezing Mac's shoulder.

"It's time to get back to it, son."

An endless supply of leaves drifts through the air like snow but Mac smiles back to his father and begins to rake.

•

"*Mac,* you have to drink this."

Mac opens his eyes, like rising up out of a deep, deep shaft, arriving into the regular world. Eve's hands are holding a pill and a bottle of water near his face. He feels a presence to one side and turns, catching small indeterminate figures in the corner of his eye scurrying around the park for cover. He focuses beyond them; something amid a few people entering and exiting the park draws his gaze, a man walking away, the unmistakable tilt of his gait, the familiarity of his left hand shoved deep in his pocket, his right hand swinging free. The man turns onto the sidewalk, for just an instant his profile visible, and Mac knows, without a doubt in the world, that he has just seen his father.

(52)

Julian Sanders sits in his suite watching a twenty-four-hour news channel. He thought of switching hotels but this was the only way Mac Wells could get in touch. Roderick and Ben had called in reinforcements, two people they knew in the business, a white woman named Lipinski and a tall black man named Webster. The woman didn't look like much; she had a slight build, but Roderick assured him that she could more than hold her own.

Julian looks at the phone on the glass coffee table. Five hours since he met Wells at Salmon's apartment and he has been staring at the phone since then. For the twentieth time he wills it to ring.

It does.

He knocks a magazine to the floor reaching for the receiver. Roderick and everyone else sit up.

"Hello, Julian Sanders here."

"Mr. Sanders, this is Ann Audorian, we met at that convention last week . . ."

There was no convention. "Right, right. Ann, I've been waiting for your call." Sanders grips the phone.

"I've got that information we discussed, the children's day-care situation, the whole business." The voice has a trace of a southern accent, maybe black.

"So we should meet."

"In half an hour."

"I'll be there."

Julian gets to One hundred tenth Street and West End Avenue early and has the limo circle the block to check things out. He notices there are no cameras on the corner and has his driver park.

A Ford Taurus pulls alongside and the Taurus's window lowers. Julian lowers his own window and sees inside the Taurus an attractive black woman.

"Mr. Sanders, get in my car, please."

Julian is immediately struck by the woman's voice, soft and graceful. "I don't go anywhere without my guards."

"One can come with you."

Julian nods to Roderick and they exit the limo and climb into the Taurus, Julian taking the front seat. The moment they shut their doors Lisa drives away.

"So where are we going."

"To a safe place."

"What's the plan?" Despite the situation Julian can't keep from staring at the woman. Something about her, an almost indefinable gentility mixed with unflinching resolve, reminds him of his mother.

"Do you have contacts at the *New York Times*?"

"A couple good friends."

"In four hours we want to come in to the New York Times Building. We want safe haven at their offices until the story is printed."

"But miss, wouldn't you and your associates be safer if you

just revealed the information from a distance and remained at an unknown location?" Julian notices the woman drives slowly, careful not to attract attention. The car is heading south.

"The only way to ensure long-term safety is to draw as much attention as possible. If my friends just hand over what they have, the story will take on a life of its own, eventually leave them behind, and someone might still be after them. But if they are highly visible, if their stay at the paper is part of the story, they will be a lot safer. The people after my friends are experts in 'accidents' and 'natural deaths.'"

"I don't mean to be rude, but how do I know this story is—"

"You won't be disappointed, Mr. Sanders."

"Call me Julian."

No one speaks for the rest of the ride. Julian watches as they cross the Brooklyn Bridge, makes a mental note of the streets they take. The car turns down a back street, a narrow road that runs behind a block of well-kept row houses with small square backyards.

Lisa parks next to a large white fence. She had debated whether or not to use her mother's house but she hadn't had time to move her mother, and entering behind the house provided hidden access; one could walk to the house totally unseen between a shed and a hedgerow. Plus the previous owner had soundproofed the basement, something to do with his wife's hatred of sports on TV.

She leads Julian and Roderick through the dark backyard to the basement entrance. She knocks softly and a moment later a lock turns inside. She lifts the heavy metal door and motions Julian down the wooden steps into the ground.

The first thing Julian sees as he steps onto the cement floor of the basement is the attractive blonde woman he met at Salmon's apartment, pointing a gun at his chest. Lisa is right behind him.

"It's okay, Eve."

The blonde woman lowers the gun, relief filling her expression, and sticks out her hand. "I've admired you for years, Mr. Sanders."

"Thank you."

Roderick stands at the bottom of the steps by the door and Eve leads Julian over to an ancient couch with a pattern of large orange flowers where an older woman, an aged version of Lisa, sits next to Mac Wells who looks pale and exhausted. Before Eve can introduce Lisa's mother, Julian bends down so his face is only slightly above Valerie's. "You must be Lisa's lovely sister."

Julian Sanders is a hero to Valerie, someone who has fought more than most living public figures for the rights of minorities and the disadvantaged, someone whom Valerie never in her wildest dreams expected to meet. Valerie Washington smiles at the compliment; she has always appreciated the attention of a man, even if he is twenty years younger, and lying.

"Mr. Sanders, if you tell me you've come to help my daughter and Mac and Eve, I will start crying."

"I am here to do whatever I can."

Valerie lives up to her word and the tears begin to flow. Lisa is quickly at her side. Julian sees that the blonde woman, Eve, has tears in her eyes also and for the first time he truly feels how frightened and tired these people are, how desperate their situation is.

Mac gets shakily to his feet and puts out his hand. Julian takes it and Wells's grip is firm. He can tell that Wells is drugged, there's something off in his expression.

"Mr. Sanders, I've often disagreed with you on political issues but I always knew you were a good man. Thank you for coming. When you hear our story, you'll be glad you did."

"We don't have much time," Lisa says from behind and Julian turns, noticing a video camera in her hand. "I need Mac, Eve, and Mr. Sanders on the couch."

Eve sits next to Mac on the couch, taking one of his hands in both of hers. Julian helps Valerie move to the old La-Z-Boy and sits down next to Eve.

"Mr. Sanders, Mac and Eve are going to tell you their story. We're taping it so there is a record, so we have insurance." Lisa presses the Record button.

Julian has done many interviews over the years, both asking questions and answering them, but he has never done anything as remotely strange as this.

"Why don't you just start from the beginning, Mr. Wells," he says.

Mac looks into the camera. He feels Eve squeeze his hand. He takes a deep breath of the cellar air, which is damp and smells like wet stone. "This whole thing began seven days ago when I accidentally shot my partner, Sam Mullane. . . . "

Julian listens, up until this moment not knowing what the story would be. Drugs? police corruption? illegal surveillance? As Mac retells the events that have led him to be a fugitive in a fellow PEACE officer's basement, Julian Sanders is, indeed, glad he came.

(53)

1:00 A.M., five hours later. In front of the New York Times Building, the rain that began half an hour before pours down as if it is in a hurry. The streets are empty. To a casual observer the whole area would appear desolate, but in a cardboard box above a grate, behind two pillars in the heavy shadows, men wait. A darkened food stand, closed for the night, sits on the corner. Inside, a pair of night-vision goggles, casting the rainy night in an eerie green glow, scan up and down the street.

Two figures in large hooded raincoats, a man and a woman, judging from their sizes, hurry down the sidewalk, holding hands.

"Probable male, female approaching sector one. Positive ID impossible."

The agents have been on duty for four hours and are anxious to get to it. The rain means that any reasonable target must be intercepted. The two people approaching are more than reasonable.

At the back of the building four more men, two in the shadows at the doors and two on either side of the alley, listen to the communications.

"The targets are turning into the building. Repeat, the targets are turning into the building. That is a go . . ."

Five men close on the two hooded figures in seconds. Their hoods are pulled back and in the pouring rain flashlights are shined in the faces of the two bodyguards, Robert Webster and Pam Lipinski.

At that moment the two men at the back door are approached by a black man and woman.

The two government men step in front of the doors, blocking the way. "Sir, ma'am, excuse me, we're the new security. We need to see ID after nine P.M."

"Really?" Roderick says. "I'm glad the building's finally getting its security operations up to speed. Let me see . . . " Roderick reaches into the breast pocket of his coat. When he pulls his civilian issue stun gun the two men in front of him have no chance, but the men hidden in the sides of the alley do, stepping out, Roderick an easy shot. Lisa pivots toward them, her tranq-gun ready. Within seconds it is over.

Roderick scans the side street, no opposition left and presses the button on a beeper. Twenty seconds later Julian's limousine skids up onto the curb and Mac, Eve, and Julian step out of the back.

"I've arranged everything with the managing editor, Norm Goldwin," Julian says. "We go back a long way. He doesn't know the details but he's waiting for you."

"We can't thank you enough, Julian," Mac says. He shakes Julian's hand and Eve gives him a hug. Inside the car, Valerie takes in everything wide-eyed.

Eve and Mac start down the alley and Roderick tips his hat as they pass. Mac swipes the key card in the lock slot and the doors unlock. He turns to Lisa.

"You sure you won't come in with us? It'll be safer."

"No, I gotta make sure my mom's all right. Julian's going to find us somewhere to lay low."

Both Mac and Eve hug Lisa.

Roderick walks with Lisa back toward the limo, his stun gun still in hand. Standing next to the door Julian watches Lisa approach. A friend of his owns a huge summer place on a private lake up in the Adirondacks and he will insist that Lisa and her mother stay there with him until things are safe. It is a good place to hide and has an indoor pool, a sauna, all the amenities two lovely women could want.

Lisa and Roderick reach the car and Julian, rain pouring down his face, holds the door for Lisa.

Mac and Eve walk down a hallway to a bank of elevators. Eve presses the button for the eighth floor. She looks at Mac and she smiles.

"You feel better?"

"Yeah. Wiped out, like there's a fog covering my senses, but no more, you know, voices or anything."

"Here." She pulls the bottle of Masic from her pocket and hands Mac a pill. No one knows how they work exactly, just that they do. He downs it.

The elevator doors open and Mac and Eve step in. As the elevator rises Mac watches the numbers glowing from floor to floor. The exhaustion, a side effect of Masic, is so overwhelming in his body he just wants to lie on the floor and go to sleep. After the story gets printed he will lie down and sleep a few weeks.

He takes Eve's hand and can see she is as tired as he is, just not drugged. The elevator stops suddenly between the seventh and eighth floors. It begins to descend. He can feel Eve's hand pull away, tense, her shoulders hunching up. He unholsters his tranq-gun and the .45. He leans heavily into the wall, his aim a little shaky.

The elevator stops and the doors open to an empty fifth floor. Eve lets go with a nervous laugh. Mac motions to her to be quiet. The doors close and the elevator descends to the fourth floor. The doors open to an empty floor.

Suddenly an arm is pointing a gun in from the side at Eve and Mac recognizes John Codd's voice. "Mac, put the guns on the ground or I'll shoot her."

Mac lays the guns on the floor. "They're down."

Codd peeks around the corner and steps into the elevator. He smells of alcohol. He presses a button and the elevator begins to descend. He will have to search them after they are dead, safer in a deserted area like the basement.

"It's a pity that you went to all this effort, Wells. They wouldn't have printed it anyway."

Mac meets Codd's eyes.

"That's right. There's not a closet big enough to hold the skeletons for the people up there. We had you either way."

The elevator stops and the doors open to the basement, a wide ramp leading down to a large pile of stacked garbage bags.

"Step out of the elevator, please." Codd backs down the ramp. Mac and Eve step out onto the cement. Codd raises his gun at Mac. "'Bye."

The sound of two silenced gunshots fired in rapid succession echo off the concrete walls and a fixed looked of surprise freezes on John Codd's face. He drops to the floor and rolls down the ramp into the trash.

Scott Joyce steps out from behind a column as Mac is about to step back into the elevator for the tranq-gun.

"No. Stay still," Joyce says, approaching, his gun aimed from the hip.

Joyce sees Mac glance at Codd, his blood making a half-moon on the floor.

"He talked too much. He was supposed to have a heart attack, but you know, two birds with one stone. Now ma'am, if you would slowly, carefully pick up the guns on the floor behind you and toss them this way."

Eve picks up the .45 and the tranq-gun and slides them down the ramp.

Mac calculates the distance to Joyce. He would be shot closing the span but he might be able to get to Joyce before he died, might be able to spare Eve. A metal railing lines each side of the ramp. There is no cover, there is no other option.

He is about to launch himself when the arrow above the elevator next to theirs lights up and a tone sounds. The doors open and a nighttime custodian steps out of the elevator. He sees Joyce and stumbles back into the elevator as Joyce moves forward, firing two quick shots through the closing doors. Mac pulls Eve back into the elevator and punches the Door Close button as Joyce swings back to them, firing six shots. Mac feels one bullet hit the front of his shoe, another skimming his side just below his ribs. The doors close. He scrambles to hit the button for the eighth floor. The elevator begins to rise. Mac watches the numbers climb, hears Eve saying "please" softly over and over again. Just before the sixth floor the elevator stops again, the lights going out, a small emergency bulb casting the closed space in red.

Out in the long sixth floor hallway, a tall, thin custodian backs up slowly, buffing the floors to the beat of the Bee Gees on a walkman.

Over the hum of the buffer, he sings along out of tune, "*Night fever, night fever. . . .*" He does not see Scott Joyce step into the hall from the stairway. Joyce walks to the elevator bank, inserts a key into the keyhole in the button panel, and the elevator doors open. He carefully steps forward to the elevator, the compartment stopped so that only its top half is visible, the roof of the car at his eye level. He fires three shots down into the interior. He peers down into the elevator but no one is there.

On a lateral brace above the elevator, Mac and Eve are holding onto cables, Mac shielding Eve with his body. Before Joyce can look up, Mac drops down, his heel stomping Joyce on the top of his forehead. Joyce stumbles backward as Mac throws himself out of the shaft onto Joyce. Mac feels Joyce's knee raised into his gut, the air knocked out of his lungs. Joyce's gun goes off and the bullet hits the elevator control panel, all the doors in the elevator bank opening and closing like an elaborate game of peekaboo. Mac and Eve's elevator begins to descend and Eve jumps to the floor. Mac knows that, exhausted and drugged, he can't beat Joyce, he is just trying to get Eve a chance to escape. He grabs Joyce's gun hand in both of his hands and with his strength ebbing slams it over and over against the wall, the gun coming free, dropping to the floor, Joyce's foot accidentally kicking it into an elevator shaft. Joyce puts his hands around Mac's neck, choking him, and Mac feels his air passage being crushed, no strength left to break Joyce's grip.

Eve screams at the custodian for help but his back is to her as he buffs the floor in his own disco universe. Mac feels the hallway begin to recede.

Eve jumps on Joyce's back, her fingernails raking his face, trying to find his eyes. Joyce lets go of Mac and easily flings Eve against the wall, her head smashing the glass of a display window.

Mac on his hands and knees, barely able to keep from blacking out, sees Eve hit the wall, glass crashing in large shards around her head and something snaps deep inside him. He feels a rage flare and force his body to its feet. He isn't aware when he grabs Joyce around the neck, isn't aware when Joyce delivers hard, repeated blows to his face. They mean nothing as he forces Joyce toward an open elevator door, blind anger pulsing in every ounce of his body, then pushes Joyce with all his might into the open shaft.

Joyce grabs at Mac's sweatshirt, almost pulling him in, and even as Joyce is falling, his hands reaching out and missing the cables, his face is calm.

The sound of his impact on the top of the elevator continues to echo even as his body, all at wrong angles, blood seeping out from every side, lifts past them.

Mac wants to go to Eve but falls to one knee, woozy but conscious, as a set of feet come rushing up, the custodian and Eve helping him to his feet. The custodian supports Mac up the stairs to the eighth floor.

Through a long glass window Mac can see, through eyes swelling shut, an older man sitting at a desk. Eve knocks on the glass and Norm Goldwin comes running over, opens the door.

Unsmiling, Goldwin looks Mac and Eve up and down. "This man needs a doctor."

Mac and Eve look at the skeptical expression on Goldwin's face, Codd's words still in their ears.

"I don't know exactly what story you two've dragged in here," Goldwin says, holding the end of his tie, "but I've gotten calls from people who aren't screwing around. The dirt they have is deeply damaging, it could scar people's lives." Goldwin pauses a moment, looking at the pattern on his tie, small Liberty Bells, and Eve thinks she will begin to cry.

Goldwin breaks into a big smile. "You must have something great."

(54)

The moment the word comes in, about the decoy at the front of the New York Times Building, the men down at the back entrance, William Kane presses the button on his pager, his wife Martha interrupted in the middle of preparations to send Elizabeth out on her first date. Perhaps there would simply be a regrouping, perhaps the situation could be survived, even overcome. But he is tired of watching his back. He knows everything. He is a liability.

When the small black box in Martha's pocket, where she always keeps it, begins to vibrate, she is so startled she screams a little and Elizabeth stops the blow-dryer to ask her what is wrong. Martha presses in the confirmation number and the message is clear.

Within twenty minutes Martha and a protesting Elizabeth have loaded into the family four-by-four and driven off into the night.

Kane walks out the side of the building in Harlem. When he gets to the corner two eighteen-wheelers and a black four-by-four with tinted windows speed past and pull in at the building to haul away the equipment, to clean up the zoo. Orders already given in his absence. Kane begins to walk, the first step out of a death sentence. Even if he isn't scheduled to have an "accident," continuing on as before, having to keep secrets of the magnitude of paradigm shifts in the country's consciousness, is too much. He would never get to be a professor now. He taps the envelope in his pocket; a ticket for a train, more anonymous than plane travel, up to Boston, then a private charter down to the small island in the Bermuda Triangle.

A good place to disappear.

55

Four weeks later. A lone car moves north along a country road somewhere in Connecticut. Eve is driving, talking on the phone. Mac sits in the passenger seat, a pile of newspapers in his lap. The top one, the Sunday edition of the *New York Times,* flutters in his hands, the headline for the lead article, "PEACE System Side Effects—President Continues to Deny Involvement on Eve of Election." A bottle of Masic rolls back and forth on the dash and Mac reaches forward and drops it in the door pocket.

Eve raises her voice into the phone, "No. How much? From who? My God, you're kidding." Eve covers the phone, glances over at Mac. "We can get a much bigger place in Maine than we thought."

Mac smiles.

"I gotta go." Eve hangs up and puts a hand over Mac's. "Have you taken your pill?"

"I forgot." Mac reaches down and pops one in his mouth. Without water it leaves a bitter taste. He turns the paper over and looks at the bottom half of the front page.

"They appointed an independent investigator."

P. E. A. C. E.

"Who?"

"Some Washington big shot, I guess. Never heard of him though." Mac holds the paper up for Eve to see. Next to the article is a picture of a smiling George Angelson.

There is the revving of an engine behind the car as a blue Ford Contour suddenly tailgates them. Mac looks over his shoulder and, through the glare-covered windshield, sees three people in the car wearing sunglasses, one in the passenger seat talking into a walkie-talkie, one in the backseat holding a gun.

Mac glances from Eve, looking at the road ahead, oblivious, to the backseat where his gun is packed in a tote bag.

The Ford suddenly speeds up, passing, and Mac is about to dive in the back for the gun but sees it is just a man, a woman on a car phone, and a kid in the backseat with a water pistol. The kid points the gun at Mac.

Mac aims back with his finger and fires.

About the Author

Guy Holmes attended Kenyon College and received his MFA in writing at Columbia University. He lives in Santa Fe.